Clements Robert Markham

A Life of John Davis, the Navigator

1550-1605 - Discoverer of Davis Straits

Clements Robert Markham

A Life of John Davis, the Navigator
1550-1605 - Discoverer of Davis Straits

ISBN/EAN: 9783744693684

Printed in Europe, USA, Canada, Australia, Japan

Cover: Foto ©Raphael Reischuk / pixelio.de

More available books at **www.hansebooks.com**

A

LIFE OF JOHN DAVIS,

THE NAVIGATOR,

1550—1605,

DISCOVERER OF DAVIS STRAITS.

BY

CLEMENTS R. MARKHAM, C.B., F.R.S.

LONDON:

GEORGE PHILIP & SON, 32 FLEET STREET;

LIVERPOOL: 45 TO 51 SOUTH CASTLE STREET.

1889.

EDITORIAL PREFACE.

The story of the world's exploration is always attractive. We naturally take a keen interest in the personality of the men who have dared to force their way into the unknown, and so unveiled to us the face of mother earth. The interest in the work of exploration has been particularly strong and widespread in recent years, and it is believed that a series of volumes dealing with the great explorers and explorations of the past is likely to prove welcome to a wide circle of readers. Without a knowledge of what has been accomplished, the results of the unprecedented exploring activity of the present cannot be understood. It is hoped, therefore, that the present series will supply a real want. With one or two exceptions, each volume will deal mainly with one leading explorer, bringing out prominently the man's personality, telling the story of his life, and showing in full detail what he did for the exploration of the world. When it may be necessary to depart somewhat from the general plan, it will always be kept in view that the series is essentially a popular one. When complete the series will form a Biographical History of Geographical Discovery.

The Editors congratulate themselves on having been able to secure the co-operation of men well known as the highest authorities in their own departments ; their names are too familiar to the public to require introduction. Each writer is of course entirely responsible for his own work.

THE EDITORS.

CONTENTS.

———◆———

LIST OF ILLUSTRATIONS AND MAPS.

LIFE OF JOHN DAVIS.

CHAPTER I.

HOME AND BOYHOOD.

THE knowledge of the varied regions of our earth is due to the devoted labours of a few great men. It is to the pioneers of old, who first opened the gates leading to the unknown, who first threw their light on discoveries which were completed by those who followed it—it is to these worthies that mankind owes its knowledge of the earth, and all the consequences which have followed from such knowledge. Every region on the earth's surface connects itself with one or a few great names—the names of men who first threw a clear light over an unknown tract, or who were mainly instrumental in illuminating the previous darkness. Hence it is that the life-history of a chief among explorers embraces the geography of the region with which his name is associated. The connection is inseparable. Around the story of a great explorer's life the facts relating to his discoveries are naturally grouped. The skill and fortitude, the dangers and hardships, the aspirations and successes, of the man breathe life and human interest into the physical aspects and scientific facts connected with the region upon which

A

his labours threw light.   Biography is the best vehiclo
for the conveyance and retention of geographical knowledge.

The Arctic Regions are connected with many a talo
of chivalrous daring, with many a heart-stirring episode ;
and such deeds are interwoven so closely with the phy-·
sical conditions of the locality, that the one cannot bo
related without a knowledge of tho other.   This is so in
all parts of the world, but it is moro especially tho caso
in the wild regions of tho North.   Foremost in tho front
rank of Arctic worthies stand the names of the Elizabethan seamen Davis, Hudson, and Baffin; and their .
life-histories cannot be studied and stored in our memo-
ries without a sound geographical knowledgo of the
region upon which their labours threw a flood of light,
and the complete discovery of which is but the following
up of routes first pointed out by thom.

The England of Queen Elizabeth was just awakening
to a sense of her greatness, and of the possibilities of
her future.   Men were in earnest in thoso days.   The
examplo of tho great Queen filled them with passionate
loyalty.   Elizabeth called upon them to fight for tho
liberty of their neighbours, and they doggedly faced the
matchless infantry of Spain until tho cause of freedom
triumphed.   Their Queen and their country were syno-
nymous terms.   For Elizabeth and for England they
traversed unknown seas, visited the ends of the earth,
and mastered all the knowledgo of their adversaries.
In after years, when England was disgraced under the
feeble tyranny of the Stuarts, men looked back with
bitter regret to the days of the great Queen.   The uni-
versal feeling found eloquent expression from that illustrious victim of Stuart malignity, that martyr of our

liberties—Sir John Eliot. "Elizabeth, that glorious star," he exclaimed, "was glorious beyond any of her predecessors. The Great Council of the Parliament was the nurse of all her actions, and such an emulation of love was between that senate and the Queen, as it is questionable which had more affection, the Parliament in observance unto her, or she in indulgence to the Parliament. And what were the effects? Her story told them. Peace and prosperity at home, honour and reputation abroad, a love and observation in her friends, consternation in her enemies, admiration even in all. The ambitious pride of Spain was broken by her power, the distracted French were united by her arts, the distressed Hollanders were supported by her succours. Violence and injury were repelled, usurpation and oppression counterwrought, the weak assisted, the necessitous relieved, and men and money into divers parts sent out, as if England had been the magazine of them all. She was most just and pious to her subjects, insomuch that they, by a free possession of their liberties, increased in wealth and plenty." In another speech he pointed out how the great Queen "made them our scorn who now are made our terror."

Brave Sir John Eliot and his contemporaries might well regret the days of Elizabeth. Happy they who were privileged to labour for their country during that glorious reign, and to achieve undying fame in the service of the Queen. Her sailors and discoverers, after long and diligent training, added largely to geographical knowledge, and to the greatness and prosperity of their country. They hailed from all parts of England, but certainly there was a brilliant and numerous band of illustrious seamen who were natives of the West

Country. The Boroughs from Bideford, the gallant Hawkins, mariners of Plymouth, Drake, Seymour, Oxenham, Chudleigh, the Gilberts, Raleigh, and Davis, all came from Devonshire, and all added to the glories of the reign of the great Queen.

In the Elizabethan age there was activity and capacity, and consequent achievement on all sides. It was the age of Shakespeare and Spenser, of Bacon and Cecil, of Hakluyt and Camden ; but it was also the age of Vere and Norris, of Raleigh, Drake, and Hawkins. The greatest among these steadfast workers rise above their fellows as beacon-lights for future generations. As the Elizabethan statesmen raised England to the first rank among the nations, as the poets attained an excellence never since surpassed, as the soldiers founded a school which opens our modern military history, so among the mariners there were men who serve as beacons and centres for the study alike of maritime discovery and of geography. Drake and Cavendish were our first circumnavigators; the opening chapter of our connection with the East Indies is headed by the name of Lancaster ; Guiana and Virginia are coupled for ever with the name of Sir Walter Raleigh, and the Arctic Regions with that of John Davis,—one of the ablest, and certainly the most scientific, of the Queen's West Country sailors. It is with John Davis, his discoveries, and the stirring history of his sea-services, that we now have to do.

John Davis was born at Sandridge, on the left bank of the Dart, between Totnes and Dartmouth, in about the year 1550, and his brother Edward was a year or two younger. They were the sons of a yeoman who owned a small freehold in Sandridge, a manor in the

JOHN DAVIS'S BIRTHPLACE AT SANDRIDGE.

parish of Stoke Gabriel, of which a branch of the Pomeroy family had been lords since the days of Edward III.

Stoke Creek is the little harbour for Stoke Gabriel. To the south are the wooded slopes of Sandridge, rising from the river. At the head of the creek is the old church, with its spreading yew-tree in the churchyard. A graceful screen of carved oak, with figures of saints painted in the lower panels, separates the chancel and its aisles from the nave, and there is an old pulpit carved with grapes and vine-leaves. Mural tablets preserve the memory of the Pomeroys, and in the worm-eaten parish register are the records of the marriage of John Davis and the baptisms of his children. The little village clusters round the church, and a Devonshire lane leads by walls covered with valerian and pennywort, and past a pond full of yellow iris, to the woods and meadows of Sandridge, approaching them from the landward side.

The manor-house of the Pomeroys stood on an eminence overlooking the river, surrounded by woods, near the site of the present seat of the Baroness de Verte, which was built by Lord Ashburton about eighty years ago. This site is flanked by a ravine, at the head of which a farmhouse faces bright green pastures, which slope gently down to a creek of the river. On the left are the Sandridge woods, rising from the beach up steep slopes, with masses of honeysuckles and dog-roses hanging over the branches and almost touching the water. To the right are groves of splendid old elms and oaks, which separate the grounds of the manor-house from the small freehold, as it was then, which was the home of John Davis in his boyhood.

The house at Sandridge was only separated from the cove by two or three pastures, and when the two boys, John and Edward Davis, ran down to their boat and pushed out into mid-stream, a lovely scene met their view. The Dart, in this part of its course, widens out, and has all the appearance of a lake surrounded by wooded hills. Along the northern side are the woods of Sandridge and Wadditon, with the hills rising into craggy ridges to the east. Here the leafy boughs touch the water at high tide, and when the river is low, there is a beach where fishermen spread their nets and haul up ten and twelve-pound salmon. On the west side there is a bold promontory; and the picturesque village of Dittisham, surrounded by plum-orchards, runs along the lowland of the isthmus from one reach of the river to another. The view to the south is closed in by the richly wooded heights crowned by Greenway Court, the ancestral home of the Gilberts. Here the river narrows at Anchor Rock, and flows down for two miles and a half to Dartmouth. At high tide this lake-like reach between Saudridge and Greenway is one expanse of water. When the tide is low, there is a dry flat in the centre, along the edge of which herons may be seen fishing; and if disturbed by a boat, they rise on the wing, and flap lazily away to their nests in Sharpham Wood.

Kind friends and neighbours dwelt around this reach of the Dart. The Davis boys in their skiff had a sure welcome, whether they steered west, or east, or south. Many a time they pulled across, or round the flat if it were low tide, and landed under the wooded height of Greenway—home of a brotherhood of naval heroes. John and Humphrey Gilbert were some years older

ST. PETROX, DARTMOUTH.

than John Davis, but their younger brother, Adrian,
was nearly the same age, and the half-brothers Carew
and Walter Raleigh were a few years younger. When
boys together, Humphrey and Adrian Gilbert, Walter
Raleigh, and John Davis must often have made excur-
sions down the river to Dartmouth. In those days the
landlocked little harbour was much frequented, and
ships were built in the dockyard at Hardness. The
boys might sit on the stone steps and parapets of the
wharf, and listen for hours to the tales-of-mariners from
all parts of the world, till their young hearts thrilled
with longing to seek honour and fame on the great
deep. The voyages of English ships were being extended
in several directions. When the young friends on the
Dart were still at school, John Hawkins was visiting
the coast of Guinea and the West Indies, while the servants of the Muscovy Company were striving to "pur-
chase perpetual fame and renown" by wrestling with
the ice-floes in the Kara Sea. There were old sailors
who had made voyages to Guinea and to the White Sea
many years before. Dartmouth was a great resort of
sailors, and the boys would have had many opportunities
of listening to their yarns. They would see the tall
ships appearing between the beetling cliffs at the harbour mouth, and the weather-beaten crew landing at
the quay with many a strange curiosity from foreign
shores. They would be impressed by the sight of the
God-fearing among them—and there were not a few
such—wending their way to the little church of St.
Petrox to offer up thanks for their safe return. Standing on the edge of the cliff, where the ships rounded
the point and ran into the landlocked haven, St.
Petrox—dedicated to a native Devon saint—seemed to

be the first to welcome their return. Its parapet wall
was a fine look-out, whence the boys could descry the
white sails on the horizon, and the great expanse of sea
which they longed to sail over, and so get their chance
of "purchasing renown both to themselves and their
country."

Greenway Court and a trip to Dartmouth with the
Gilberts was not the only attraction for young Davis.
When he shot his boat out of Sandridge Creek, while
Greenway was in full view on one hand, the tower of
Dittisham church rose from a valley full of plum-
orchards on the other; and on the hill, about a mile
away, stood the manor-house or barton of Bozomzele.
This old house is still standing. The doorways have
pointed arches, and it contains a large hall. It is now
a farmhouse, and is one of the meets for the beagles of
the *Britannia* cadets. In the sixteenth century it was
the pleasant seat of Sir John Fulford, who inherited it
owing to his great-grandfather, Sir Baldwin Fulford,
having married the heiress of Sir John Bozom. Here
Sir John often resided with his wife Lady Dorothy,
daughter of John Bourchier, Earl of Bath, and his six
children. The visits both of John Davis and of Adrian
Gilbert were welcome at Bozomzele to children of about
their own age. The sons were John and Andrew, and
there were four blooming daughters—Faith, Elizabeth,
Anne, and Cecilia. The eldest is not mentioned by the
Heralds of King James in their Visitations, probably
owing to a reason which will be referred to farther on,
and which would make her brother at Great Fulford
unwilling to allude to her; but the name is given by
Westcote, whose local information was far more complete
than that of the Heralds.

This intimacy at Bozomzele led to the marriage, in after years, of Faith Fulford with John Davis, and of the widow of Andrew Fulford with Adrian Gilbert. Another neighbour of the Sandridge folks was Richard Holway of Watton or Wadditon, who afterwards sold his estate to, or, as some say, was cozened out of it by one Adams, the husband of another of the Fulford girls.

John Davis certainly received a classical education, but he was not in the same social position as the Gilberts and Fulfords. The Grammar-school at Totnes was founded in 1554, and he may have attended there; but it seems clear that he went to sea at an early age, and was probably absent from home for many years. We first get sight of him again in 1579, when he was twenty-eight years of age. During the interval Davis had not only become an experienced sailor, specially expert in the scientific branch of his profession, but was also a man whose capacity was recognised beyond the limits of his own West Country circle. The character of his services is unknown to us, and there is no record preserved of his early life at sea. He appears suddenly, at the age of twenty-eight, as a captain of known valour and conduct, in whom merchants and other adventurers were willing to repose trust and confidence.

His comrades at Greenway had also made their way in the world. John, the eldest of the Gilberts, was established at Greenway and Compton as an active magistrate. Humphrey, after an education at Eton and Oxford, had served with distinction in Ireland, had gallantly led the volunteers at Flushing and Goes against the flower of the Spanish infantry, and had finally devoted his energies to schemes of discovery and colonisation. His famous discourse on the North-West

Passage displays much classical learning, a thorough knowledge of the then conditions of the problem, and a noble spirit of patriotic devotion. In 1578 he made his first voyage to the West; soon afterwards he obtained a patent for colonising newly-discovered lands, and in 1583 he sailed with five ships with the object of forming a settlement in Newfoundland. One vessel deserted him, another was lost. The return voyage had to be made in the *Golden Hind* and the little *Squirrel* of ten tons. Gilbert was urged to go on board the larger and safer ship, but he replied, " I will not forsake my little company going homeward, with whom I have passed so many storms and perils." The *Hind* kept as near her consort as possible, but a violent storm arose off the Azores. Captain Hayes of the *Hind* saw Sir Humphrey sitting abaft with a book in his hand, and heard him cry out, " Courage, my lads ! we are as near to heaven by sea as by land." The same night the little *Squirrel's* light suddenly disappeared, and nothing more was ever seen of her. A squirrel was the crest of the Gilberts. Thus did one of the boys who had listened so eagerly to the yarns of sailors on Dartmouth quay win his way to fame. He died prematurely, but not before he had made his name immortal. It was as he would have desired. " He is not worthy to live at all," he exclaimed at the close of his discourse on the North-West Passage, " who for fear or danger of death shunneth his country's service or his own honour, since death is inevitable and the fame of virtue immortal."

The other boys lived on, strengthened and invigorated in their struggle for fame by the glorious example of their comrade. Adrian Gilbert was a man of considerable learning, a doctor of medicine, a mineralogist, a very able mathematician, and an ardent promoter of geographical discovery.   Walter Raleigh was three years at Oxford with Hakluyt and Camden, and went in 1569 to serve with the Huguenots in France, fighting at the battles of Jarnac and Moncontour, and not returning home until 1575.   He probably undertook a voyage to the West Indies in 1577, made the voyage with his brother Humphrey Gilbert in 1578, and did good service in Ireland in 1580.   In the year 1582 Raleigh had become a favourite of the Queen, and was placed in a position to do still more valuable service to his country.   A learned scholar, with ripe experience both as a soldier and a sailor, and full of zeal for discovery, this comrade of Davis's boyhood had also won his way to a front place in the ranks of the Elizabethan worthies.

John Davis returned home in 1579, and passed the next six years partly at Sandridge and partly in London.   Adrian Gilbert was then living in a house at Sandridge.   He probably rented the manor-house of the Pomeroys.   He married the widow of Andrew Fulford, and was in constant companionship with the friend of his boyhood.   The young ladies at Bozomzele were still single, and John Davis, now a gallant sea-captain, was able to renew the happy friendships of his boyish days.   The visits to Bozomzele bore fruit. The parish register at Stoke Gabriel records the marriage of John Davis and Faith Fulford on September 29, 1582, and the fact that John Davis had a child christened Gilbert on the 27th of March 1583.   The other Miss Fulfords were married in the neighbourhood, Anne to Master English of Totnes, Elizabeth to Thomas Cary of Cary Barton, and Cecilia to Master Adams of

Wadditon.   Adrian Gilbert, as we have seen, was married to the sister-in-law of Davis's wife.

The spirit-stirring discourses of Sir Humphrey Gilbert, followed so quickly by his glorious death at sea,
must have made a deep impression on his brother and
on Davis. They too were filled with the desire to extend
the trade and power of England through discoveries in
unknown regions, and especially by the solution of the
North-West Passage problem. As early as 1579 they had
made the acquaintance of the famous philosopher at
Mortlake, and had discussed with him the prospects of
a Northern voyage of discovery.   Dr. Dee mentions in
his journal that on June 3, 1580, " Mr. Adrian Gilbert
and John Davys rode homeward into Devonshire," after
having had conferences with the learned mathematician
on subjects in which they were all deeply interested.
This was before the last voyage of Humphrey Gilbert,
and his death only inspired the friends with fresh zeal
to fulfil his wishes, and take up the great work where
he had left it.   Sir Walter Raleigh joined them, not
only with sympathy and encouragement, but with more
substantial aid.   Thus were the comrades who had
shared in many a boyish adventure along the banks of
the Dart, and who had passed so many happy days of
their youth speculating on the wonders of foreign countries, now joined together in a great and memorable
enterprise.   Then they were boys, full of inquiry and
curiosity, who longed for the time when they too might
add to the renown of England. Their early enthusiasm,
aided by capacity for hard work and the desire to do
well, had borne rich fruit.   Now they were qualified to
become the pioneers of English discovery in the Arctic
Regions.

CHAPTER II.

PREPARATIONS FOR THE NORTH.

THE house of Dr. Dee at Mortlake contained one of the finest private libraries then existing in England, including valuable manuscripts, maps, and charts, while among instruments was the cross-staff used by Chancellor in his famous voyage to the White Sea. Here the philosopher was frequently visited by sea-captains and men about to undertake distant enterprises, and he was. consulted by statesmen as well as by the Queen herself. He drew up a memoir on her Majesty's right to Norumbega and to the unknown parts adjacent, and in 1583 he had prepared a learned report on the reform of the calendar.

On the 23rd of January 1584 two men were sitting in the library at Mortlake engaged in earnest conversation. One was in the prime of life, tall and handsome, with an eager, intelligent countenance, and equipped for a journey. The other was an elderly man, with a long beard as white as milk, and a clear, sanguine complexion, dressed in a loose gown with hanging sleeves. His eyes were unnaturally bright and wandering, as if they were used to peer into occult and forbidden mysteries. Dr. Dee and Adrian Gilbert were deep in the consideration of the new pro-

13

ject for Arctic discovery, when a visitor was announced.
It was the Secretary of State, Sir Francis Walsingham,
who had called on his way down the river to Greenwich.
Walsingham was a sedate and cautious man, yet he
became so interested in the conversation when it was
continued in his presence, that he expressed a desire to
hear the subject of Northern discovery discussed before
him in all its bearings. It was arranged that there
should be a meeting at the house of Mr. Beale, a mutual
friend, on the very next day. Accordingly, Dr. Dee,
Adrian Gilbert, and John Davis met the Secretary of
State on the 24th of January in an interview where,
as Dr. Dee tells us, "only we four were secret, and we
made Mr. Secretary privie of the North-West Passage,
and all charts and rutters were agreed upon in general."
In other words, the experienced sailor and his friend,
with the help of the profound mathematician and cosmographer, placed before the statesman the then existing knowledge of the northern regions derived from
the results of former voyages, and thus enabled him to
grasp the subject, and come to a conclusion respecting
the wisdom of undertaking such an enterprise. If we
now take a similar review of what had been done before
the voyage of Davis, we shall be able to understand the
point of view from which the great navigator and his
supporters arranged their plans and based their hopes
of success, as well as the grounds on which they obtained
the support of Sir Francis Walsingham.

Our Elizabethan ancestors knew nothing of the sagas
of the Norsemen, which were brought to light by Professor Rafn in our time, and showed that Greenland
and the eastern coast of North America were visited
and colonised from Iceland several centuries before the

first voyage of Columbus. They had dim traditions of the wonderful discovery made by Friar Nicholas of Lynn, and of voyages to Iceland from Lynn and Bristol; but no positive information could be derived from these stories. Nor were the more recent voyages of John and Sebastian Cabot of· much more use. For the charts and papers of Sebastian had been taken from him in the time of Queen Mary, and intrusted to a certain Master Worthington, who probably handed them over to Philip

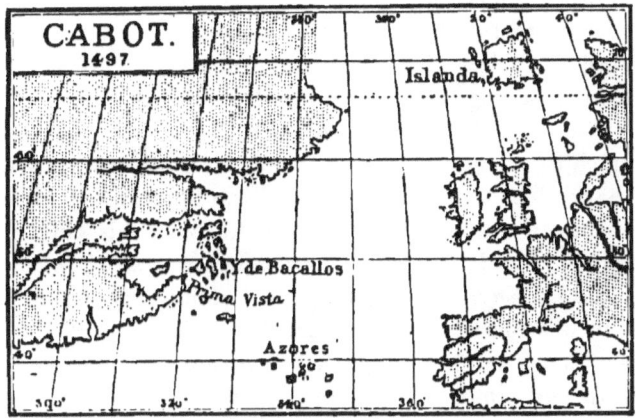

FROM CABOT'S MAPS.

of Spain. All that was accessible in England was comprised in the famous *mappemonde* drawn by Sebastian Cabot himself, a copy of which, executed by Clement Adams, was hung up in the privy gallery at Whitehall. It showed the "Prima Vista" of Cape Breton, being the first land seen by John Cabot in 1497, the land of Bacalhaos or Newfoundland, and the coast of Labrador to about 60° N. A knowledge of these coasts had been improved by subsequent voyagers. In 1500 the Por-

tuguese navigator, Gaspar de Cortereal, sailed along the
coast of Labrador, a name derived from the natives
he brought to Lisbon, who were believed to be good
labourers. The land he visited is shown on a Portuguese chart of 1504 as "Terra de Corte Real." The
name of Bacalhaos (which means codfish) is given to
Newfoundland. Estevão Gomez, in a Spanish ship,
also made a voyage to the fisheries. Many vessels from
England, France, Portugal, and the Basque Provinces
of Spain, following these pioneers, yearly undertook
voyages to the fishery of Newfoundland; and in 1534
Jacques Cartier discovered the insularity of Newfoundland by sailing through the straits of Belleisle.

Although the voyages of the Cabots did not add
much to a practical knowledge of the American coasts,
the conduct of the operations of the Company of Merchant Adventurers by Sebastian Cabot in his old age
was of essential service in advancing and opening a new
route for English commerce. In December 1551 Sebastian was constituted governor of this Company for life,
and in 1553 a fleet was set forth under his supervision,
with Sir Hugh Willoughby as admiral and Richard
Chancellor as chief pilot. In his instructions to the
leaders of this expedition, Cabot was the first to establish
rules for keeping a logbook at sea. Willoughby perished miserably on the coast of Lapland with all his
people, but not before he had discovered the coast of
Novaya Zemlya. Owing to the absence of any means
of fixing the longitude, this coast appeared on the charts
for a long time as *Willoughby's Land*, between Spitzbergen and Novaya Zemlya. Chancellor reached the
White Sea and opened a trade with Russia. From
that time ships were regularly dispatched to St.

Nicholas.   The third voyage of the Muscovy Company
in 1556 was conducted by Stephen Borough, a Devonshire sailor of great ability, who discovered the entrance
into the Kara Sea, and wintered with the Russians at
Kholmogro.   Borough also commanded the seventh
voyage of the Merchant Adventurers in 1560; but
.from 1563 until his death in 1584, he was in the
Queen's service as chief pilot in the Medway.   His
discovery of a strait between. Novaya Zemlya and the
mainland gave rise to projects for finding a North-East
Passage to China, which engaged the attention of the
Merchant Adventurers during several years.   An attempt was made in 1568, of which no account has been
preserved; and in 1580 the Company fitted out two
vessels, commanded by Arthur Pet and Charles Jackman.   The former passed through the strait into the
Kara Sea, and made several attempts to penetrate the
heavy pack-ice and reach the mouth of the river Ob.
Jackman and his ship were never heard of again, and
Pet returned with a report on the reasons of his failure.
The disappointing result of Pet's voyage caused the
abandonment of attempts in that direction, and concentrated the attention of explorers on a passage by
the north-west ; although Anthony Jenkinson continued
to advocate a North-Eastern Passage.

The four able men who were considering the subject
with close attention in Mr. Beale's house on that January afternoon three hundred and five years ago would,
therefore, have turned away from the eastern parts to
take stock of what was known respecting the routes
on the American side.   In those days great importance
was attached to a curious map, with an accompanying
narrative, published at Venice in the year 1558.   The

D

history of this map, which long misled our navigators, is interesting.

Nicolò Zeno, the representative of one of the noblest. and most ancient families in Venice, was born in the year 1515, and he appears to have succeeded to the property, including the Zeni Palace and its archives, when he was very young. He says that he was but

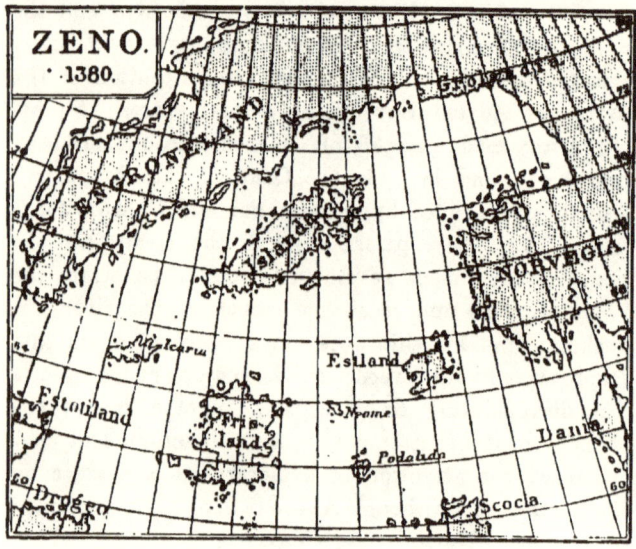

THE ZENI MAP.

a child when the papers of his ancestors fell into his hands, and that he, not knowing what they were, "tore them in pieces, as children will do, and sent them all to ruin." In after years he looked over some fragments that remained, and found them to be family records of the deepest interest. Ever afterwards he looked back upon the destructiveness of his childhood with the

greatest sorrow. In the fourteenth century the family
was represented by three brothers, Nicolò, Antonio, and
Carlo. Nicolò went on a voyage of curiosity into the
northern seas, and was wrecked on an island which he
called Frislanda in 1390. He was befriended by a
chief named Zichmni, into whose service he entered as
pilot of his fleet, and wrote to his brother Antonio to
join him. Antonio reached the distant Northern land,
lived there with his brother Nicolò for four years, remained ten years after Nicolò's death, and then returned
to Venice, where he died. During his absence Antonio
wrote letters to the third brother, Carlo.

It was these precious letters which the younger Nicolò,
a hundred and fifty years afterwards, tore up during his
childhood. The fragments he recovered in after years
were parts of the letter from Nicolò the elder to Antonio,
and of the letters from Antonio to Carlo, as well as a map
rotten with age and damp. The letters give an account
of a visit of Nicolò Zeno to a land he calls Greenland,
and information derived from fishermen respecting distant western lands called Drogeo and Estotiland. The
younger Nicolò strove to repair the errors of his mis-
chievous childhood by preparing these surviving fragments for the press. He also made a copy of the
decaying map, adding his own conjectural emendations
where the original could not be deciphered. This,
compilation was published at Venice by Nicolò Zeno
in 1558.

The misleading map of Nicolò Zeno became a document of great importance, and its errors more or less
influenced cartographers for at least a century. Greenland, called Engroneland, Tramontana, and Grolandia,
is here connected with Norway, and in the bay thus

formed a large island called Islanda is placed, rather
to the north of the latitude of Iceland. Due south of
Islanda there is another large island called Frisland;
and half way between Frisland and the south point of
Engroneland a third island of considerable size is placed,
called Icaria. At the western extreme of the map, in
the same latitude as Frisland, Estotiland appears, and
Drogeo is in the S.W. corner of the map. These two
latter names were very generally assumed to be Newfoundland, and the " Prima Vista " of Cabot. Islanda, of
course, was Iceland, and the outline of Greenland is not
very incorrectly drawn. But the two islands of Frisland and Icaria were very puzzling to the Elizabethan
cosmographers. There was certainly no such island as
Frisland of the size and in the position where it is
placed on Zeno's map. It was accordingly shifted farther
to the west, where it appeared in numerous charts; the
Greenland coast was occasionally mistaken for it, and it
was a source of endless confusion.

The geographers at Mr. Beale's house would have
called Walsingham's attention from a study of the
narrative and map of the Zeni to a consideration of
the much more recent voyages of Martin Frobisher, the
first of which was commenced simultaneously with the
appearance of Sir Humphrey Gilbert's discourse of a
North-West Passage. Except Frobisher himself, and
Michael Lok, his chief helper and adviser, no one was
better able to narrate the history of Frobisher's enterprises than Dr. Dee, who was constantly consulted, and
who gave instruction to the officers selected to serve in
the expedition, in navigation and nautical astronomy, as
it was then understood. Frobisher had entertained the
idea of discovering a North-West Passage for many

years, but it was not until he had secured the aid of
Michael Lok, an influential merchant and an indefatigable geographer, that he was in a position to fit out an
expedition.

Two new vessels, of about twenty tons burden, called
the *Gabriel* and the *Michael*, having been supplied with
necessaries and with a crew of thirty-five men and boys,
bold Martin Frobisher set sail from Blackwall on the
7th of June 1576, and shaped a course for the Shetland
Islands. But meeting with a gale of wind, the *Michael*
deserted her consort, and returned home with a false
report that the *Gabriel* had gone down in a terrible
storm. Frobisher pushed onwards, and came in sight
of land which he supposed to be the Frisland of Zeno's
map; but he could not approach owing to the quantity
of ice which was pressed upon it. After encountering a
furious gale and heavy sea, in which the little *Gabriel*
was nearly lost, he persevered for some days in a westerly
course, and on the 20th of July high land was sighted,
which he named Queen Elizabeth's Foreland. Here
much ice was again encountered, and as the ship was
detained off an inlet between two headlands, Frobisher
determined to explore it. He was under the impression
that the coast on one side of this inlet was America, and
that the land on the other side was the continent of Asia.
He gave the name of Frobisher's Strait to his discovery,
and returned to England in October. The first land he
saw must have been the east coast of Greenland, near
Cape Farewell; and sailing across the channel which
was destined to bear the name of Davis, he reached his
inlet on its western shore. Unluckily one of the crew
brought home a shining piece of mica, which was believed to be gold ore. " This kindled a great opinion in

the hearts of many to advance the voyage again," and thus the interests of geography were lost sight of in this foolish quest for mineral wealth.

A company was formed, a charter was granted to Michael Lok and Martin Frobisher, and a second expedition was soon ready for sea. It consisted of three vessels—the *Aid*, of 240 tons, lent by the Queen, the *Michael*, and *Gabriel*. On board the *Aid* were the admiral himself, Martin Frobisher, his lieutenant, George Best, who was the historian of the voyage, and Christopher Hall, the master. The *Gabriel* was commanded by Edward Fenton, with William Smyth as master, and the *Michael* by Gilbert Yorke. Sailing in June 1577, they sighted the same coast which had been taken for Frisland in the former voyage, early in July. Frobisher made several ineffectual attempts to force his way through the ice in a boat and effect a landing. He was baffled by dense fogs, and on the 8th of July the voyage was resumed. It is curious that Frobisher's officers should have found this rugged and inaccessible coast to agree very well with the island of Frisland as described by Zeno in his narrative and shown on his map. Leaving it, the expedition steered westward, and reached the inlet called Frobisher's Strait on the 17th of July. There was a good deal of intercourse with the Eskimos, but all exploring work was abandoned for the sake of the search for ores, and this second expedition returned without adding anything to geographical knowledge. The Queen gave the name of " Meta Incognita " to the land discovered by Frobisher.

The reports of the assayers who examined the stones that were brought home still further excited the cupidity of speculators. A third expedition was fitted out on a

large scale, and it was actually intended to leave a
colony of a hundred men to watch over the imaginary
ores of "Meta Incognita." A fleet of fifteen sail was
assembled at Harwich on the 27th of May 1578, including the *Aid*, commanded by Frobisher himself;
the *Judith*, Captain Fenton ; the *Thomas Allen*, Captain
Yorke ; the *Ann Frances*, Captain Best ; the *Moon*, the
Gabriel, and *Michael*, and the *Emma*, a buss of Bridgewater. This time Frobisher took the route down
Channel, and sighted his supposed Frisland on the 20th
of June, to which he gave the name of "West England."
He succeeded in effecting a landing, and took possession
in the name of the Queen. Natives were seen, with
dogs and tents, closely resembling those of "Meta Incognita." This gave rise to the suspicion among some of
the officers that the so-called Frisland was really the
mainland of Greenland. They also conjectured that
"Meta Incognita" and Greenland might be connected
by a coast-line forming a deep bay. The great numbers
of icebergs would not be met with, they thought, if there
was an open sea to the north. Thus we see the sound
natural sense of practical mariners struggling against
the errors and absurdities of Zeno's map.

"Meta Incognita" was reached on the 23rd of June,
there being a fair wind across the channel, and as the
lofty mountains of Greenland, which Frobisher believed
to be Frisland, and called "West England," faded from
view, the last peak that was in sight received the name
of "Charing Cross," "from a certain similitude." Very
bad weather was encountered off Frobisher's Inlet, and
the expedition was a complete failure ; but one of the
vessels, the little buss of Bridgewater, added to the
confusion of existing maps by the report of her captain

touching another imaginary island. He declared that he had sighted a great island to the south-east of Frisland, and sailed three days along the coast, the land seeming to be fruitful, full of woods, and a champaign country. Accordingly one more island, called "The Land of Buss," appeared on charts of the North Atlantic, to increase the confusion caused by Nicolò Zeno. Many a sailor, in the years to come, kept a fruitless and anxious look-out for "the sunken land of Busse." Frobisher returned in October 1578, having lost forty men during the voyage. Unfortunately he abandoned his real work for the search of imaginary gold ore, and all his gallant efforts were wasted. The question was still unsolved, and his work remained undone. The misunderstood discoveries of Frobisher added to the perplexities of the Zeno map.

If we remember that our ancestors laboured under great difficulties in ascertaining the longitude of any position, it will easily be seen that it was only by very sagacious reasoning from several points of view that an error could be detected. Accepting Frobisher's own belief that the first land he sighted was Frisland, and relying on the map of Zeno, the conclusion at which Davis and his friends arrived was inevitable. After leaving Frisland, the next land Frobisher came to would, according to these data, be Greenland. Consequently Davis looked upon Frobisher's Inlet as a strait through the southern part of Greenland. Looking farther west, he saw the open channel on Zeno's map to the west of Greenland, only bounded to the west by Estotiland, which was generally accepted as Newfoundland. A coast-line was believed to extend farther north, which had been partially examined by Cabot, and afterwards by Cortereal and other Portuguese some years later.

This was the coast of Labrador. It was to the wide channel between the west side of Greenland and the Labrador coast that the attention of Davis and his friends was turned, as an important route for future discovery. As Frobisher's Strait was assumed to be on the eastern side of this channel, the information collected during the three voyages commanded by Sir Martin Frobisher appeared to furnish no guidance to explorers intending to adopt a more western route, except as regards the general remarks on the nature and position of the ice. It is right to observe that this does not appear to have been the view of Michael Lok, or of Frobisher himself. In the map published by Lok, Frobisher's Strait is shown as the actual North-West Passage, although a study of the narratives fully justified the conclusion of Davis.

Respectful attention would certainly have been given to that famous discourse on the North-West Passage by Sir Humphrey Gilbert, which saw the light at the time when Frobisher's first expedition left the Thames. To the four men who sat in council at Mr. Beale's house it would have seemed like a voice from the dead—as a call to duty from one of England's most illustrious sons. It was a learned and eloquent state paper. Gilbert's argument was that America was an island, widely separated by oceans from any other continent, and that consequently it could be circumnavigated. He referred to the description of Atlantis in the "Critias" and "Timæus" of Plato, and argued that the great island of Egyptian tradition could be no other than America : an opinion which he shared with the most eminent cosmographers of the continent, including Sebastian Münster of Ingelheim, Apianus of Leipsig, Gemma Frisius, and Ortelius.

He then alluded to the voyage of Other along the north-
east coast of Europe, as described in the translation of
Orosius by King Alfred, in order to show how the route
taken by the ancient navigator had been rediscovered
by Englishmen centuries afterwards, who, in his day,
were accustomed to make annual voyages to the White
Sea. These observant seamen had described the currents and the accumulations of ice in the Kara Sea,
and their reports led Gilbert to the conclusion that a
voyage by the north-west would be a shorter and easier
route to Cathay and India.

In considering the route along the north coast of
America, Sir Humphrey collected all available evidence
respecting the distance between America and Asia. He
quoted from Gomara, the Spanish historian, who declared both America and Greenland to be islands; and
strengthened his arguments by the evidence of Chinese
geographers, who affirmed that their coast-line trended
to the north-east as far as 50° N. These conclusions
respecting the insular character of America were confirmed in part by Jacques Cartier, the French discoverer
of Canada, and by Nonnius, the great Portuguese geographer.

Gilbert next appealed to the evidence of Sebastian
Cabot, who was remembered by many then living.
Cabot described the passage on his charts, which were
to be seen in those days in the Queen's privy gallery at
Whitehall. Cabot is also said by Sir Humphrey Gilbert
to have affirmed that he reached the latitude of 67° 30'
N. along the coast of Labrador, where the sea was still
open, and that he would have completed the voyage to
Cathay if he had not been prevented by a mutiny in
his ship. Gilbert believed the reports that the passage

had actually been made. Pliny, quoting from Cornelius Nepos, mentions the arrival of Indians on the coast of Germany, who were presented to the Roman proconsul of Gaul, Quintus Metellus Celer, by the King of Suevia. Moreover, in 1160, during the reign of Frederick Barbarossa, certain other Indians 'arrived on the coast of Germany. Gilbert discussed the various routes by which they might have come, and decided in favour of the North-West Passage. Gemma Frisius had affirmed that three brethren had actually sailed through the strait; a friar of Mexico, named Urdaneta, whose chart had been seen by gentlemen of good credit, also claimed to have made the passage. It had been attempted by Cabot and by the Portuguese Cortereal, the Labrador coast being known certainly as far as 62° N., and the west coast of Greenland being supposed to extend to 72° N. The discourse of Sir Humphrey Gilbert reviewed all these stories and reports, discussed the question of currents, and concluded with an eloquent peroration on the importance of discovering a shorter route to India and Cathay, and on the patriotic duty which called upon Englishmen to undertake it.

The discourse had been more than ten years before the world at the date of Walsingham's conference with the geographers, but it had lost none of its freshness and persuasive earnestness. It had the true ring in it, and was one of the most valuable of the documents to be considered.

There were also recent maps and charts of importance. The great map of Mercator was published in 1569, and was the result of the careful study of numerous maps and charts now lost to us. On Mercator's map the coast of Labrador is shown with some approach

to accuracy, and is called "Terra Corterealis." He
makes its eastern coast run from 53° to 60° N., and
shows the entrance to Hudson's Strait and Ungava Bay.
His new information appears, from the names, to have

ARCTIC MAP FROM ATLAS OF ORTELIUS.

been derived from Portuguese sources.   The atlas of
Ortelius was published in 1570.

Walsingham was a statesman of enlightened views,
and he had always been favourable to voyages of discovery. The thorough examination of all the arguments,
in his conference with Dr. Dee and his friends, had the

effect of confirming his former opinion, and of securing a powerful friend to the projected undertaking.   He was fully alive to the value of a route to the Indies which would be free from Spanish or Portuguese claims ; but he also desired to foster the spirit of enterprise in his countrymen, and to encourage all voyages which were calculated to serve as training-grounds for hardy and expert seamen.   Such a policy is the true policy of this country, and statesmen worthy of the name have recognised its importance.   In time of peace the attitude of an Administration with regard to Polar exploration is an infallible test of its worth and patriotism.   Cecil and Walsingham were alike able and patriotic, and in their days Polar discovery received hearty encouragement. When the conference at Mr. Beale's house broke up, official countenance and good-will had been secured for the contemplated expedition.

The next point was to interest the wealthy merchants of the City of London in the new attempt to discover a shorter route to Cathay.   On the 6th of March John Davis and Adrian Gilbert had an interview with several City magnates, and set forth the commercial importance of the enterprise.   Alderman Barne, who was Lord Mayor in 1586, Mr. Towerson, Mr. Yonge, and Mr. Thomas Hudson were the merchants to whom Dr. Dee introduced his friends.   The meeting probably took place at Mr. Hudson's house at Mortlake — a circumstance of peculiar interest to Arctic students ; for Thomas Hudson is believed, on good grounds, to have been the uncle and guardian of the great navigator, Henry Hudson ; so that it is quite possible that the young Henry may have been present when his illustrious predecessor in Arctic discovery met the merchants in his uncle's house,

and may have listened with intense interest to the
address in which Davis explained his plans.

Having sown good seed in this interview with the
merchants of London, Davis and Gilbert did not allow
the grass to grow beneath their feet. On the 17th they
lodged at the house of Mr. Radforth in Chelsea, and
next day they set out on the long ride to Devonshire.
Their object was to induce the merchants of Exeter and
their own neighbours at Dartmouth to join the enterprise. They were fairly successful. Subscriptions were
obtained at both places; but an event occurred while
they were still in the West country which threatened to
derange their plans.

This was the loss of Dr. Dee's advice, owing to his
unexpected departure from England. The philosopher
of Mortlake, although his learning was sound and extensive, was the victim of spiritualistic delusions. He
became more and more absorbed in chemical experiments to find the philosopher's stone and in imaginary intercourse with angels. He possessed a crystal
globe with miraculous powers. During his labours in
the cause of maritime discovery in concert with Davis
and Gilbert, he was already deep in the study of forbidden arts. In March 1582 he engaged a medium who
could communicate with spirits by means of the crystal
globe. At about the same time Dr. Dee made the
acquaintance of Albert Laski, a Bohemian nobleman,
who proposed that both the philosopher and his medium
should return with him to his country, where they would
be furnished with ample means for continuing their
mysterious researches. Dee, whose expensive pursuits
had loaded him with debt, accepted the offer, and in
September 1583 he left Mortlake privately and em-

barked for the continent. On his departure, a mob broke into his house and destroyed a great part of his library, believing him to be a magician whose dealings were with the evil one.

This sudden disappearance of their influential friend must have caused considerable anxiety and consternation in the minds of the partners at Sandridge. But they were not dismayed. Gilbert's half-brother was at the height of his influence at court, and when they turned to him for help in their need, they were met more than half-way. Sir Walter Raleigh entered into their plans with characteristic ardour. He received the honour of knighthood in the end of 1584. He was rapidly becoming wealthy through the lucrative appointments and gifts conferred upon him by the Queen, and he spent his fortune nobly in schemes for the advancement of commerce and the promotion of discovery. He induced the Queen to grant a charter in the names of himself, Adrian Gilbert, and John Davis "for the search and discoverie of the North-West Passage to China." Thus were the three boys who had so often rowed and sailed on the Dart together, and who had listened eagerly to the stories of sailors on Dartmouth wharf, now associated as grown men, to make their own great effort for their country's glory. Raleigh himself mainly devoted his energies to the equipment of the expeditions to Virginia, dispatched in the same years as those which saw the discoveries of Davis. But Raleigh was not absorbed by his Virginian schemes. He found time to give most efficient aid to his old schoolfellows.

The most useful help, due to the friendship of Sir Walter, was the recommendation of his associates to the good offices of Master William Sanderson. This eminent

merchant was one of the most liberal and enlightened
adventurers of his time.   In those days there were men
to be found in abundance who were willing to spend
their profits lavishly on public objects, and especially on
promoting maritime discovery.   Sanderson was a merchant of great wealth, and he was married to a niece of
Sir Walter Raleigh.   Before embarking on the venture
of Gilbert and Davis, he carefully studied the subject in
all its bearings, and, with other information, a discourse
on voyages to the north-east between 1553 and 1583
was prepared for him by Mr. Henry Lane.   The result
of his deliberations was, that he resolved to give liberal
support to the proposed expedition.   He superintended
all the preparations, advanced the largest share of the
funds, and his relative, Mr. John Janes, went out as
supercargo to represent the great merchant's interests.

In the spring of 1585 John Davis was busily engaged
in the work of fitting out his expedition at Dartmouth.
It was a memorable year.   In 1585 the Queen hurled
defiance at Philip of Spain, and resolved to assist the
people of the Netherlands in their struggle for freedom.
In 1585 Raleigh sent out his first expedition, and gave
the name of Virginia to the coast he was resolved to
colonise; so that it was the remote birth-year of the
great American Republic.   In 1585 the first Englishmen arrived in India.   In 1585 Raleigh's former play-
fellow realised the wildest dreams of his boyhood.   He
was to be the leader of an attempt to make discoveries
beyond the great ocean, for the glory of his native land.
Living at Sandridge, and actively assisted by his neighbour and lifelong friend, Adrian Gilbert, the work at
Dartmouth was actively pushed forward.

The expedition consisted of two small vessels, the *Sun-*

shine of London, of fifty tons, and the *Moonshine*, built at
Dartmouth, of only thirty-five tons. By the beginning
of June they were ready for sea. Davis commanded
the *Sunshine*, with William Eston and Richard Pope as
his master and master's mate, Henry Davy and William
Crosse as gunner and boatswain, and Mr. John Janes
as merchant and supercargo. The crew consisted of a
carpenter, eleven seamen, four musicians, and a boy.
The *Moonshine* was commanded by William Bruton,
with John Ellis as master.

On the 7th of June 1585 the two ships sailed out of
Dartmouth harbour on their daring voyage to discover
a route to China and India by the north-west. It was
a private venture, undertaken by merchants of London
and Exeter under the lead of Master Sanderson, but it
was dispatched to secure great national objects, and it
was under the direct patronage of Sir Francis Walsingham, the Secretary of State, and of Sir Walter Raleigh.
John Davis was the right man to command such an
expedition—"a man very well grounded in the prin-
ciples of the art of navigation," as Mr. Janes described
him, full of enthusiasm, brave and daring, but prudent
and cautious. As he passed the church of St. Petrox,
and waved his last farewell to Adrian Gilbert and his
other friends, how vividly must the daydreams of his
boyhood have returned to him! He must have remembered how often he had sat with Raleigh and the
Gilberts on that very parapet of St. Petrox, and longed
for the time to come when he too could sail away to
discover unknown lands. At last the time had come!

CHAPTER III.

THE FIRST AND SECOND ARCTIC VOYAGES.

JOHN DAVIS was in the prime of life, just entering upon his thirty-sixth year, when he sailed out of Dartmouth harbour in command of the *Sunshine* and *Moonshine*. Brought up under excellent influences at his lovely home on the banks of the Dart, enjoying the companionship of kindred spirits, and drinking in the love of adventure from his earliest boyhood, he entered upon the profession of the sea with great advantages. His studies at school, probably at Totnes, had given him some classical knowledge, and he had a natural bent for mathematics and nautical science. He had now been some twenty years at sea, and was accounted one of the most experienced and accomplished seamen of his time. Besides his old play-fellows, Raleigh and the Gilberts, he had formed many friendships in the West Country, chief among them being that of the adventurous Master Chudleigh of Broad Clyst, who warmly sympathised in his aspirations, and was himself destined to lead forth an expedition and to become a martyr to science. Sir Francis Walsingham, Secretary of State, Sir Edward Dyer, afterwards Chancellor of the Garter, the Earl of Warwick, who was Master-General of the Ordnance, and

34

Mr. William Sanderson were his patrons. Young students of rank at the universities, who were interested in cosmography and the mathematics, had sought the society of the famous seaman; among whom were George Clifford, Earl of Cumberland, and young Lords Lumley and Darcy of Chiche. In recent years Davis had become well known, and had formed many valuable acquaintances, who all wished him God-speed. He left behind him, in his home at Sandridge, a wife and little boy, surrounded by friendly neighbours, several of whom were near relations. All seemed to prosper with him. This was the turning-point of his destiny, and he knew how to seize the right moment. Ably and zealously assisted by loving friends, it was to his own perseverance and energy that the dispatch of the expedition was mainly due. He was resolute and brave, skilled and experienced in all a sailor's art, and full of enthusiasm. At the same time Davis was a God-fearing man, gentle and courteous, considerate and thoughtful of the welfare of his crew, and beloved by his men—a very perfect specimen of an English sailor of the days of the great Queen.

On the first day at sea, the captain, in consultation with the master, formed the crew into messes and arranged the scale of provisions. In the small cabin of the *Sunshine*—a little vessel of fifty tons—there was a mess consisting of seven persons. Here the captain had his charts and instruments, his globe, with the aid of which he worked out most of his nautical problems, and his few books. William Eston, the master, was an experienced seaman, devoted to his chief, and doubtless an old shipmate. His mate was named Richard Pope. Mr. John Janes, a nephew of Master William Sander-

son, came on board as merchant, to watch the interests
of the adventurers.   He formed a close friendship with
Captain Davis, and assisted him in his calculations.
Henry Davy, the gunner,. appears to have been an
Exeter man.   His namesake, John Davy, served the
office of mayor of Exeter in 1584, and was mortgagee
of some of the property of Davis's friend Chudleigh.
William Cross, the boatswain, and Robert Wats, the
carpenter, completed the number of seven officers.   Many
a night at sea must these earnest explorers have pored
over the charts, listened eagerly to the explanations of
their chief, and discussed the chances of success.   They
were waited upon by the only boy in the ship, young
Kit Gurney.

The seamen were told off into two messes, five in
each, and there was another mess of one seaman and
four musicians, who had been engaged to entice and
secure the good-will of any savages that might be met
with on the voyage.   One of the seamen may probably
have been the son of his namesake, John Ellis, master
of the *Moonshine*.   Another, Luke Adams, was a young
apprentice, related to the owner of Wadditon, the next
estate to Sandridge, who married a sister-in-law of
Captain Davis.

Captain Davis and Master Eston surveyed the whole
stock of provisions, and carefully calculated how long
they would last.   They consisted of cod and salt meat,
bread and pease, butter and cheese, with beer.   The
clothing was entirely woollen, and adapted for the cold
weather; and in all respects thought had been taken
for the comfort of the men by their generous employer,
Master William Sanderson. ·

A strong south-west wind obliged the two vessels to

take shelter in Falmouth harbour for five days. They
made sail before a northerly breeze on the 13th of June,
but the wind again shifted, and Captain Davis anchored
at the Scilly Islands until there should be a fair wind for
Greenland.   He was detained for twelve days, and, ever
anxious to perform useful work whenever an opportunity
offered, he employed his time in making a survey of the
Scilly Islands.   Accompanied by the master and Mr.
Janes, he visited every part of the group in his boat, plot-
ting and describing the positions of all the islands, rocks,
and anchorages, and making a regular survey for the
use of navigators.   Davis was thus usefully employed
until the 28th, when the expedition weighed and made
sail before a light easterly breeze, for the voyage across
the ocean.   On the two following days they were hin-
dered by a dense fog ; but on the 1st of July they were
well out on the Atlantic, with a clear horizon and a
school of porpoises playing round the ship.   To many
on board this was a novel sight, and when the master
sent for his harpoon, and began to throw it, as the porpoises sported past the ship within range, there was
great excitement.   He missed them several times, but
at last the iron went home; the crew manned the line,
and the porpoise was hauled on to the deck.   Mr. Eston
pronounced it to be a "darlie-head," and, whatever it
was, the flesh was served out next day, and was considered to be as good as mutton.   On the 3rd, the
monsters of the deep promised still better sport, and the
master succeeded in striking one of them ; but the creature was so strong that it went off with harpoon, line,
and all, disappointing their hopes and spoiling their
fun.   Then they tried the boat-hook, but all was of no
use, and at last they gave it up, and allowed the great

porpoises to play around them in peace. The number
of whales seen during the rest of the voyage across the
Atlantic would be considered extraordinary now. But
in those days the *Balœna Biscayensis* had not yet been
hunted almost to extinction. Not only were these
great whales, which were provided with whalebone, and
differed very slightly from the *B. Mysticetus* of the
Polar seas, often met with in the Atlantic, but they
frequented the coasts of the Bay of Biscay, and were
hunted in boats from the villages of Biscay and Guipuzcoa. It is many years since those villages were
enriched by the bone and oil of the Biscayan whales,
but they still occur in municipal coats of arms, and the
old harpoons, long since disused, still hang on the walls
of houses whose owners have been fishermen for generations. In the days of Davis, the Basque sailors throve
on the whale-fishery, and "great store of whales" was
seen by those who crossed the Atlantic.

At the end of three weeks the coast of Greenland
was very near. On the 19th of July, the sea being
calm and a dense mist obstructing the view, "a mighty
great roaring" was heard. The captain of the *Moonshine* was ordered to hoist his boat out and go ahead
to sound, but there was no bottom at 300 fathoms,
though the noise was like the breaking of waves on a
beach. Then Davis, taking Master Eston and Janes
with him, and ordering the gunner to fire a musket as
a signal to show the ship's position at the end of every
half-hour, pulled away in the direction of the mysterious noise. He soon found that the ships were close
to a stream of pack-ice, and that the noise was caused
by the large pieces grinding together. He returned
before nightfall, with his boat laden with ice, which

made excellent fresh water.   Next day the fog rose,
and the rugged mountains of Greenland, covered with
snow, stood out before them, a wide extent of pack-ice
intervening between the ships and the shore.   Davis
called it the " Land of Desolation," for, as he said, " the
irksome noise of the ice and the loathsome view of the
shore bred strange conceits among us."   He had probably reached the east coast somewhere near Cape Dis-
cord.   Being almost beset, Davis shaped a southerly
course and got clear of the pack.   On the 22nd he again
hoisted out his boat and pulled inshore to examine the
ice.   Many seals were seen and quantities of birds were
on the water, which induced the men to get their lines
out, but no fish were caught.   The ice prevented a close
approach to the land, and when the captain returned on
board, he continued his southerly course, intending to
round the southern point of Greenland.

The cold had increased owing to the ships being near
the ice, so Davis resolved, in order to encourage his
men, to increase their allowance, every mess of five
persons receiving half a pound of bread and a can of
beer each morning for breakfast.   Rounding the point
afterwards called Cape Farewell by Davis, the expedition lost sight of land and steered to the north-west for
four days, hoping to discover the passage.   Davis knew
that he was well to the westward of Frisland, that he
had rounded the south point of Greenland, and that he
was in the channel shown by Mercator to exist between
Greenland and Labrador.   On the 29th of July he
sighted land in 64° 15' N., and as the wind was foul
for a north-westerly course, he bore in for it, finding it
to consist of many islands and deep inlets.   He was at
the entrance of the fiord on the shores of which the

Danish settlement of Godthaab is now situated, and he

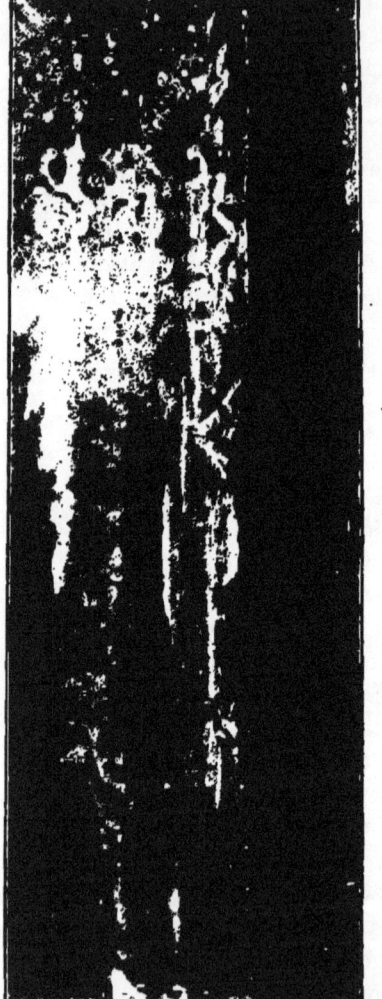

GODTHAAB DISTRICT.   (From Original Sketch by the late Dr. E. L. Moss in the Royal Geographical Society.)

named the place of his anchorage Gilbert Sound, in memory of his friends at Greenway, and especially of his colleague and neighbour, Adrian. He had given the same name to his first-born child.

Captain Davis, with Eston and Janes, had landed on a small island to look for wood and water, when they saw a number of natives shouting and making signs from a short distance. On the Greenland coast the small granite islands are scattered in great numbers at the entrances of the deep fiords, pretty well clothed with moss, grasses, and wild-flowers in the summer-time, and embosomed in a deep blue sea, on which masses of ice float here and there, and become distorted by refrac-

tion on the horizon.   Nature does not present a more
lovely scene; and here the explorers had their first interview with the Eskimo.   Hearing the shouting and noise,
Captain Bruton and Master Ellis, of the *Moonshine*,
manned their boat, took the four musicians on board,
and hurried either to rescue their chief or co-operate
in his attempt to conciliate the natives.   When they
arrived, Captain Davis caused the musicians to play,
while he and his companions danced and made signs of
friendship.   Ellis was appointed to go down to the
water-side and win their confidence, in which he succeeded by carefully imitating their signs.   A good un-
derstanding had been established before the explorers
returned on board that night, and next morning a number of *kayaks* were darting about round the ships, and
natives stood on the nearest islands and made signs to
induce their visitors to land.   Again the boat went on
shore, and perfect confidence was established.   Five
kayaks were purchased and specimens of native clothing;
the impression left on the minds of Davis and Janes
being that the Eskimos were a tractable people, whom
it would be easy to civilise.   Great numbers of seals
were seen, and the vegetation, consisting of dwarf
willow and birch, and of the berry-bearing *Empetrum
nigrum*, was observed.

On the 1st of August, the wind being fair, Davis left
Gilbert Sound, and shaping a north-west course in pursuance of his discovery, sighted the land on the opposite
side of the channel in 66° 40′ N. on the 6th.   Here he
cast anchor in a place which he called Totnes Road,
while a lofty cliff overshadowing the anchorage received
the name of Mount Raleigh.   The large bay nearly surrounding Mount Raleigh was called Exeter Sound, the

point to the north was christened Cape Dyer, and that
to the south Cape Walsingham.   The explorers had
their first encounter with Polar bears under Mount
Raleigh.   Four were seen from the ship, and the boat
was quickly manned by eager sportsmen.   Janes, who
was on shore, loaded his gun with buckshot and a
bullet, and hit one in the neck.   It took to the water,
and was killed by the boat's crew with boar-spears,
as well as two others; and a few days afterwards
another bear was secured after a long and exciting
encounter.   Dwarf willows were found on shore, and
a yellow flower which they took for a primrose.   It
must have been either the *Ranunculus glacialis* or
Papaver Alpinum.

The expedition left Totnes Road on the 8th of
August, and the men having complained of the insufficiency of their food in such a climate, Captain Davis
framed a new dietary.   Each mess of five men was to
receive four pounds of bread daily, twelve quarts of
beer, six stock-fish, and an extra gill of peas on salt-
meat days.

The next service performed by the expedition was the
examination of Cumberland Gulf.   The northern point
of the entrance was named the Cape of God's Mercy,
and the two ships went up the gulf, discovering an
island in mid-channel.   The *Sunshine* sailed up on one
side of it, the *Moonshine* took the other channel, and a
very complete examination of the gulf was effected, but
without sighting the end of it.   Various indications
inclined Davis to the belief that it was a strait, but a
strong north-west wind obliged him to shape a course
towards the open sea.   On the 23rd of August he anchored on the south shore of the gulf, and on the 26th

he resolved to wend his way homewards, arriving at Dartmouth on the 30th of September.

John Davis was not disheartened by the result of his first voyage. He considered that his discoveries had materially increased the amount of knowledge which must be collected before the passage was likely to be found, unless by some fortunate accident. On leaving Greenland he had steered westward, and although he had been stopped by a coast-line, he had discovered an open-ing (Cumberland Gulf) which he supposed to be the passage, though the season was too late to enable him to continue the voyage. His vessels were only pro-visioned for six months. He was warmly welcomed and encouraged by his steadfast friend, Adrian Gilbert. Three days after his arrival he addressed a most hope-ful letter to Sir Francis Walsingham. He assured the Secretary of State that "the North-West Passage is a matter nothing doubtful, but at any tyme almost to be passed, the sea navigable, voyd of yse, the ayre tolerable, and the waters very depe." Davis also pointed out the trade in oil and furs that might be opened with the lands actually discovered.

As soon as the explorer "could take order for his maryners and shipping," he hurried up to London, to give a personal account to the Secretary of State and to Mr. Sanderson, and to induce the adventurers to under-take a second expedition. The merchants of Devonshire subscribed liberally, and owned two of the ships which were fitted out for the new attempt. The exploring fleet consisted of the *Mermaid* (120 tons), the *Sunshine*, *Moonshine*, and a pinnace called the *North Star*, of ten tons. The conduct of the expedition was again intrusted to John Davis, who sailed in the *Mermaid*, with William

Eston again as his master. Richard Pope, who had
been master's mate in the former voyage, now received
command of the *Sunshine*, with Mark Carter as his
mate, and Henry Morgan as purser. Morgan was a
servant of Mr. William Sanderson.

Davis was more than ever impressed with the importance of the service, and as a larger squadron had been
intrusted to him, he resolved to attempt a more extensive examination of the unknown northern region by
dividing his ships and sending Captain Pope on a
separate duty. On the 7th of May 1586, the three
exploring ships and the little pinnace sailed from Dartmouth harbour for the discovery of the North-West
Passage. Coasting along the southern shore of Ireland,
the squadron was off Dursey Head, the northern point
of Bantry Bay, on the 11th. Thence the General, as
the commander of a fleet was then called, shaped a
course for Greenland, and on reaching 60° N. latitude,
he gave his instructions to his second in command, and
the *Sunshine*, with the pinnace *North Star* as a tender,
parted company. Captain Pope was to search for a
passage northward between Greenland and Iceland as
far as 80° N., if he was not stopped by land. He started
on this important mission on the 7th of June, the
Mermaid and *Moonshine* continuing their voyage, and
coming in sight of the southern extremity of Greenland
on the 15th. The pack-ice, extending for several leagues
off the shore, rendered it impossible to land; so Davis
gave it the name of Cape Farewell, and made sail in
order to get a good offing, once more entering the strait
which bears his name. Here he encountered severe
gales of wind during the next fortnight, and it was
not until the 29th that he again sighted the frowning

mountains of Greenland near Gilbert Sound, his discovery of the previous year. He at once resolved to
take shelter among the islands which skirt the coast,
and there to put together a small pinnace, which had
been brought out in pieces on board the *Mermaid*, to
examine the indentations of the coast and act as a scout.
Davis accurately described the coast as "very high and
mountainous, having before it, on the west side, a mightie
companie of isles, full of fayre soundes and harboroughs.
The land was very little troubled with snowe, and the
sea altogether voyd of yce."

A boat was sent away to sound for a suitable anchorage,
and was soon surrounded by *kayaks*. As soon as the
Eskimos recognised some of the men who had been there
in the previous year, "they hung about the boat with
such comfortable joy as would require a long discourse
to be uttered." Davis then landed on one of the islands,
with eighteen knives, and gave one to each native. They
offered skins in exchange, but it was explained to them,
by signs, that "the knives were not solde, but given
them of curtesie."

Next day the pinnace was landed at a convenient
place on one of the islands, and while the carpenters·
were employed in putting it together, the people paid
continual visits, sometimes as many as a hundred
kayaks arriving together. They brought seals, skins,
fish, and birds; and Davis visited their summer tents.
He was anxious to explore the country as far as possible, and sent boats up the fiord for ten miles, which
discovered a comparatively level tract with grass and
moss, like an English moorland. Davis himself, with his
boat's crew, walked several miles inland, seeing nothing
but falcons, ravens, and some small land birds. On the

3rd of July he made another boat expedition, attended by fifty Eskimos in their *kayaks*. He climbed to the top of a high hill in order to obtain a view, the natives being very friendly, and helping the strangers up and down the rocks. Having satisfied himself with regard to the nature of the country, he organised some athletic sports. In long jumps the English beat the natives. This was followed by wrestling-matches, when the strangers found their match. The Eskimos were strong and nimble, and they threw some of the English sailors who were held to be good wrestlers.

The pinnace was launched on the 4th of July, forty of the Eskimos willingly giving their assistance. On the same day the master of the *Mermaid* discovered a grave on one of the islands, in which several bodies were interred, with a cross laid over them. It is possible that this may have been a relic of the Norsemen, or that the tradition of the use of the cross may have been preserved by the Skrællings from the wreck of the Norse colonies. A few days afterwards, Captain Davis went for another long boat expedition up one of the fiords. These fiords run up towards the interior glacier of Greenland for distances of fifty or even a hundred miles. The frowning granite cliffs rise on either side to a great height, while in several places there are breaks where small valleys are formed, bright with mosses and wildflowers during the short summer. In the far distance an occasional glimpse is caught of the white gleaming line of the glacier.

On the return of the General from one of these expeditions, he found that the natives had shown their propensity for thieving in a very persistent way. They had stolen an anchor, attempted to cut the hemp cable,

cut away the boat from the stern, and had displayed
their hostility by throwing large stones on to the decks.
The crews were very angry, and said that Davis's "lenity
and friendly using of them gave them stomach for mis-
chief." But he still forbore, and endeavoured to regain
the good-will of the natives by giving them more presents. That night they made another attack, and the
boatswain of the *Moonshine* was knocked down by a large
stone. The patience of the General was at length exhausted. He chased their *kayaks* in a boat, but, of
course, to no purpose. Next day, however, a native was
captured, and signs were made that he would not be
liberated until the anchor was restored. Within an hour
the wind became fair, and the two ships hastily weighed,
taking the Eskimo with them. He died during the
voyage. Davis wrote a very graphic account of these
people in his journal, and collected a vocabulary of their
language.

Up to this time the health of the crews had been
excellent. Only one young man had been taken ill, and
he died at sea on the 14th of July. On the 15th he
was cast overboard, "according to the order of the sea,
with praise given to God by service."

When to the southward of Gilbert Sound, in 63° 8' N.,
Davis fell in with an enormous iceberg on the 17th of
July. Its extent and height were so extraordinary that
the pinnace was sent to ascertain whether it was land
or really ice. The report that it was indeed one gigantic
mass of ice floating on the sea, with bays and capes,
plateaux and towering peaks, excited great astonishment. Soon other masses began to collect round the
ships, while the ropes and sails were frozen and covered
with frost, and the air was obscured by fogs. This was

the more disheartening because in the previous year the
sea was free and navigable in the same latitude.

Progress was checked, and the men began to despond.
They came aft very respectfully and advised their General
that he should regard the safety of his own life and the
preservation of his people, and that he should not through
over-boldness run the risk of making children father-
less and wives desolate. The gallant seaman was much
moved. On the one hand, he had to consider the welfare of those intrusted to his charge; on the other,
he was bound to recognise the importance of achieving
the great business on which he was employed : "where-
upon," he tells us, "seeking help from God, the fountain
of all mercies, it pleased His Divine Majesty to moove
my heart to prosecute that which I hope shall be to His
glory, and to the contentation of every Christian mind."
After much reflection, he finally resolved that, although
the *Mermaid* was a strong and sufficient ship, yet not
so serviceable as a smaller vessel for this service, and
being also a heavy expense to her owners, he would
send her home and continue the voyage in the *Moonshine*.
Having come to this decision, he steered eastward for
the land with a fair wind, and anchored in an excellent
road in latitude 66° 30' N. on the 2nd of August. This
place, on the west coast of Greenland, is called Old
Sukkertoppen by the Danes. The *Moonshine* was repaired and re-victualled, while, according to his invari-
able custom, Davis caused the surrounding country to
be explored.

William Eston, the master, went away in a boat, and
returned with a report that all the land seemed to consist of islands. The heat was very great, and those
who went on shore were much tormented by mosquitos.

Friendly relations were established with the natives, commencing in a curious way. A recently killed seal, with bladders tied to it, was floated down to the ships with the flood-tide; this Davis looked upon as a friendly present, and on the next day the natives appeared and began to barter without fear. Leaving the *Mermaid* at anchor preparing to commence her long voyage home, Davis weighed on the 15th of August, and continued the work of exploration in the *Moonshine*. Sailing across the strait, he once more sighted the Cape of God's Mercy; and noticing a current to the west, great hope was conceived that there might really be a passage by way of Cumberland Gulf. But on the 19th of August it began to snow, and foul weather continued all night with much wind. The *Moonshine* was obliged to heave-to off the shore. In the morning, the weather clearing up, she ran in, and was anchored in a safe roadstead. Next day the General continued his examination of the coast to the southward, searching for a passage.

Davis surveyed this western coast from the 20th to the 28th of August, laying it down from the 67th to the 57th parallels of north latitude. He found enormous numbers of birds breeding in the cliffs, which led him to suppose that there must be a similar abundance of fish in the sea. So he hove the ship to for about half an hour, and in that short time the men caught a hundred cod. He then anchored in a roadstead on the Labrador coast, remaining there until the 1st of September. Davis, as was his wont, made an expedition into the interior, and found a wooded country with abundance of game. His people succeeded in bringing down numbers of birds with bows and arrows, and they caught many more cod at the harbour's mouth.

D

On the 1st of September the *Moonshine* was got under
weigh, and continued to sail along the coast, with fine
weather, for three days. It then fell calm, and the
vessel was brought-to with a kedge-anchor in 54° 30' N.
Again the lines were put overboard, and immense quantities of cod were secured. "The hook was no sooner
over the side, but presently a fish was taken." On the
4th Davis anchored again, having passed a great opening which seemed to offer another hope of a passage.
It was probably the Strait of Belleisle; but the wind
was dead against him, and he could not enter it. While
they were at anchor, men were sent on shore to fetch
some fish which had been laid out on the rocks to cure.
The place appears to have been somewhere on the north
coast of Newfoundland. Several Micmac Indians were
lurking in the woods, and, without previous warning or
parley, they opened a murderous fire on the English
sailors with their bows and arrows. When he saw this
from the ship, Davis quickly slipped his cable, set his
foresail, and ran in towards the shore, discharging
muskets at the savages, which put them to flight. But
two of his men were killed by the arrows, two seriously
wounded, and only one escaped by swimming off to the
ship, with an arrow through his arm.

The troubles of the explorers were increased by a
furious gale of wind which sprang up from the N.N.E.
that evening, and lasted for three days. Some of the
strands of the cable of the sheet-anchor were torn asun-
der, but the others held, and the *Moonshine* weathered
the storm. Then, on the 11th of September, with a fair
W.N.W. wind, the gallant Davis shaped his course for
England, arriving in the beginning of October 1586.

Meanwhile the *Sunshine* and *North Star*, having parted

company with Captain Davis on the 7th of June, proceeded northward in pursuance of their instructions.
Captain Pope anchored in one of the ports of Iceland
on the 11th, where he found another English ship from
Ipswich. After remaining there a few days, he resumed
his voyage, and sighted the east coast of Greenland on
the 7th of July. Unable to approach the shore owing
to the closely packed ice extending for several leagues,
he coasted along it until he came in sight of the mountains which Davis had named "The Land of Desolation"
during the voyage of the previous year. Rounding
Cape Farewell, they reached the rendezvous at Gilbert
Sound on the 3rd of August. The crew of the *Sunshine*
appear to have had several games of football with the
Eskimos. Two other places on the Greenland coast were
visited, and there was an unfortunate encounter with
the natives, three of them being killed. Captain Pope
finally commenced his voyage home on the 31st of
August. Three days afterwards they encountered a
severe gale, which obliged the *Sunshine* to lay-to, and the
little pinnace was lost sight of, and never seen again.
Captain Pope waited four days, but nothing more was
ever heard of the *North Star*. The *Sunshine* arrived
safely in the Thames on the 6th of October. The account
of her voyage was written by Master Henry Morgan,
the purser.

This second voyage was looked upon by Captain Davis
as very satisfactory. An immense extent of unknown
coast-line had been explored, several wide openings leading to the westward had been seen, and he was more
resolute than ever in his desire to continue the great
contest with Nature until the victory was won. Davis
had lost faith in Cumberland Gulf, but he had dis-

covered another great opening (Hudson Strait) which he
thought might be a passage; and his observations had
led him to the correct conclusion that " the north parts
of America are all islands." The evidence that these
tentative voyages might be made to pay their expenses
by bringing home cargoes of fish, was another encouraging result of this second attempt. Davis had been
unprovided with fishing gear, had been obliged to
make hooks out of bent nails, and to use his sounding-
lines to fish with; while his small stock of salt only
enabled him to bring home about thirty couple of cod.
Yet he had had ocular demonstration of the wonderful
abundance of fish on the coast of Labrador.

The explorer addressed a letter to Mr. William Sanderson from Exeter, on the 14th of October. His own
ship had brought home a cargo of cod-fish, and the *Sunshine* had on board 500 sealskins and 140 half-skins. He
wrote in feeling terms about the loss of the pinnace.
" God be merciful unto the poor men and preserve them,
if it be His blessed will." He assured Sanderson that
the extensive knowledge he had acquired of the Northern
regions had convinced him that the passage must be in
one of four places, or else that it did not exist. He
promised that if the attempt were continued there should
be some profit for the adventurers, and he declared that
he would forfeit all his hopes for the future, and even
his portion of his beloved Sandridge, rather than fail to
see the end of this great business. If all others fell
away, there would be no failing, no turning from the
plough where this good man and true was concerned.

CHAPTER IV.

DAVIS, as soon as he landed from his second voyage, proceeded to Exeter, to give an account to the West Country
merchants and urge them to continue the enterprise.
But they had lost heart. Their expectations of large
returns were not fulfilled. Davis wrote sadly that "all
the westerne marchant-adventurers fell from the action."
He would meet with a better reception in London,
but meanwhile he had an interval of rest at Sandridge. His wife had brought him another little boy
during his absence, who was named Arthur. For a
short time he enjoyed the pleasures of home, discussing
the prospects of the discovery with his neighbour and
lifelong friend, Adrian Gilbert, and inspiring the people
of Stoke Gabriel with some of his own enthusiasm.

During the winter Davis and Gilbert rode up to London together, to organise a third expedition with the
help of their unfailing friend, William Sanderson. This
merchant-prince was himself an accomplished geographer,
and a munificent patron of geographical research. His
great influence secured the support of a sufficient number
of adventurers in London to enable Davis to fit out a
third expedition, and the enterprise was encouraged by
the Lord Treasurer and Sir Francis Walsingham.

The winter and spring of 1587 was a busy time at
Dartmouth. The old *Sunshine*, having been battered by
the ice during two previous voyages, was in sad want of
repair, and another vessel was fitted out at Dartmouth,
called the *Elizabeth*. It was felt that there must be an
attempt to make the expedition at least pay its expenses,
and with this object two vessels were to be prepared
for the fishery. One of these was the *Sunshine ;* the
other was a clincher-built pinnace of about twenty tons,
called the *Ellen*. Her staunchness and sailing powers
were much praised by her former owners, but there
were some who felt doubtful about her from the first,
"falling into reckoning that she was a clincher." A
boat is clincher-built when the outside planks overlap
each other, an unusual build for a sea-going vessel even
in those days, and most dangerous in ice navigation.
The "clincher" was destined to give her crew a good
deal of trouble. A smaller pinnace was also framed by
Pearson, the carpenter, to be put together and used for
exploring when they reached the Greenland coast.

Captain Davis was a most popular commander. Men
who had once served with him always wanted to enter
again, and his shipmates soon began to share his enthusiasm for discovery. In the third voyage, William Bruton, who had been master of the *Moonshine* in 1585, now
entered as master of the *Elizabeth*. John Janes, the
author of the narrative of the first voyage, sailed again
as merchant for Mr. Sanderson, but really as friend and
counsellor of the commander. Davis also had the pleasure of being able to appoint a native of his own village
as pilot of the *Ellen*. The Churchwards were one of the
principal families of Stoke Gabriel. The name is the
first in the old parish register, which commences in

1550, and it continues to occur frequently down to the present time. John Churchward, like Davis and other natives of Stoke Gabriel, had adopted a sailor's life, and now took service under his fellow-townsman. Pearson, the carpenter, had shown ability and resource in the work of fitting out, and many of the seamen had already served with Davis. But the men of the *Sunshine* had been entered for fishing and not for discovery—a mistake which led to misunderstandings—and the old vessel could only be partially repaired.

At midnight on the 19th of May 1587 the *Sunshine*, *Elizabeth*, and clincher *Ellen* weighed their anchors and sailed out of Dartmouth harbour before a fresh gale from the north-east. On the 21st the expedition met the *Red Lion* homeward bound from Spain, and requested her captain to take a packet of letters directed to Master Sanderson. It was attempted to throw the parcel, with a weight attached to it, on board the homeward-bounder, but it fell short, and so only a message could be sent. Next day the Scilly Islands were sighted, and on the 25th the squadron was obliged to heave-to, while the *Sunshine* searched for a leak, which could only be kept under by five hundred strokes at the pump during each watch. The clincher proved a sad failure, and had to be towed, having lost her foremast.

During the voyage the master of the *Sunshine* had trouble with his crew, because they wanted to proceed at once to the fishery, while he insisted upon keeping company with the explorers until he received orders. He was afraid the men would shape a contrary course while he was asleep; but at length, after much discussion, the crew consented to keep company until Greenland was reached. On the 14th the rugged mountains, with the loom of the glacier between their peaks, was sighted, and in the afternoon of the 16th of June the squadron came to an anchor in Gilbert Sound.

Considering the importance of making the voyage pay its expenses, with a view to inducing adventurers to continue their efforts, Davis came to a resolution which was little less than heroic. He determined to dispatch both the *Sunshine* and the *Elizabeth* to the fishery, and to continue his voyage of discovery in the little clincher-built pinnace *Ellen*, of barely twenty tons. It was first necessary to put the small pinnace together, and the carpenters set to work, under Pearson's superintendence, on one of the islands. During the night of the 20th, when she was nearly ready for launching, the Eskimos came and tore away the two upper strakes for the sake of the iron. A blank cartridge was fired from a saker (a gun about ten feet long, firing a ball of four to seven pounds) to frighten them away, and the master of the *Elizabeth* went on shore immediately afterwards. But the boat had been seriously injured, and it was decided that she should be handed over to the *Elizabeth* to do service at the fishery.

A more serious disaster was reported on the following day. John Churchward, who was pilot in the *Ellen*, came to the captain with the alarming news that she had sprung a leak, and that it required three hundred strokes of the pump during a watch to keep her free of water. In this wretched little craft the explorers were to hazard their lives. All felt the crisis to be serious. Several hesitated. John Davis considered the matter, and his decision was worthy of him. He told his people that it would be better to end their lives with credit than to return with infamy and disgrace. The crew at once

accepted his words as final, and resolved to live and die
together.   So at midnight on the 21st the squadron finally
departed from Gilbert Sound, "our two barks for our fish-
ing-voyage, and myself in the pinnace for the discovery."

The *Ellen* proceeded northwards along the west coast

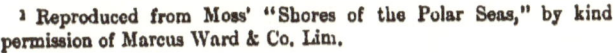

SANDERSON HIS HOPE.[1]

of Greenland, to which Davis gave the name of the
London Coast, occasionally bartering with Eskimos who
passed in their *kayaks*.   An observation taken by Davis
on the 30th showed them to be in latitude 72° 12′ N.,
with the sea quite open to the northward and westward.

1 Reproduced from Moss' "Shores of the Polar Seas," by kind
permission of Marcus Ward & Co. Lim.

It was the most northern point reached by the great
explorer. A lofty perpendicular cliff, which is in reality
one of several small islands off the coast, was named,
after the friend and chief promoter of the expedition—
"Sanderson his Hope;" for here it was that there
seemed to be the greatest hope of a passage. A very
grand sight was before the discoverers on that memorable 30th of June 1587. A bright blue sea extended to
the horizon on the north and west, obstructed by no ice
floes, but here and there a few majestic icebergs, with
snowy peaks shooting up into the sky, floated on the
bosom of the deep. Near the horizon, in the far distance, these icebergs, distorted by the refraction, were
raised up into the most fantastic and beautiful forms
imaginable. To the eastward were the granite mountains of Greenland, and beyond them the white line of
the mightiest glacier in the world, upheld by the mountain buttresses like huge caryatides. Rising immediately
above the tiny vessel was the beetling wall of Hope
Sanderson, with its summit 850 feet above the sea-level.
Its surface is slightly broken by narrow ledges, on which
hundreds of thousands of guillemots rear their young;
and when disturbed, they fly out in dense clouds, and
return after circling many times over the water. At its
base the sea was a sheet of foam and spray. The little
clincher of twenty tons would have looked like a bird
flapping its white wings over the water from the summit of the Hope, when she came thus to christen the
mighty cliff for all time. Insignificant as she appeared
amidst that scene of calm magnificence, there were great
and swelling hearts on board the *Ellen*, on whom the
grandeur of the scene must have made a deep impression. The refracted beauties on the northern horizon

were like a scene in fairyland,—a scene so utterly un-
like anything that is ever seen in lower latitudes, so
bright and beautiful that it must have seemed like the
very reflection of embodied hope to the weather-beaten
explorers. The mighty cliff was the leading mark of
" Sanderson his hope of a North-West Passage;" with
large, open water to the north. "No ice towards the
north, but a great sea, free, large, very salt and blue,
and of an unsearchable depth."

But that night the aspect of affairs changed. The
little pinnace was obliged to alter course to the west
owing to a strong northerly wind having sprung up, and
ran forty leagues in that direction without sighting land.
Captain Davis had been indefatigable with his scientific
observations throughout the voyage. He fixed the latitude of Sanderson's Hope correctly at 72° 12' N. The
variation of the compass was 28° W., and the sun was
5° above the horizon at midnight, the weather being
warm and calm. Davis paid close attention to the
phenomena of terrestrial magnetism, a subject the importance of which was beginning to be appreciated. The
series of observations for variation at London was commenced in 1580, and in the following year William
Borough published his "Discourse of the Compass or
Magnetical Needle." This was followed in 1585 by
Robert Norman's "New Attractive," in which the "new
discovered secret and subtil propertie" of the dip of the
magnetic needle is explained. The investigations into
the properties of the magnet were well known to Captain
Davis, who did his best to increase the data on which they
were based by careful observations during his voyages.

On the 2nd of July the little *Ellen* encountered a
"mighty bank of ice," lying north and south, which

checked her progress. This was the famous "middle pack," a mass of ice drifting towards the Atlantic, and sometimes extending for 200 miles, its average thickness being eight feet. The prevalent wind is from the north-west, and the ice mass is thus steadily drifted south-wards, leaving a sheet of navigable water in its wake. The wind prevented Davis from carrying out his first intention of doubling the northern end of the pack, and reaching the "north water." He therefore coasted it to the southward, hoping to double the southern end and then run westward in search of a passage. On the 3rd and 4th the weather was foggy; but on the 6th it was very clear, and a close examination resulted in the belief that a lane of water through the pack would lead to an open and navigable sea. These appearances are too often deceptive, and they proved so in the present instance. The *Ellen* was taken up a lane of water by means of oars for a distance of five leagues westerly; but the ice had closed up, the hopeful appearances of open water had disappeared, and there was nothing for it but to retrace her steps and escape from being beset in the ice. Fortunately, it was nearly calm, and by midnight of the 8th the explorers recovered the open sea to the eastward. Coasting along the pack for three more days, in calm but foggy weather, they sighted the western coast of Davis Strait, and bartered with some natives who came out to sea in their *kayaks*.

Mount Raleigh, the lofty hill which had been dis-covered and named during the first voyage, was sighted on the 19th of July, and by midnight the little pinnace was off the entrance of Cumberland Gulf. Davis de-cided to make a second examination of this great open-ing, and sailed along its northern entrance until he

reached the group of islands at the end, which were also
named after the adventurous young Earl of Cumberland.
A large whale passed the *Ellen* while she was at anchor,
going westward among the islands. Here Davis again
observed for variation, and found it to be 30°.

Davis shaped a course on the 24th to recover the
open sea, and being becalmed at the entrance of the
gulf on the 25th, William Bruton, the master, went on
shore with a boat's crew to course with their dogs. But
the dogs had become so fat on board ship that they were
scarcely able to run. Proceeding on their voyage southward, they came to a wide opening between 62° and 63°
N. latitude, to which Davis gave the name of Lord
Lumley's Inlet; and a headland passed on the 31st was
called the Earl of Warwick's Foreland. The inlet was
clearly Frobisher's Strait, and the land was no other than
the *Meta Incognita* of that navigator. This has been
placed beyond any doubt through the discovery of the
remains of Frobisher's expedition in recent years by
Captain Hall. But the error in longitude led geographers to place the discoveries of Frobisher in Greenland. They are thus shown on the map of the world of
1600, and this was certainly the belief of Davis.

Next came the discovery of the great strait, at the
mouth of which there were confused currents, called on
the Molyneux globe, and on the "New Map" of 1599,
"the furious overfall." Davis says in the log: "We fell
into a mighty race, where an island of ice was carried by
the force of the current as fast as our barke could sail.
We saw the sea falling down into the gulfe with a mighty
overfal, and roring, with divers circular motions like
whirlepooles, in such sort as forcible streams passe thorow
the arches of bridges." Mr. Janes in his journal says:

"We passed by a very great gulfe, the water whirling
and roring as it were the meeting of tides." Thus did
Davis point out the way to future important discoveries.
His exploratory labours threw the light which marked
the way. "He did, I conceive," said Luke Fox many
years afterwards, "light Hudson into his strait." After
coasting along an ice-floe which had drifted out of the

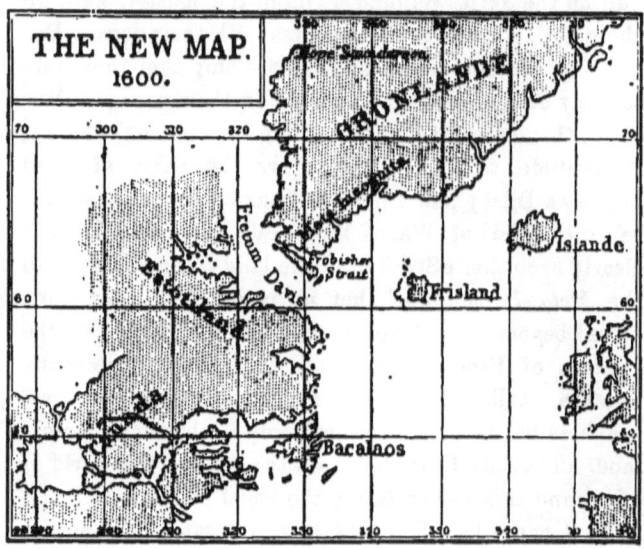

DAVIS STRAIT.

strait, Davis came to the point of land which formed its
southern entrance, and named it Cape Chudleigh (or
Chidley), after his Devonshire friend. Continuing the
voyage, they named an island off the Labrador coast
after Lord Darcy on the 12th of August.

A boat's crew landed on Darcy Island with Mr.
Janes, in hopes of securing some deer that had been

seen from the ship browsing on its slopes. After chasing them twice round the island, the deer took the sea, and swam in the direction of some other islands. The boat was unable to overtake them, but Mr. Janes shot a grey hare on Darcy Island, which was the sole result of his excursion. The rendezvous for the fishing-vessels *Sunshine* and *Elizabeth* was at the islands off the Labrador coast in 54° N., and, in looking for them, the *Ellen* struck upon a rock; and was in considerable danger, as she sprung a serious leak. Necessary repairs were effected during a gale of wind; and on the 15th of August, when in latitude 52° 12′ N., and thirty-six miles from the shore, Captain Davis " shaped a course for England in God's name." The fishing-ground had been appointed by Davis to be between 54° and 55° N. The captains of the *Sunshine* and *Elizabeth* had been ordered to erect cairns on every headland within twenty leagues of their fishing-ground, but nothing of the kind had been done. The vessels had probably returned home without carrying out their instructions. When she commenced her voyage, the *Ellen* had very little fuel left, and only half a hogshead of water. After much variable weather, the little pinnace, with her gallant crew, arrived safely at Dartmouth on the 15th of September 1587, and the discoverers landed, "giving thanks to God for their safe arrival."

· The narratives of the first and third Arctic voyages of Davis were written by Mr. John Janes; the second was written by Davis himself, the detached voyage of the *Sunshine* being narrated by Henry Morgan, the purser. Davis doubtless kept logs during all three voyages, and drew charts as the results of his surveys; but the log of his third voyage is the only one that has been preserved. The columns are headed with the months, days, hours, courses, distances run, winds, elevation of the pole or latitude, and remarks. He called it his "Traverse Book." The narratives were first published in 1589 in Hakluyt's "Principal Navigations." In his "World's Hydrographical Description" Davis gives a brief *résumé* of the three voyages and of their results.

We have no account of the return of the *Sunshine* and *Elizabeth*, nor of the result of their fishing. Captain Davis had continued a hazardous voyage of discovery, and had exposed himself and his gallant followers to great risk and danger in the little "clincher," in order that the adventurers who had promoted the voyage might not be losers. We may reasonably hope that the captain's object was secured, that the fishery was successful, and that the expedition paid its expenses, besides adding largely to geographical knowledge.

The country was in a state of preparation for a desperate struggle with Philip of Spain. Sluys had fallen, and the Duke of Parma was carrying all before him. The invasion of England was threatened, and the thoughts of every Englishman were concentrated on the defence of his native country. Davis rendered an account of his discoveries to Mr. Sanderson, to Sir Walter Raleigh, and to Adrian Gilbert. They all appreciated his great achievement, and continued to be his true and constant friends. He conferred with Master Hakluyt on the incidents of his voyages, with Master Molyneux on his surveys, and with Master Edward Wright on his scientific observations. But for the present, there could be no thought of further discovery. The country was in danger, and every faculty of her sons must be devoted to the work of diverting or overcoming it. "By reason of the Spanish fleet and the unfortunate time of Mr. Secretary's death, the voyage was omitted and never since attempted."

Once more John Davis returned to the home of his boyhood, to beautiful Sandridge. Another child had been born in his absence, and had been baptized in Stoke Gabriel Church with his father's name on the 8th of July 1587—the very day on which the admirable seamanship of that father had extricated his vessel from the perils of the middle pack. The brave sailor now had three little boys playing round his knees, and his wife Faith was still true and loyal. Alas! that those sweet bells should ever have become jangled and out of tune.

We may now take stock of the Arctic discoveries achieved by John Davis. Norsemen had settled in Greenland centuries before, and had disappeared. Cabot had been on the Labrador coast; Cortereal and other Portuguese had followed in his track, and had possibly reached Ungava Bay within Hudson's Strait. Frobisher had, more recently, collected imaginary ores on the shores of *Meta Incognita*, but the position of his discovery was unsettled. No navigator, however, had previously entered those seas whose scientific knowledge could be compared with that of John Davis. All the coasts and seas not actually discovered were laid down and mapped afresh, and must be considered to have been rediscovered and first brought within the actual knowledge of his generation by him.

The great continent of Greenland, though indicated on the Zeno map, was rediscovered and made known by Davis. Including the work of Captain Pope in 1586, the east coast was traced from the latitude of the

E

northern point of Iceland to Cape Farewell. The west
coast was laid down by Davis himself, from Cape Farewell
in 60° N. to Sanderson's Hope in 72° 12′ N., a distance of
732 miles. But he did not merely define the coast-lines
and make certain the existence of the great mass of land
which had long been vaguely known as Greenland. He
collected information respecting the physical conditions
of land and sea. He found that heavy floes of ice were
pressed upon the east coast and the southern part of
the west coast, so that it was impossible to approach the
land within several leagues. This is the ice brought
down by the great *southerly* current, which, flowing down
the east coast of Greenland, is checked in its passage by
the Gulf Stream flowing athwart its course. Its ice-
encumbered waters are thus diverted, and made to turn
round Cape Farewell and up the west coast, until they
are met by the current flowing south from Baffin's Bay,
and again diverted. Thus it was that Davis was baffled
in all his attempts to reach the land until he arrived at
the part of the west coast to the north of this diverted
southerly current. Gilbert Sound was found to be clear
of ice long before the coast to the southward. In all
three voyages, Gilbert Sound, in 64° N., was the first
land reached, while the places to the southward could
not be visited until much later in the summer.

The continent of Greenland is 1400 miles in length
by about 400 miles in its widest part, and, except a rim
of granitic mountains along the coast, which is broken
by deep inlets or fiords fringed with numerous islands,
it is covered by one enormous glacier. The glacier re-
ceives the snowfall from year to year, and its vast mass
is pressed outwards in all directions. At certain points
it reaches the heads of the deepest fiords, and is forced

down them until the outer ends float on the water, and
are broken off, forming icebergs. These offshoots of the
main glacier at the heads of fiords are called "discharging glaciers," and they send forth the great harvest of
icebergs which float on the surface of Davis Strait, and
are drifted into the Atlantic during the early summer.
John Davis observed these natural phenomena with
admiration and astonishment. He saw the blink of
the glacier beyond the granite mountains; he examined
some of the largest icebergs, and correctly divined their
origin.

The mountains forming the rim which confines the
inland glacier present a magnificent aspect from the
sea. The long narrow promontories running out from
them and the innumerable islands are all of the same
primitive formation. Davis examined these rocks with
care, and noticed the same shining veins of mica which
Frobisher had mistaken for ores of the precious metals.
He made long boat expeditions up the fiords, and
climbed several hills to obtain a correct idea of the
nature of the country. He also noticed the character
of the vegetation, enumerating the dwarf willow, the
birch, the cloud-berry, and several humble flowering
herbs. The driftwood which comes down with the East
Greenland current was puzzling, and he was unable
to account for its appearance.

The animal life, which is so abundant in Arctic seas,
was observed with great interest by Davis and his companions. The fish, the numerous seals, the "great
store" of whales, and the white bears were seen in
great quantities; and boats' crews were sent away in
chase whenever a chance offered; while reindeer, hares,
and foxes were hunted on the promontories and islands.

Most of the Arctic birds are referred to in the narratives
of Davis's voyages, and the incredible numbers of gulls
and guillemots, breeding on the cliffs or dotted over the
calm surface of the sea, was another cause for admiration, as well as a means of supplementing the allowance
of provisions.

Davis took special pains to describe the Eskimos,
their superstitions and customs, their habits and mode
of life, their tents and _kayaks_ or sealskin canoes; and
he collected a vocabulary of their language.

In Denmark there was a tradition, still tolerably fresh
in men's minds, of a lost colony in Greenland; but the
Sagas recording that interesting episode were known to
few. They relate how, in the tenth century, a Norse-
man settled in Iceland, named Erik Rada, had discovered
a land to the westward and named it Greenland; how
he had returned and brought back settlers, who established themselves on the shores of the deep fiords; how
churches were built and a bishopric created. They tell .
how Lief, the son of Erik, and his brothers, discovered
countries still farther to the westward, named Vinland,
Markland, Helluland; believed to have been Massachu-
setts, Nova Scotia, and Newfoundland. Later chroni-
cles record that after the middle of the fourteenth century, when the black death spread havoc over Europe,
all communication with the Greenland colony ceased,
and that the Norse settlers were supposed to have been
destroyed by a small race of men coming from the north,
called Skrællings.

Two centuries had elapsed, and Davis was the first to
revisit the sites of the old Norse colonies. He found
the Skrællings, afterwards called Eskimos, in undis-
puted possession. Of the Norsemen he had never heard,

and he saw no sign of them. He gave a full description
of the people he met with, and he also mentioned the
discovery of a grave with a cross upon it. Other Norse
graves have since been discovered with runic inscrip-
tions. To Davis is due the honour of having rediscovered Greenland after that great region had been
buried in oblivion for more than two centuries.

Davis also explored that sea which has ever since
been known as Davis Strait. He found it open and
navigable along the west coast of Greenland as far as
72° 12' N. He discovered the position of the middle
pack of ice, its character and drift. Not content with
coasting along its edge, he forced his way into the pack,
and was beset for several days in a most perilous position.

In his "World's Hydrographical Description" he gives
an account of the different kinds of ice met with in the
Arctic regions. He explains how icebergs are formed
by being detached from the glaciers bordering on the
deep sea in the fiords, and how they carry off great
boulders of rock. He tried experiments to ascertain the
flotation of ice, and showed the reason that the icebergs
"calve" and turn over.

His extensive discoveries and surveys along the
western shores of Davis Strait were equally important.
He ascertained the existence of three great openings,
one of which he twice explored. These were the
Earl of Cumberland's Gulf, Lord Lumley's Inlet, and
the great opening to which he gave no name, but
which was Hudson's Strait. Cumberland's Gulf has
since been proved to extend for 160 miles, and Lumley's
Inlet is now known to be identical with the so-called
Frobisher's Strait. But Hudson's Strait is one route,
by Hecla and Fury Strait and Bellot's Strait, to Bering's

Strait, and consequently a North-West Passage. Sanderson's Hope, the limit of the northern discoveries of Davis, is the portal of another passage by way of Barrow and Peel Straits. It is the route taken by Sir John Franklin, and by which that great navigator would have achieved his object if he had been aware that King William's Land was an island. In his letter to Master Sanderson, Davis said that there were four openings discovered by him, any one of which might turn out to be the long-sought passage. Modern research has proved that no less than two of these actually are North-West Passages.

. Davis also examined and laid down the whole coast of Labrador from Cape Chidley to Newfoundland. A recent writer has correctly observed that "it is to Davis that we owe the most exact knowledge of the Labrador coast until modern times."[1] Cabot, Cortereal, and others are known to have visited this coast, but it is to Davis that we owe its first intelligible delineation. The practical results of the great seaman's work were the opening of a most lucrative whale and seal fishery in Davis Strait, the extension of the cod-fishery to the coast of Labrador, and the eventual recolonisation of Greenland. All these benefits may be traced in their origin to the discoveries of Davis. His scientific observations were made with regularity and care. He fixed his latitudes by meridian altitudes of heavenly bodies, and took a regular series of observations for the variation of the compass, and probably also for the dip of the magnetic needle. His diligently worked system of dead-reckoning, combined with astronomical observations, enabled him to prepare

[1] Professor Packard, Bulletin of the American Geographical Society, vol. xx. No. 2, p. 225 (June 1888).

charts of his discoveries, and his nautical experience suggested improvements in methods of observing and working which were of great service during that and the next generation to his brother seamen.

Davis converted the Arctic regions from a confused myth into a defined area, the physical aspects and conditions of which were understood so far as they were known. He not only described and mapped the extensive tract explored by himself, but he clearly pointed out the work cut out for his successors. He lighted Hudson into his strait. He lighted Baffin into his bay. He lighted Hans Egede to the scene of his Greenland labours. But he did more. His true-hearted devotion to the cause of Arctic discovery, his patient scientific research, his loyalty to his employers, his dauntless gallantry and enthusiasm, form an example which will be a beacon-light to maritime explorers for all time to come.

CHAPTER V.

WAR SERVICES.

DURING the three years following his return from the Arctic regions, John Davis, like every other British seaman of distinction, was engaged on services connected with the war with Spain.

Queen Elizabeth had entered upon a war for the defence of the Netherlands in 1585. Philip II. determined to make a great effort to destroy the power of England by invading his enemy's country, and enforcing his claim to the crown as the legitimate representative of the House of Lancaster. Preparations were made in the ports of Spain on a gigantic scale, ships and men being collected from all parts of Philip's European dominions. The great reliance of Spain, as regards her navy, was on the hardy seamen of the Basque provinces. Sebastian del Cano, who was born on the shores of the Bay of Biscay, was the first to circumnavigate the globe, and Basques, or "Biscayners," as the English called them, were the earliest pioneers of the whale-fishery. They were equally efficient in maritime warfare, and the squadron of Guipuzcoa under Don Miguel de Oquendo, and of Biscay under Don Juan Martinez de Recalde, formed the backbone of the Spanish Armada. At Bilbao and Santander, twelve of the finest ships in

Philip's navy had recently been built, and named after the twelve apostles. The squadron of Andalusia was commanded by Don Pedro de Valdez, an officer well acquainted with the navigation of the British Channel, and Don Hugo de Monçada was chief of the galleasses. The Castilian admiral was Don Diego Flores de Valdez, who lost his nerve. He had under his command several brave and noble captains, including the Marques de Peñafiel in the *San Marcos*, Don Diego de Pimentel in the *San Mateo*, Don Agustin Mesia in the *San Luis*, Don Francisco de Toledo in the *San Felipe*, Don Diego Enriquez in the *San Juan*, and Don Antonio Pereyra in the *Santiago*. Martin de Ventendona, Gaspar de Sousa, and Diego Tellez Enriquez led the Italian contingents in the *San Juan de Sicilia* and the galleon of Florence. The land forces consisted of 20,000 soldiers. They were led by Don Alonzo de Leyva, a brilliant and dashing cavalier, who had commanded a regiment of noblemen at Gemblour. He embarked on board the *Rata*, and had Maurice Fitzgerald, Caly O'Connor, and other Irish rebels in his company.

The whole Armada consisted of 129 vessels, seven of which were upwards of 1000 tons, manned by 8000 sailors and 1000 gentlemen volunteers, and seventy-two galleys rowed by 2080 galley-slaves. The ships were built with very high poops and forecastles, and were inferior to the English in sailing qualities and in the weight of their broadsides. The whole Armada was under the command of the Duke of Medina Sidonia, a nobleman of the highest rank and of tried courage and conduct. He hoisted his flag on board the *San Marcos*, with orders to sail up the Channel, form a junction with the Duke of Parma at Dunkirk, and convoy his army

across to the shores of England. The Armada assembled
at Ferrol, and on the 2nd of July the mighty fleet sailed
for the English Channel.

England was not unprepared. She had already
entered upon her third campaign against Spain in
the Netherlands, and Lord Willoughby, with the pick
of the English companies, was at Bergen-op-Zoom.
Under the fostering care of Sir John Hawkins, the
Queen possessed a navy, provided with ordnance, which
was quite equal to that of Spain, placing her in the
first rank as a fighting naval power. The largest guns,
called cannons, threw a shot of 66 lbs.; and of these
there were twenty-six, distributed among the ten largest
ships. The demi-cannons were 32-pounders, and of these
there were fifty-four in the twelve largest ships; and
the *culverins*, with shot weighing 17 lbs., were distributed among the sixteen largest ships. The heaviest
armament consisted of four *cannons*, four *demi-cannons*,
twelve *culverins*, and twenty-two smaller pieces. The
small vessels were armed with *demi-culverins* having $9\frac{1}{2}$-
pound shot, and *sakers* throwing shot of $3\frac{1}{2}$ lbs. Great
improvements had also been made in the construction
of the Queen's ships. In 1583, under the able superintendence of Sir John Hawkins, five new ships had been
built. These were the *Triumph*, of 1100 tons, the *White
Bear*, and *Elizabeth Jonas*, of 900, and the *Ark* and *Victory*, of 800 tons. The improvements consisted in their
sterns and forecastles being lower, their keels longer,
and their lines generally finer and sharper. The *Hope*,
of 800 tons, was a ship of the same class, but some years
older. Three ships were of 600 tons, namely, the *Lion*,
Elizabeth Bonaventure, and *Mary Rose*, and were of an
earlier type. The famous old *Revenge*, built in the year

1579, was one of four 500-ton ships, the others being
the *Nonpareil, Rainbow,* and *Vanguard.* The *Dreadnought* and *Swiftsure* were 400 tons, the *Antelope, Swallow,* and *Foresight* from 350 to 300 ton ships. These
eighteen large vessels formed the line of battle. There
were also the *Aid* of 240 tons, and fifteen smaller vessels
from 160 to 20 tons.

The preparations of the Spanish Armada were reported
in England, and aroused vehement patriotic feeling
throughout the land. Noblemen, wealthy merchants,
and seaport towns came forward with money and volunteer ships, and all seamen eagerly sought for employment against the enemy. The Queen's ships were placed
in commission under the Lord Howard of Effingham,
Lord High Admiral, whose flag was on board the *Ark
Royal,* with Roger Townshend as his flag-captain. He
obtained the command of two of the finest new ships,
the *White Bear* and the *Elizabeth Jonas,* for his nephew
Lord Sheffield and his son-in-law Sir Robert Southwell,
while his cousin Lord Thomas Howard had the *Lion.*
Lord Henry Seymour and the Earl of Cumberland had
the *Rainbow* and the *Elizabeth Bonaventure.* Eight ships
were commanded by sailors whose names are honourably
known to geographers, and Arctic men were of course
well to the front. Martin Frobisher had the *Triumph,*
the largest ship in the navy, Captain Fenton was in the
Mary Rose, and John Davis in the *Black Dog.* Sir John
Hawkins, to whose ability and zeal the efficiency of the
fleet was mainly due, embarked on board the *Victory,*
one of the ships of his new design, and he had sufficient
interest to obtain the command of the *Swallow* for his
gallant young son Richard. Sir Francis Drake, the
renowned circumnavigator, had the *Revenge,* and a

number of armed merchant-vessels were under his command. His old colleague, Sir William Winter, was in
the *Vanguard*, and Captain Fenner had the *Nonpareil*,
with his two brothers Edward and William in the command of the *Mary Rose* and *Aid*. Robert Cross, who
was afterwards a commander of great distinction, Sir
George Beeston, and Sir Henry Palmer had the *Hope*,
Dreadnought, and *Antelope*, while Christopher Baker was
in the *Foresight*. One other officer of the fleet was
destined to be well known both as a gallant sea-captain
and as an intelligent writer on naval matters, but he
had no separate command. This was Sir William
Monson, who was serving on board the *Charles*, a
little vessel of 70 tons with an armament of sixteen
sakers.

Lord Howard took the sea with Sir Francis Drake
as his Vice-, and Sir John Hawkins as his Rear-Admiral.
Lord Henry Seymour, with the *Rainbow*, *Vanguard*,
Antelope, and a squadron of smaller ships was stationed
off Calais to watch the movements of the Duke of
Parma, whose army was assembling at Dunkirk. The
Lord Admiral with the rest of the fleet cruised to the
westward, with head-quarters at Plymouth. When,
early in July 1588, Lord Howard signified to the Queen
the great difference in power between the English and
Spanish, and advised her to send more aid to the sea,
the patriotic enthusiasm rose to boiling-point. Many
noblemen and gentlemen, the names of fourteen of
whom are recorded by Stowe and Camden, fitted out
vessels at their own expense, and put to sea as a
volunteer squadron under the command of Sir Walter
Raleigh. London sent sixteen ships and four pinnaces,
the Merchant Adventurers sent ten, while Bristol, Exeter,

Plymouth, Barnstaple, and Dartmouth all sent their contingents.

So zealous and patriotic a seaman as John Davis could not be less forward than his fellows in those busy times. From his home at Sandridge he could give the benefit of his knowledge and experience either to the officials at Plymouth or to his neighbours at Dartmouth, who were busily fitting out two vessels, the *Crescent* of 70 and the *Hart* of 30 tons, commanded respectively by John Wylson and James Houston, as their contingent towards the defence of their country. For active service afloat, Captain Davis would be in demand as an expert pilot. We have seen how zealously he seized the opportunity of a few days' detention to make a survey of the Scilly Islands. He was also a Channel pilot, and had constructed a chart of the *Slieve* (as the English Channel was then called), with soundings, mainly from his own surveys. His ability and zeal were well known; and although he had not sufficient interest to obtain the command of a large ship, he was appointed to a hired vessel of twenty tons, called the *Black Dog*, to act as a tender to the Lord Admiral. She had a crew of ten men and an armament of three *sakers*. Her duty would be to remain near the flag-ship, to act as a cruiser and dispatch-vessel, and to pilot the Admiral in case of need. She served throughout the campaign, with the crew receiving the Queen's pay. The *Ark Royal* and the rest of the fleet were in Plymouth Sound, except the squadron under Seymour off Calais, when Captain Fleming arrived in hot haste to report having sighted the Armada off the Lizard on the 20th of July 1588.

Soon the stately Spanish ships were seen rounding

Rame Head, and the English fleet at once put to sea.
Lord Howard allowed the long line to pass, and then
made a furious attack on the *Rata*, which was commanded
by Don Alonzo de Leyva, and brought up the rear.
The *Ark Royal* was supported by the *Triumph*, while
the squadron of Biscay under Don Juan Martinez de
Recalde, the Vice-Admiral, rallied to the support of
Leyva. The English fought until their ammunition
was nearly exhausted. It would be on such occasions
as these that the services of Davis would have been
valuable, to run in for stores and provisions, and to act
as a scout when the combatants drew off.

The night of the 21st was disastrous to the Spaniards.
The *Ark Royal*, *Bear*, and *Mary Rose*, with their tenders
in advance, followed the hostile fleet. In the dead of
night the sky was lighted up from the blaze of a Spanish
ship. It was the flag-ship of Oquendo, the Admiral of
Guipuzcoa, who turned her adrift and shifted his flag
on board another vessel. In coming to her assistance,
the *Capitana* of Don Pedro de Valdez ran into the
Santa Catalina, losing her foremast and bowsprit. Having been left behind, and the ship not being under con-
trol, he surrendered to Drake, and was towed into
Dartmouth, while the abandoned Guipuzcoan flag-ship
was taken into Weymouth. It was not until the evening of the 22nd that Drake rejoined the Admiral.

During the 23rd the wind blew from the north, and
both fleets, as they sailed up Channel, manœuvred to
gain the weather-gage. A desperate action was fought
all the afternoon until evening, Lord Howard trying
conclusions with the Marques de Peñafiel, who was in
the *San Marcos* of 792 tons. Many other ships were
engaged, including several volunteers, and Camden

mentions "*Solus Cockus Anglus in sua, inter medios hostes, navicula cum laude periit.*" All honour to "Cockus Anglus!" concerning whom we know nothing more than his glorious death. It was almost a dead calm on the 24th, and Lord Howard was occupied in organising his fleet in four divisions.

A fiercely contested action was fought off the back of the Isle of Wight on the 25th, when the Admiral in the *Ark Royal* led his division, consisting of the *Lion* under Lord Thomás Howard, the *Bear* under Lord Sheffield, the *Elizabeth Jonas* under Sir Robert Southwell, and the *Victory* under Sir John Hawkins, into the centre of the Spanish fleet. It was the whole Howard connection. Admiral Oquendo, in his new flag-ship of 900 tons, engaged the English flag-ship and rammed her stern, unshipping the rudder. The *Triumph* under Frobisher, the *Nonpareil*, and *Mary Rose* then joined in the fray, captured a Spanish ship, and towed the *Ark Royal* out of action; but the *Triumph* was seriously injured. For their gallantry in this action Lord Howard knighted Lord Thomas Howard, Lord Sheffield, Hawkins, Frobisher, and his flag-captain, Roger Townshend.

There were no hostilities on the 26th and 27th, and these no doubt were busy days for the Lord Admiral's tender, passing to and fro with ammunition and stores. Lord Howard went to Dover himself on the 27th, and forming a junction with the squadron of Lord Henry Seymour, he followed the Spanish fleet to Calais Roads, which they had reached on the same day. The two fleets were anchored within half a mile of each other.

During the whole of the 28th of July Lord Howard was preparing to send fireships down into the Spanish fleet. "He emptied eight of his basest barkes," says

Stowe, "and put therein combustible matter, which in
the evening were subtillie set on fire, and, with advantage of wind and tide, guided within reach of cannon-
shot before the Spaniards could discern the same. Then
the flames grew fierce with sudden terror to the enemy,
in which fear they were all amazed with shrikes and
loud outcryes, to the great astonishment of the neare
inhabitants. Some cut cables, others let the hawsers
slip, and happiest they could first begone, though few
could tell what course to take." The Duke of Medina
Sidonia kept his head, ordering the fleet to weigh and
rendezvous at Gravelines; but the other commanders
appear to have been completely demoralised. The *San
Lorenzo*, under Hugo de Monçada, went on shore at
Calais, all hands being lost.

While still in disorder, the Spanish fleet was attacked
by the bulk of the English ships, led by Howard and
Drake, on the 29th. Recalde, Oquendo, and Leyva
gallantly strove to keep a squadron together for the
protection of the transports. But it was to no purpose.
The *San Mateo, San Felipe*, and others were driven on
shore on the coast of Flanders. On the 30th there was
a hard gale from the N.W. which shifted to the S.W.,
and the Duke, after a council of war, resolved to return
to Spain by running before the storm and rounding the
North of Scotland. Thus the victory was completed by
the elements, and only fifty-four ships escaped. The
barbarous treatment of the Spaniards who were shipwrecked on the coast of Ireland is an indelible stain on
the British scutcheon, and, to some extent, throws a
shade on the brilliant record of that eventful year.

The *Black Dog*, relieved of her duties as tender to the
Ark Royal, went back to Plymouth, and Captain Davis

returned home after ten days of hard and most memorable service.   It was doubtless in memory of this service
under the Lord High Admiral that he dedicated his
work on navigation, entitled "The Seaman's Secrets," to
Lord Howard of Effingham.   He was at Sandridge when
his fourth child was born.   It was seldom that his active
service in distant seas allowed the brave sailor to be
present at family ceremonies.   But he stood at the font
in Stoke Gabriel Church when this child was baptized
with the name of Philip on the 9th of February 1589.

The total overthrow of the great Armada of Spain
was immediately followed by numerous enterprises,
undertaken for the purpose of harassing and destroying
Spanish commerce, and ships were fitted out by noblemen and merchants, with the approval, and often with
the assistance, of the Government.   John Davis had a
firm friend in Sir Walter Raleigh, and he deservedly
retained the full confidence of Master Sanderson.   He,
therefore, had good reason to hope that he would receive
a command with the object of carrying on the war with
his country's enemies.

George Clifford, the young Earl of Cumberland, had
been fond of mathematics and geographical science ever
since he was a student at Oxford, and in those early
days he had formed the acquaintance of Captain Davis,
who had named a deep inlet on the west side of Davis
Strait in his honour.   He had grown up to be a nobleman of a most adventurous disposition.   He had commanded the *Elizabeth Bonaventure* with credit in the
repulse of the Spanish Armada.   In the following year
he determined to lead an expedition at his own expense
to prey upon Spanish commerce.   The Queen lent him
one of her ships, the *Victory*, of 800 tons, and he fitted

F

out three small vessels, called the *Margaret* and the *Meg*, and a caravel. His chief reliance was on Captain Christopher Lister, a neighbour in Yorkshire, a man of great resolution; and he also had with him, as captain of the *Meg*, the same William Monson who had served on board the *Charles* in the fleet that repulsed the Spanish Armada, and who was destined to rise to high rank in the navy. The eminent mathematician and cosmographer, Master Edward Wright, was induced to accompany the Earl, and he was the historian of the voyage. Several gentlemen volunteers embarked in the enterprise, and there were rather less than 400 soldiers and sailors. The Earl of Cumberland's expedition sailed from Plymouth on the 18th of June 1589.

John Davis succeeded in obtaining employment of the same kind. He fitted out a ship called the *Drake* and a pinnace, the owner of which was, in all probability, his old friend Master Sanderson, the intention being to unite his forces with those of the Earl of Cumberland. Davis had for a consort a ship called the *Barke of Lime*, owned by Sir Walter Raleigh, and commanded by Captain Markesbury. The destination of these ships was the Azores in Mid-Atlantic; but we can only derive any knowledge of the proceedings of Davis from the allusions to them in Master Wright's narrative of the voyage of the Earl of Cumberland, which, therefore, must needs be our guide.

Leaving Plymouth on the 18th, the Earl captured three French vessels on the 21st of June, which were found to be Leaguers, and consequently lawful prizes. Two were sent to Plymouth, and the third conveyed all the French crews to one of their own ports. Next he met some ships of Rotterdam and Emden bound for

Rochelle, which were dismissed; and then some English vessels returning from the expedition to Portugal. They were supplied with provisions and water. Thus he proceeded on his course to the Azores, challenging every ship he met, fighting if they resisted search, dismissing friends, making prize of Spaniards or French Leaguers, and seizing property belonging to an enemy. On the 1st of August he sighted the Island of St. Michael's, and cut three ships out from under the guns of a castle, creating uproar and confusion in the principal port. The ships were laden with wine, pepper, and salad-oil, and on the 7th another small vessel was captured between St. Michael's and Terceira, with a cargo of good Madeira wine, woollen cloth, and silk. When the predatory little squadron arrived at Flores, the most westerly island of the Azores, the Earl was able to keep on friendly terms with the inhabitants by paying for their fresh water and provisions in oil, wine, and pepper. Mr. Wright went on shore at Flores, and found the town of Santa Cruz in ruins, owing to attacks of English privateers. In returning to the ship, a huge fish, with jaws gaping a yard and a half wide, pursued his boat, and he feared it would be capsized, "but by rowing as hard as we could, God be praised, we escaped." The learned mathematician, who had gone to sea to observe the practical working of problems in nautical astronomy, was passing through strange experiences.

Captain Davis joined the Earl of Cumberland's squadron between Flores and Fayal in the *Drake*, and his Lordship's force was increased at the same time by the *Barke of Lime* under Captain Markesbury, and by a small vessel called the *Saucy Jack*.

The Azores are divided into three clusters, Flores and

Corvo to the west; Fayal, Pico, St. George, Terceira, and Graciosa in the centre; St. Michael's and St. Mary in the east. Fayal is a beautiful island, so named from the beech forests with which it was covered at the time of its discovery in the fifteenth century. The hills rise from the seaside to high moorlands in the centre, cut here and there by deep ravines. The lower slopes are cultivated, while the hill-tops and moorlands are covered

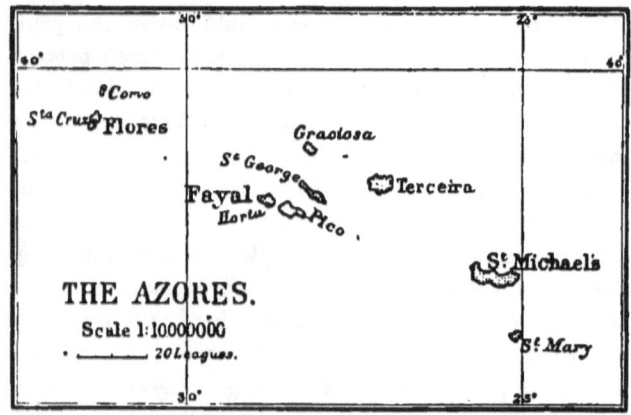

THE AZORES.

with myrtle and other flowering shrubs. Fruit orchards abound in the neighbourhood of villages, and the vegetation is like that of the Riviera. The chief town, called Horta, is built along the stony shore of a road-stead which is much exposed to the prevailing winds, and from the sea-wall, or the steep hills overhanging the town, there is a magnificent view of the volcanic peak which forms the adjacent island of Pico. Fayal was colonised by Flemings in the days of the Portuguese Duchess of Burgundy, and their descendants had

as yet mingled their blood but slightly with that of
the inhabitants of the Iberian peninsula.

Cumberland's squadron reached Fayal Roads on the
27th of August; and seeing some vessels at anchor, the
Earl sent Captains Lister and Monson, with the *Saucy
Jack* and some skiffs, to cut them out. A ship of 250
tons with fourteen guns was moored under the fire of
the castle. One English boat's crew boarded her over the
quarter, another in the hawse. Most of the Spaniards
jumped overboard. The prize was towed clear under a
heavy fire from the castle, and was found to be laden
with sugar, ginger, and hides from Puerto Rico. Three
smaller vessels were also captured, with cargoes of elephants' teeth, grain, cocoa-nuts, and skins from Guinea.
They were sent to England as prizes, and on the 31st
the squadron made sail in the direction of the island
of Terceira. Next morning a boat under sail was
sighted coming out from under the land. It proved to
be manned by eight Englishmen who had escaped from
imprisonment. Finding a boat on the beach, they
shoved off and put out to sea, with no other yard for
their mainsail than two barrel-staves fished together,
and no provisions but what they could take in their
pockets and bosoms. They brought certain intelligence
that the rich West Indian galleons, for which the Earl
of Cumberland was in search, had sailed for Spain a
week before.

For ten days the ships were delayed by calms or
light and baffling winds in sight of Pico; and it was
not until the 10th of September that they entered
Fayal Roads again, with the intention of attacking the
town of Horta. Some of the leading inhabitants came
on board the *Victory*, and were told that they must

either surrender the castle until a ransom was paid
for the town or abide the hazard of war. Don Diego
Gomez, the governor, refused to surrender, and hostilities commenced.   All boats were sent on shore,
manned and armed, and the troops were landed on a
small stretch of sandy beach about half a league from
the castle, with the Earl of Cumberland at their head.
Armed men, both horse and foot, were formed on a hill
called the Cerro de Carneiro, which overlooks the town,
and two companies of foot, with ensigns flying, were
drawn up on the seashore in front of the castle.   The
guns of the castle opened fire on the invading force as
they were forming on the beach ; while the ships of the
squadron continued to return the fire of the castle until
the cross of St. George was seen flying over its ramparts.
As the Earl advanced, the opposing force dispersed.
IIe marched through the town without meeting any resistance, and took possession of the castle, which had
been evacuated.

   The town of Horta then consisted of about 300 houses,
well built of stone and lime, with roofs of red tiles.
Every house had a cistern with a garden at the back.
Vines with ripe clusters of grapes covered the walls,
and afforded agreeable shade.   Fig-trees, both green and
red, orange, lemon, peach, and quince trees formed the
orchards; while potato roots and the tobacco plant,
which was already well known and used in England,
were cultivated in the fields.   The Earl gave strict
orders that none of the churches or religious houses
should be pillaged, and sentries were stationed to protect them ; but the sailors and soldiers ransacked the
private houses. The occupation continued for three
days, when the inhabitants paid a ransom of 2000

ducats, chiefly in church-plate. The castle was then set on fire, and the ordnance was either taken or rendered unserviceable. It consisted of fifty-eight iron guns, of which twenty-three had been mounted on a platform facing the sea.

Peace was thus restored. The governor only came once to parley about the ransom, and declined all friendly intercourse; but four of the principal inhabitants of Horta, doubtless men of Flemish descent, accepted an invitation to come on board the *Victory* to dinner. They were hospitably entertained, and solemnly dismissed to the sound of drum and trumpet and a peal of ordnance. A letter was given to them from the Earl of Cumberland, requesting all Englishmen who should visit the place in future to refrain from molesting them, except for fresh provisions and water. Next day a strong breeze sprang up from W.S.W., the prevailing quarter at that time of year, and the ships were obliged to weigh and stand along the land. The gale continued, with heavy rain, for several days, while the squadron worked off and on or lay-to in sight of St. George Island.

On the 23rd of September the Earl of Cumberland returned to Fayal Roads to recover an anchor, and was received as a friend. The officers landed to see the town of Horta, and to buy anything they wanted, just as if they had been in England, while the inhabitants helped the sailors in the work of filling their water-casks. Here John Davis and Edward Wright may have met, and most probably did meet, though doubtless not for the first time, conversing under the pleasant shade of vines, or during walks in the vicinity of the town. One was the best practical observer among the

seamen of his time, the other was the most accomplished
mathematical student.   Davis invented an improved
instrument for observing the heavenly bodies.   Wright
discovered the method of constructing charts on Mercator's projection by the use of tables of meridional
parts.   The town of Horta must have had a special
interest for these accomplished geographers; for it was
long the home of one of the most eminent of their predecessors.   Martin Behaim of Nuremburg, the inventor
of an astrolabe for use at sea, and the constructor of
the earliest globe now extant, was a contemporary of
Columbus.   A century before Davis and Wright met
at Horta, Behaim married the daughter of its founder,
and was settled there for several years.

On the 25th a gale sprung up so suddenly in the night,
that the Earl himself aroused the men, worked at the
capstan with them, and afterwards cheered them up with
wine.   On the 1st of October they were off Graciosa,
and Captain Davis was sent in, with two boats full of
empty casks and about fifty men, to fill up with water.
They met with a determined resistance, and as they
pulled along the shore, seeking for a safe landing-place,
troops of men followed with ensigns displayed.   Thirteen
of the boats' crews were wounded by their fire, and three
by the fire of a great piece which the country-people
dragged about with oxen.   A retreat became necessary;
and as it would be dangerous to attempt a landing, the
Earl sent a message on shore that he would excuse their
conduct for the sake of his friend King Antonio.[1]   Next

[1] Philip II. had seized Portugal as heir to the Cardinal Henry,
the last king.   Antonio, Prior of Crato, was an illegitimate son of
one of old King Henry's brothers.   He was a pretender, and was
acknowledged as King of Portugal by England and Holland.   He
married a sister of Prince Maurice of Orange.

day a flag of truce came from the shore with excuses,
and the chief inhabitants offered to supply wine and
fresh provisions.   They said that they only had rain-
water stored in cisterns, and that they would sooner give
two tons of wine than one ton of water.   Captain Davis
remained at anchor before the town to receive the promised provisions from the people of Graciosa, while the
Victory went for a short cruise, and captured a French
ship laden with fish from Newfoundland.

From this time the squadron began to suffer seriously
from the difficulty of getting fresh water.   Attempts
to land for water on the island of St. Michael's were
repulsed by the inhabitants.   They next went to St.
Mary's, the easternmost island of the group.   The Earl of
Cumberland had been joined by a most valuable officer
in the person of Captain Amyas Preston, who had
behaved with distinguished gallantry at Calais Roads in
the previous year.   He had come out in his own ship,
but had lost sight of her one night, perhaps when dining
with the Earl, and was now forced to stay on board the
Victory.   At St. Mary's Captains Davis, Lister, and
Preston were sent in with their boats, and a friendly
letter asking to be allowed to water.   Resistance was
made to their landing, on which Davis boarded a ship
at anchor.   She was fast aground, and he was obliged to
retire before a heavy fire from the shore.   One prize,
laden with sugar, was towed out, but the English lost
two men killed and sixteen wounded.   On the 25th of
October about six tons of water were obtained from a
stream falling over a cliff on St. George Island; and on
the 31st the *Margaret*, as she was leaking badly, and
the prize taken at St. Mary's, were sent direct to England with the sick and wounded.   Captain Davis kept

company with the Earl of Cumberland in a cruise towards the coast of Portugal, and they were so successful in the capture of important prizes, that, by the middle of November, they were unable to man any more, and consequently made sail for England.

No account of the voyage home of the *Drake* has been preserved, but Master Wright has given a graphic description of the sufferings of the people on board the *Victory* from want of water. Strong easterly gales delayed their return for weeks. They were driven to leeward, and could not fetch any part of Ireland. The allowance was reduced to half a pint, then to a quarter. At last they could only have three or four spoonfuls of vinegar at their meals, or some liquor wrung out of the wine-lees. They remained in this condition for a fortnight, when a fall of hail relieved their sufferings. "We ate the hailstones more pleasantly than if they had been the sweetest comfits in the world. Raindrops were carefully saved; sheets, napkins, and clouts being hung up to receive them." At length, on the 2nd of December, they anchored in Ventry harbour, and the Earl hurried on shore to get fresh water and provisions for the refreshment of his people. On their passage to England they were delayed by light winds, and "were faine to keep a cold Christmas with the Bishop and his Clerks." * They landed at Falmouth two days after Christmas, and received the melancholy intelligence that their best prize had been shipwrecked on the coast of Cornwall, and that their gallant comrade, Captain Lister, who went home in charge of her, had been drowned.

The Earl of Cumberland's squadron captured thirteen prizes, and John Davis of course received his share of

* Rocks off St. David's.

the prize-money.   Davis continued his cruises during the
following year, with ships under Captains Middleton and
Harvey as consorts.   Middleton was probably the same
officer who brought the news of the approach of the
Spanish fleet to Sir Richard Grenville at Flores in 1591,
when—

> " His pinnace like a fluttered bird
> Came flying from far away."

One of their prizes, called the *Uggera Salvagnia*, became
the subject of a lawsuit, the goods being claimed by
Philip Corsini and other Italian merchants in London.
Sir Walter Raleigh acted on behalf of Davis, and in
February 1591 the matter was settled by a compromise.

These services, performed with a view to harassing
the Queen's enemy and destroying his commerce, were
satisfactory in their results, by enriching Captain Davis,
and enabling him to join in the conduct of an enterprise
which was far more to his taste.   He was again placed
in a position to undertake an expedition having geographical discovery for its main object.

CHAPTER VI.

PREPARATIONS FOR THE SOUTH.

John Davis was so successful during his cruise to the Azores, and in the capture of Spanish prizes generally, that he was able once more to turn his attention to the great work of discovery. He now possessed means which placed him in a position to take his share in the expense of equipping an expedition. Circumstances led him to conceive the idea of making the dreaded voyage through Magellan's Strait, of navigating the South Sea, and of discovering the northern passage from the western, instead of the eastern side. For he was ever faithful to the project of increasing the wealth and prosperity of his country by discovering that passage by one way or the other. His bold conception of achieving the great enterprise from the Pacific side appears to have been partly due to his acquaintance with Thomas Cavendish, who was then anxious to undertake a second voyage through Magellan's Strait, and partly owing to his sharing the knowledge which his friend Sir Walter Raleigh had acquired from special sources at about the same time. We may, therefore, imagine John Davis holding consultations with Sir Walter Raleigh and Adrian Gilbert during the spring of the year 1591, at which they would have passed in review all that was known of Magellan's Strait, and the arguments for and against the hazardous attempt. In order that we may be able to understand and appreciate the views of Davis, it will be well that we too should take stock of the knowledge within his reach, and cast a glance over the history of previous voyages to the South Sea.

Ever since Columbus, in his fourth voyage, had failed to discover a strait after diligent search along the Spanish Main, the quest had been continued from time to time along the east coast of South America. The announcement of Vasco Nunez de Balboa that there was indeed another ocean, gave still greater importance to the discovery of a navigable route from the Atlantic to that vast South Sea, the navigation of which must lead to India and the Spice Islands. Charles V., therefore, received a proposal from Fernão de Magelhães (Ferdinand Magellan), a distinguished Portuguese navigator, to attempt the discovery of a passage, with complacency. Magellan argued that by continuing the passage southwards along the east coast of South America, either the land must come to an end, or there must be a strait through it. He was intrusted with the command of an expedition consisting of five vessels, the *Trinidad* and *San Antonio*, of 130 tons each, the *Victoria*, *Concepcion*, and *Santiago*, of 90 tons; and on the 20th of September 1519 he sailed from Seville.

Magellan was placed in a very difficult position owing to his Portuguese nationality. The captains of the other ships were all Spaniards, who regarded the elevation of a foreigner to command them with thinly disguised jealousy and resentment. There were several misunderstandings on the way out, and one of the captains had been actually superseded by a Portuguese adherent of

Magellan, when the fleet arrived at Port St. Julian, on the coast of Patagonia, in April 1520. Here a mutiny broke out, but its suppression was prompt and ruthless. One Spanish captain was stabbed to death on his own quarter-deck, another was strangled, and a third was put on shore and abandoned to his fate. Of all the leading Spaniards, there only remained the chief pilot, Juan Rodriguez Serrano, and Sebastian del Cano, the pilot of the *Victoria*. Serrano was sent to examine the coast to the southward of Port St. Julian in the *Santiago*, and he discovered the mouth of the Santa Cruz river. But his vessel was forced on shore and wrecked. He and his men succeeded in making their way back to Port St. Julian by a land journey.

It was not until the middle of October that Magellan resumed his southerly course with his fleet of four ships, and on the 21st he was off a headland where the coast turned to the west. He seems to have assumed at once that he had found the long-sought-for strait. It was the Feast of St. Ursula, and he called the cape which appeared to point the way to his famous discovery by the name of the Ten thousand Virgins. The smaller vessels were sent on ahead, and they reported a strait with very deep water. When Magellan anchored a few leagues within it, he had three months' provisions left.

For many days Magellan sailed on through the strait. He saw fires at night on the southern side, and named the land " Tierra del Fuego." Then he came to coasts bordered by woods of tall trees and dense underwood, while far to the south he beheld a snowy peak piercing the stormy clouds. He gave it the name of " Campana de Roldan,"—the bell of Roldan,—calling it after an officer of artillery, one of the few who were destined

ever to return home. The length of the strait alarmed
the people, and there were murmurs against continuing
the voyage. When the channel appeared to branch into
two openings, and the *San Antonio* was sent to examine
one of them, she took the opportunity of deserting her
consorts and returning to Spain. Magellan was a man
of a cruel and savage disposition; he was harsh and
unconciliatory; but his perseverance was indomitable,
his nerve of iron. He was hated and feared by his
followers. He now told them that they should eat the
chafing-mats on the rigging before they should return,
and that no man should speak of going back on pain
of death. After having been thirty-seven days in the
strait, Magellan entered the South Sea on the 27th of
November 1520, naming the headland to the south
Cape Deseado. He reckoned the length of the strait to
be 110 leagues, which was not very far from the truth.
He then stretched boldly across the Pacific Ocean, and
reached the islands of the farther east. There the man
who had so ruthlessly slaughtered his own comrades at
Port St. Julian was himself butchered by the natives,
while the high honour of circumnavigating the globe for
the first time was reserved for one with cleaner hands
and a better conscience.

Sebastian del Cano was a Basque from the picturesque
little town of Guetaria, on the shores of the Bay of
Biscay. Steeped in the heroic traditions of his native
land, brave, enthusiastic, and loyal, the young Basque
pilot was at the same time so courteous and considerate
that he was generally beloved. He sailed as pilot on
board the *Victoria*, and when that ship alone remained
out of the fleet of five vessels which originally sailed
from Seville, Sebastian del Cano was unanimously elected

to be the commander who should bring her home, and be the first to sail round the world. He arrived at Seville on the 6th of September 1522, after an absence of four years all but fourteen days. It was a memorable achievement, and marks an epoch in maritime history. A knowledge of it was slow to spread among the countries of Europe, but wherever this first circumnavigation became known, and especially in England, it created a deep impression. The Spanish Government at once perceived the immense significance of the discovery of this western route to India, and ·resolved to fit out a second expedition with all possible dispatch.

A fleet consisting of six ships and a *pataca*, or small tender, was got ready under the orders of Garcia Jofre de Loaysa, while Sebastian del Cano was his second in command and chief pilot. As Cano was a native of the north of Spain, and recruited from the Biscayan and Galician ports, the fleet was assembled at Coruña. Loaysa was on board a vessel of 300 tons named the *Santa Maria de la Victoria*, while Cano commanded a smaller vessel of 200 tons called the *Santo Espiritu.* The other four ships were the *Anunciada*, of 170 tons, under Pedro de Vera, the *San Gabriel*, commanded by Rodrigo de Acuña, and two small vessels of eighty tons each, called the *Santa Maria del Parrel* and the *St. Lesmes*, under Jorge Manrique de Najera and Francisco de Hozes. The fleet sailed from Coruña on the 24th of July 1525 under very happy auspices ; for the men were loyal to their officers, the most cordial relations were always preserved between Loaysa and his captains, and the expedition had the great advantage of being piloted by the first circumnavigator. In the first days of 1526 the fleet was off Cape Virgins ; but unfortunately the

Santo Espiritu was wrecked near the point, and Sebastian del Cano was taken on board the admiral.   The *Lesmes* ran before a gale as far south as 55°, and her captain, Francisco de Hozes, was the discoverer of the long island on the east side of Tierra del Fuego which has since been known as Staten Island.   Bad weather obliged the fleet to return to the Santa Cruz river, but on the 8th of April 1526 three ships entered the strait.   Observations were taken of the currents of the part of the strait where the tides meet, of the number of sounds and inlets on either coast, and of the vegetation on the sea shores.   On the 26th of May, after having been forty-eight days in the strait, the fleet entered the South Sea and began the long voyage to the Moluccas.   But Loaysa died at sea on the 26th of July, and Sebastian del Cano followed his chief only four days afterwards.   They were buried in the midst of the Pacific Ocean, and thus Cano found a grave in the centre of the great discovery in which he had a part.   For he it was, and not Magellan, who first circumnavigated the globe.   His expedition, which was well conducted, deserved a better fate. The ships eventually reached the Moluccas, and their presence acted as a spur to the Peninsular Governments to complete negotiations for the settlement of their boundary dispute.

A treaty was concluded between Spain and Portugal in 1525, whereby the region west of a meridian 17° E. of the Moluccas was recognised as belonging to the latter power, which was thus secured in quiet possession of the Spice Islands, Spain retaining the Philippines. Hence the third Spanish expedition fitted out for the Strait of Magellan was not ostensibly intended to cross the Pacific, but to explore the southern coasts of South

G

America. Two ships were dispatched from San Lucar under the command of Simon de Alcazova, who sailed on the 21st of September 1534. His voyage was a complete failure. After reaching the entrance of the strait, Alcazova returned to a port in Patagonia called "Puerto de Leones y Lobos"—the harbour of sea-lions and seals—whence he undertook an exploring expedition inland in March 1535. But he was very corpulent and in ill-health. He returned to his ship, and was soon afterwards murdered by some mutineers, who were repressed and punished by the loyal part of the crew. One ship was lost on the Brazilian coast, and the other eventually reached St. Domingo in the West Indies.

The wonderful advance of Spanish discovery along the west coast of South America from Panama led to the entrance of Magellan Strait from the western side. Pizarro conquered Peru in 1533. On the 18th of January 1535 the city of Lima was founded, and five years afterwards Pedro de Valdivia had extended the dominions of Spain over Chile. In 1551 he founded the town of Valdivia at the southern extremity of the Chilian province. This intrepid conqueror had formed a plan of returning to Spain by the Strait of Magellan, and he dispatched two vessels from Valdivia, under the command of Francisco de Ulloa, on a voyage of reconnaissance. Ulloa discovered the western coasts of the archipelago of islands which skirts the South American continent between Chile and the Strait of Magellan. But the death of Valdivia, the conqueror of Chile, in that famous battle with the Araucanian Indians which is poetically described in the epic of Ercilla, put an end to his projects.

It was not until 1557 that any further expedition was

organised in Chile. It is sufficiently marvellous that anything of the kind should have been attempted by the first settlers in the Chilian province, who were engaged in a doubtful struggle with the brave and indomitable Araucanian Indians, and who were so many hundreds of miles from their sources of supply. There is nothing that gives us a more striking idea of the extraordinary energy and pluck of the early Spanish conquerors than the fact that a mere handful of them, while engaged in a desperate struggle for life with a numerous and most formidable enemy, should be coolly engaged in equipping exploring expeditions. Yet such was the work of young Don Garcia Hurtado de Mendoza, the Captain-General who succeeded Valdivia in the government of Chile. He fitted out two vessels, called the *San Luis* and the *San Sebastian,* under the command of Juan de Ladrilleros, with the two Gallegos, Hernan and Pedro, as pilots. Ladrilleros sailed from Valdivia in November 1557, examined the coast to the southward, and wintered in the strait. He explored the channels as far as the eastern entrance at Cape Virgins, and defined the outlines of the island of Chiloe and of the Chonos Archipelago. But his survey was conducted in the face of the most appalling hardships and sufferings. Nearly the whole of his crew perished of cold and hunger. He navigated his vessel back to Chile with the aid of two survivors. Such were the deeds performed by those heroic Spaniards who made known to the world the geography of South America. The English were their rivals, and followed close in their footsteps, but no people could excel the countrymen of Sebastian del Cano and of Juan de Ladrilleros in gallantry and perseverance.

The general belief of geographers during the sixteenth

century was that the Strait of Magellan divided South America from a southern continent of vast extent. It was not until Cape Horn was rounded by the Dutch expedition of Schouten and Le Maire in 1616 that this theory was partly abandoned, and it continued to hold a place in the speculations of geographers until it was finally exploded by the voyage of Captain Cook.

It would be very interesting to know to what extent Sir Francis Drake was acquainted with the discoveries of the Spaniards, and with their voyages to the Strait of Magellan, when he undertook his own famous voyage of circumnavigation. The narrative of Magellan's voyage was written by the Italian Antonio Pigafetta, who was a volunteer in the expedition, and came home on board the *Victoria*. The earliest printed edition of his work is in French, and is believed to have been published in about 1525, and the first Italian edition, translated from the French text, appeared at Venice in 1536. Another brief narrative by Maximilian Transylvanus, who had collected his information direct from the crew of the *Victoria*, was printed at Cologne in 1523, and in Rome in 1524. There can, therefore, be no doubt that Drake was well acquainted with the history of Magellan's voyage, but he probably knew little about the voyage of Loaysa, and nothing of the expeditions sent from Chile, while the Spanish maps and charts were always jealously guarded by the maritime authorities at Seville.

Drake had already seen the South Sea from the hills of Darien, and his imagination was fired with the enthusiastic desire of emulating the achievement of Magellan. He was introduced to the Queen by his patron, Sir Christopher Hatton, and the daring seaman's enterprise received her approbation. But the ships belonged to

Drake and to private friends, who furnished the means of equipping the expedition. The fleet consisted of Drake's own ship, the *Pelican*, of 100 tons, of the *Elizabeth*, under Captain Winter, of eighty tons, the *Marigold*, thirty, *Swan*, fifty, and *Christopher* pinnace of fifteen tons. When it is remembered that, since the voyage of Loaysa, the Spaniards themselves had discontinued the use of Magellan's Strait owing to the difficulties and dangers of the route, some idea may be formed of the reckless audacity of these Englishmen in undertaking the voyage with such small vessels. On the 15th of November 1577 they sailed from Plymouth with a fair wind.

Drake's fleet anchored in Port St. Julian, the scene of Magellan's sanguinary proceedings, on the 20th of June 1578, and here a somewhat similar scene was enacted. Mr. Thomas Doughty, a volunteer in one of the ships, was accused of conspiring to create a mutiny, and was beheaded. There is no reason to doubt that Drake was convinced of Doughty's guilt, and that, under the peculiar circumstances he believed the execution to be a necessity. The fleet, now reduced to the three larger ships, sailed from Port St. Julian on the 17th, and was off Cape Virgins on the 20th of August. Here Drake changed the name of his ship from the *Pelican* to the *Golden Hind*, which was the crest of his patron, Sir Christopher Hatton. At a distance of four leagues the land was sighted, and as they approached there appeared a line of high and steep grey cliffs, full of black spots, with the sea throwing up spray along their bases like the spouting of whales.

Drake then entered the strait, and passing through the *Angosturas* or Narrows, he came to what appeared like "a large and main sea." Still advancing, he met with sinuous windings, numerous islands, and contrary. winds, obliging him to anchor frequently. The explorers acknowledged that Magellan's account was true as to the good harbours and abundance of fresh water, but the gales were so frequent and the anchorages so precarious, that "a ship navigating the strait had need to be freighted with nothing else but anchors and cables." Nevertheless, Master Fletcher, the historian of the voyage, was enraptured with the beauty of the scenery. He mentions the lofty peaks towering above the clouds, the evergreen trees, the variety of plants, the climate like that of England, "a place no doubt that lacketh nothing but a people to use the same to the Creator's glory and the increasing of the Church." Drake entered the Pacific on the 6th of September, having only been sixteen days in the strait. He estimated its length at 150 leagues.

A furious gale was encountered on the day after leaving the strait, and the ships were separated. The *Golden Hind* was driven far to the south, and Drake was probably the first to sight Cape Horn. The *Marigold* parted company, and was never heard of again, and Captain Winter, with the *Elizabeth*, re-entered the strait, abandoned his chief, and returned to England. Winter was three weeks in the strait on his way home, recruiting the health of his crew. His sojourn is rendered memorable, according to Clusius, owing to his having discovered the medicinal virtues of an aromatic bark of which he made use as a cure for scurvy during his homeward voyage. The tree was first accurately described by Forster, the botanist of Cooke's second voyage, in 1773. The bark was called *Cortex Winteranus* by Clusius, and is well known as " Winter's bark." Forster named the tree *Drimys Winteri.* It grows abundantly to a height of forty feet in the strait, but becomes a shrub ten feet high on the western shores.

Having lost both her consorts, the *Golden Hind* continued her lonely course along the western coast of America. Drake's discovery of the coast of North America, beyond the farthest point reached by the Spaniards at Cape Mendocino, had a special interest for Davis and his friends in studying the events of the voyage; for this newly-discovered coast seemed to be the portal to a passage round the northern shores of America from the Pacific side. Drake left Guatalco, on the Mexican coast, on the 16th of April 1579, and was many days at sea working to the northward. His reckoning showed that the *Golden Hind* had gone over 1400 leagues without seeing any land. It became very cold, and the explorers at length sighted the coast of America at a point as far north as 48°, a little to the south of the Straits of San Juan de Fuca. The land appeared to be of moderate height, and every hill was covered with snow in the month of June. For many years this was the most northerly known point on the west coast of America. Mr. Fletcher here states that " though we searched the coast diligently even unto the 48th degree, yet found we not the land to trend so much as one point in any place towards the east."

Drake, as is well known, circumnavigated the globe, and arrived safely at Plymouth on the 26th of September 1580. The Queen, to show her approval of his conduct, and her sense of the value of his achievement, dined on board his ship at Deptford, and conferred upon the illustrious seaman the honour of knighthood.

There was a Spanish voyage, the particulars of which

became known in England through its having been translated by Linschoten, which also had a special interest for John Davis in connection with the northern discoveries of Drake on the west coast. In the year 1582 Francisco Gali (or de Gualle) sailed from Mexico to the Philippines, and in 1584 he returned. Gali reported that the currents east of Japan flowed to the north in a wide sea, and he concluded that there must consequently be a passage between Mexico or California and Asia. He reached the American coast in 37° 30′ N. This report of Gali, combined with Drake's testimony that the American coast was still trending northwards in 48°, furnished the arguments by which Davis formed his conclusion that a passage might be found from the Pacific round the north side of America. Of this he felt little doubt. But he was impressed with the difficulties connected with the navigation of Magellan's Strait, and his misgivings on this point were not lessened by a consideration of the voyages subsequent to Drake's circumnavigation.

It was believed by the Viceroy of Peru, Don Francisco de Toledo, that Drake would attempt to return by the way he came, and it was resolved that an expedition should be sent to the Strait of Magellan to intercept him. Advantage was to be taken of the opportunity to execute a careful survey of the strait, and to report upon the best means of fortifying it, so as to prevent its use by the enemies of Spain. At that time there was an able and experienced seaman in Peru, who was admirably fitted for the command of such an expedition. Pedro Sarmiento de Gamboa was an accomplished scholar, a scientific geographer, and an intrepid explorer. He had been many years in Peru, and his first maritime

attempt had been inspired by the accurate knowledge
he possessed of the ancient traditions of the Incas. He
learnt from the Peruvian *Amautas*, or learned men, that
one of the Incas, named Tupac Yupanqui, had sent a
fleet of the boats used by the aboriginal natives of the
Peruvian coast to sail towards the setting sun ; that
they reached two islands called *Ahuachumbi* and *Nina-
chumbi*, and returned. Cabello Balboa, an author who
wrote in about 1586, mentions the same tradition.
Sarmiento undertook an expedition from Peru to discover these islands, and succeeded. Unfortunately all
record of this interesting voyage is lost. The experience
thus acquired by Sarmiento led to his appointment to a
post in the expedition of Alvaro de Mandana, which
sailed from Callao in 1567, and discovered the Solomon
Islands. His advice as to the course that should be
steered led directly to this discovery, and he headed
exploring parties to examine the interior of Santa
Isabella, the largest island of the group. Sarmiento
was the author of a report on Mandana's voyage, and of
a history of the Incas of Peru, but both these works
are lost to posterity. Sarmiento also drew the map
accompanying the elaborate pictorial representations
of the traditions and pedigree of the Incas, which was
prepared by order of the Viceroy Toledo, and sent to
King Philip II.

Sarmiento fitted out his expedition to Magellan Strait
at Callao, the seaport of Lima. It consisted of two
vessels, the *Esperanza* and *San Francisco*. Sarmiento
himself embarked on board the former, with the pilots
Anton Pablos Corzo and Hernando Alonzo, while Juan
de Villalobos commanded the *San Francisco*, with
Hernando Lamero as pilot. There was a crew of about

fifty men on board each vessel. On the 11th of October 1579 Sarmiento sailed from Callao. After exploring some of the channels in the Chonos Archipelago, he entered the strait in January 1580; but his colleague Villalobos proved to be remiss and untrustworthy, and eventually parted company. Thus weakened in the means at his command, Sarmiento set diligently to work to survey the strait. He made numerous boat expeditions so as to delineate the coast-lines in more detail, gave names to points, islands, and inlets, and sounded the channels and anchorages. On the 11th of February he anchored in a bay which he named Bahia de la Gente, and a river which empties itself into the bay was called San Juan. The place was afterwards known as Port Famine, and here Sarmiento erected a cross, and took formal possession in the name of the King of Spain. He selected two points in the narrowest part of the strait near the eastern entrance, which seemed suitable positions for forts to command the passage, and passing Cape Virgins, he entered the Atlantic on the 24th of February 1580.

Sarmiento arrived in Spain in August 1580, and presented his journals and charts to the King at Badajos. He urged that the strait might be completely guarded by building two forts to command the channel in the eastern *Angosturas* or Narrows, and that there were suitable sites for a colony farther up the strait. Philip, after some consideration, decided on the adoption of Sarmiento's scheme. A fleet of twenty-three ships was equipped at Seville, in three divisions, the first to convey a new Captain-General to Chile, the second for Brazil, and the third, under Sarmiento, to settle a colony in the straits, but the whole fleet was first to see Sarmiento established. The command in chief was given to Don Diego Flores de Valdes, and the fleet sailed from Seville on the 25th of September 1581. But they encountered a gale of wind, and seven vessels were driven on shore or disabled, including the *Esperanza*, in which Sarmiento had surveyed the strait. The rest put back to Cadiz in a shattered condition; and when the fleet again sailed in December, it only numbered sixteen vessels. Disaster followed this ill-fated expedition from the outset. After wintering at Rio, the fleet sailed for the strait; but in December 1582 the *Riola*, one of the largest ships, with most of the stores for the colony, sprung a leak, and went down at sea with all hands. Three other ships were left behind disabled. At length the irresolute Flores got as far as the Narrows, but his ships were driven out of the strait by a gale of wind, and abandoning all further attempts for that year, he returned to Rio. Flores then gave up the command, appointing Diego de Ribera to succeed him, and to co-operate with Sarmiento in fortifying the strait.

Ribera and Sarmiento reached their destination in February 1584; but, after encountering heavy gales of wind, Ribera deserted, leaving Sarmiento with only one ship, called the *Maria*, and the charge of a number of colonists who had been landed. Sarmiento found himself with 400 men, thirty women, and provisions for eight months. The first settlement was formed near the eastern entrance, and was called "Nombre de Jesus." Here 150 men were established under Andres de Viedma. The *Maria* was then sent to Point Santa Ana, within the Narrows, while Sarmiento marched to the same place by land with the rest of the colonists. A settlement was formed close to the point, which received the name of "San Felipe," and wooden houses were erected. Sarmiento then went on board the *Maria* with the intention of returning to Nombre de Jesus, giving instructions to Viedma respecting the fortification of the strait, and then proceeding to Chile for supplies. But a violent storm drove him from his anchors, and after beating against it for three weeks, he was forced to abandon the struggle and bear up for Brazil. He procured a bark at Rio, which he loaded with meal and dispatched to the colonists. His difficulties, owing to the hostility of the local authorities, were so great, that he gave up the attempt to obtain further supplies in Brazil, and sailed for Spain in April 1585. No further succour was sent to the unhappy settlers.

Sarmiento was unfortunate to the last. On her way home the *Maria* was attacked by three English vessels belonging to Sir Walter Raleigh near the Azores, and captured. The illustrious Spaniard enjoyed the hospitalities of Durham House, and he had the honour of being presented to the Queen by his host. There was probably no man living who had so complete a knowledge of subjects in which Raleigh was interested as his illustrious prisoner. Their conversations must have been most agreeable to both host and guest, and while Raleigh acquired a knowledge of Peruvian history and of the Straits of Magellan, Sarmiento enjoyed the society of one of the most accomplished and best-read courtiers in Europe. Eventually the Queen was graciously pleased to set the great Spanish navigator at liberty, and to present him with a thousand crowns. He returned to Spain, and we last hear of him as being in command of troops at the Philippines.

English adventurers, after the successful circumnavigation of Sir Francis Drake, were stimulated to imitate his example. In 1586 the Earl of Cumberland fitted out two vessels, the *Clifford* of 260 and a bark of 150 tons, commanded by Robert Witherington and Christopher Lister, to make a voyage into the South Seas. They never reached the strait. Remaining on the Brazilian coast, they cruised for Spanish prizes, but the only valuable result of their voyage was the capture of Lopez Vaz, the historian of the West Indies and the South Sea, with his manuscript. This fortunate prize furnished detailed information of Spanish discoveries down to the abandonment of the ill-fated colony in the Straits of Magellan. The manuscript was translated by Hakluyt; but we are not informed whether the author, or only the produce of his brain, was brought to England.

Thomas Cavendish, the second English circumnavigator, was a native of Frimley St. Martin in Suffolk, of the same family as the Dukes of Devonshire. He is first heard of as captain of a ship of his own in the expedition which Sir Richard Grenville commanded for Sir Walter Raleigh, with the object of planting an expedition in Virginia. He accompanied Grenville on his inland journey, and returned to England with him in September 1585. On his return Cavendish began the equipment of an expedition of his own, to follow in the footsteps of Drake round the world.

Cavendish had three vessels, his own ship, the *Desire* of 140 tons, the *Content* of sixty, and the *Hugh Gallant* of forty tons. Mr. Francis Pretty, of Eye in Suffolk, the historian of the voyage, sailed in the *Hugh Gallant*, while some valuable sailing directions were written by Thomas Fuller of Ipswich, the master of the *Desire*.

Sailing from Plymouth on the 21st of July 1586, they anchored in a harbour in 47°. 50′ S., on the coast of Patagonia, on the 17th of December, which Cavendish named Port Desire. Pretty describes the sea-lions and the abundance of birds on an island three leagues south-east of the entrance, which was named Penguin Island. The rise and fall of the tide admitted of the ships being careened, but the great drawback was the scarcity of fresh water. Some was found by digging, but it was brackish. Cavendish left Port Desire on the 28th, and on January 6, 1587, he entered the Strait of Magellan and anchored in the first Narrow.

Next morning, Cavendish, having observed lights during the night, pulled to the shore in his boat, and saw three men who made signals with a flag. They proved to be part of the garrison which Sarmiento had landed to guard the strait. They were in dreadful distress. Cavendish offered to take them on board and land them on the coast of Peru. One man, named Tomé Hernandez, stepped into the boat. They said that, besides themselves, there were only fifteen survivors, twelve men and three women. The rest had perished of cold and hunger, through ignorance of the means of obtaining supplies of birds and fish. Cavendish told the two other men to return to their comrades, and tell them that he would take them all on board. The boat then left the shore.

When Cavendish came on board, he found that a fair wind had sprung up, so he immediately made sail, and inhumanly left the unhappy survivors of the colony of Sarmiento to their fate. Hernandez subsequently made a declaration respecting the proceedings of the colonists after the departure of Sarmiento in February 1584.

Many died during the winter, and the ensuing summer was passed in anxious expectation of the arrival of a ship to relieve them. Viedma, who was in command, built two small boats out of the trees, and embarked his people in 1585. But one was wrecked with most of the stores, and the attempt was abandoned because the remaining boat would not hold all the survivors. He determined to separate the party in small divisions, in the hope that, by spreading along the shore, they would have a better chance of finding subsistence. They tried to raise crops, but the natives destroyed them, so they lingered on, living mainly on shell-fish. San Felipe was full of dead bodies, which the living were too weak to bury. Unable to remain there, the survivors were on their way to Nombre de Jesus, when Cavendish fell in with them. He afterwards landed at San Felipe, to which he gave the name of Port Famine. After filling up with fresh water, and supplying himself with fuel by pulling down the houses in the town, he proceeded on his voyage. He had also salted down an enormous number of penguins. On the 14th of January the fleet rounded the most southern point of the American continent, to which Cavendish gave the name of Cape Froward, and next day he anchored in a cove five leagues to the westward, on the south side of the strait, where great abundance of shell-fish was found. On the 24th of February he entered the South Sea with a fair wind, having been seven weeks in the strait.

Hernandez, the survivor of Sarmiento's colony, escaped from the English when they landed to fill their water-casks in the Bay of Quintero, near Valparaiso. Cavendish completed the third navigation of the globe, arriving at Plymouth on the 9th of September 1588.

His cruel abandonment of the surviving colonists in Magellan's Strait left a stain on his character which was deepened by his ruthless cruelty at every place he visited along the west coast of America. In his first voyage he showed that he was callous to the sufferings of others; in his second he proved that his inhumanity was not redeemed either by generosity in judging of his own comrades or by fortitude under misfortunes. His success was due to good fortune and to the excellent qualities of those who served with him.

This unmerited success, so far as Cavendish was individually concerned, acted as a strong incentive to other adventurers. In the year following his return, Mr. John Chudleigh, of Broad Clyst, near Exeter, undertook a similar voyage. This Devonshire worthy was, says Prince, " a right martial, bold, and adventurous spirit. He had an honourable emulation in him to equal, if not excel, the bravest heroes and their noblest exploits, not at land so much, where is the least danger, but at sea. The famous actions of Drake and Cavendish ran so much in his thoughts, that he could not rest without undertaking to show himself the third Englishman that had encompassed the world and done noble service for his country." Chudleigh was an old and dear friend of John Davis, who named the cape at the southern entrance of Hudson Strait in his honour.

Chudleigh was on board the *Wild Man* of 300 tons, with Benjamin Wood as master; the *White Lion*, of 340 tons, was commanded by Paul Wheele, and the *Delight* of Bristol by Andrew Merrick. The account of the voyage was written by William Magoths of Bristol, who was on board the *Delight*. The three ships sailed from Plymouth on the 5th of August 1589, with the intention of passing through the Strait of Magellan and entering the South Sea. The *Delight* parted company off the coast of Barbary, and never fell in with her consorts again. She anchored at Port Desire, and during her stay Merrick succeeded in finding two little springs of fresh water on the north-west side of the bay. Merrick and his companions entered the Strait of Magellan on the 1st of January 1590, and anchored off an island covered with penguins. They killed and salted a great number, but Magoths warns his successors that "they must be eaten with speed, for we found them of no long continuance." Near Port Famine they took a Spaniard on board, who was the sole survivor of those unfortunate settlers who had been so inhumanly abandoned to their fate by Cavendish. When she got a few leagues beyond Cape Froward, the *Delight* was stopped by a head wind. For several weeks the explorers persevered in their attempt to reach the South Sea, but after losing their boats, anchors, and a number of their comrades, they became disheartened. On February 14th they again passed Cape Virgins and shaped a course homewards. Merrick and the Spaniard died on the passage home, and the ship was wrecked off Cherbourg. There is no narrative of the voyage of the *Wild Man*, but we know that Chudleigh died in Magellan's Strait, and that his ship returned in safety. Prince says that "he did not live long enough to accomplish his generous designs, dying young, although he lived long enough to exhaust a vast estate."

The records of these voyages to the Strait, from Magellan to Chudleigh, embracing a stirring period of seventy years, formed the material which John Davis and his friends had to consider in planning a new

H

expedition of discovery.   The ulterior aim of Davis was always the achievement of the northern passage.   The friends in council had before them the details of Magellan's voyage from the published work of Pigafetta and the letter of Maximilian Transylvanus.   Both had been translated by Richard Eden in his "History of Travayle," a second edition of which was published by Willes in 1577.   The manuscript of Lopez Vaz and the information from Sarmiento made them acquainted with subsequent Spanish enterprises, and they were of course fully informed respecting the voyages of their own countrymen.   Sir Walter Raleigh encouraged the enterprise, Adrian Gilbert became the joint-owner of a ship with his old friend, and, the question having been fully considered, Davis resolved to make his next attempt to discover the passage by way of Magellan's Strait and the west coast of North America.   The news of the melancholy fate of John Chudleigh had arrived in England during the autumn of 1590, but it only stimulated his friends to fresh exertions.   Thomas Cavendish, unable to rest on his laurels, was eagerly organising a second expedition, and, in an evil hour, Davis consented to unite forces.   Their fleet of four ships and a pinnace was ready for sea by the summer of 1591.

CHAPTER VII.

THE VOYAGE TO THE STRAITS OF MAGELLAN.

THE disastrous voyage of John Davis to the Straits of Magellan was commenced with bright hopes of achieving important discovery. It was only in the expectation of solving the question of the North-West Passage that Davis was induced "to go with Cavendish in his attempt for the South Sea," as he told his old Admiral, Lord Howard of Effingham, in his preface to the "Seaman's Secrets." Cavendish owned the *Desire*, the ship in which he had sailed round the world. His expedition consisted of this vessel, the *Leicester* and *Roebuck*, probably furnished by adventurers, the *Dainty*, owned partly by Adrian Gilbert and partly by Davis, and a small craft called the *Black Pinnace*.

Davis contributed a large sum to the expenses of the voyage, and, at the pressing request of Cavendish, he consented to command the *Desire* instead of the *Dainty*. He did this in opposition to the advice of his friends, who disliked his leaving his own ship, and commanding a set of officers and men selected by Cavendish, and previously unknown to him. His compliance was due to a feeling of loyalty to his chief, and to a wish to promote harmony and good-will, which is most honourable to his memory. But he only consented on the

express condition that, when they arrived at California,
he was to have his own ship the *Dainty*, and the *Black
Pinnace*, and to part company with Cavendish in order
"to search that north-west discovery upon the back
parts of America." The object of Cavendish was merely
to repeat his former exploit and enrich himself with
Spanish prizes.

Thomas Cavendish embarked on board the *Leicester*
as general of the expedition, having with him a cousin
named Locke, and several other gentlemen volunteers,
including Robert Hues, the learned geographer. His
chief supporters were his friend Sir Tristram Gorges,
Sir George Cary, who provided some of the ordnance,
and Master Cary of Cockington. John Davis was
captain of the *Desire*, 120 tons, with John Pery, an
experienced sailor and a loyal man, who had sailed with
Cavendish in his former voyage, as master. Davis was
also accompanied by his constant friend John Janes,
his old shipmate in the Arctic regions, who joined the
perilous undertaking for the sake of his former commander, and out of the affection he felt for him. He
proved a stay and support during a very trying period.
For the crew was most unsatisfactory, having been
appointed by Cavendish. Nearly all were volunteers,
artificers, or servants, and there were only fourteen able
seamen. The whole company amounted to seventy-six
souls. The ship was also badly furnished with rigging,
sails, and cables. The *Roebuck* was commanded by
Captain Cocke, the *Dainty* by Captain Randolph Cotton,
a friend of Davis and of Adrian Gilbert, and the *Black
Pinnace* by Captain Tobias.

The summer of 1591 saw Davis in the society of his
wife at Sandridge for the last time. All seemed bright

and cheerful in that lovely home, and he left it with
high hopes of achieving a great discovery and of a happy
return.   Yet already there were germs of calamity both
in the expedition and in the bosom of his family.   When
he returned, he was a ruined and disappointed man, and
he found his home desolate.   But there was no thought
of disaster when, on a bright August morning, he bade
farewell to Sandridge and joined his ship.

The second expedition commanded by Thomas Cavendish sailed from Plymouth on the 26th of August 1591.
A long and tedious voyage was before them.   On the
twentieth day the Canary Isles were sighted, and they
were becalmed on the line for twenty-seven days, where
the intense heat, combined with unwholesome food and
water, caused an outbreak of scurvy.   At length a
north-westerly wind sprung up, and in three weeks
more the coast of Brazil was sighted.   Davis was uncertain of his position, but a small vessel was captured
under the land, and the pilot pointed out Cape Frio,
and took the ships into a place called Placencia, about
sixty miles from the town of Santos.   Here a welcome
supply of fresh vegetables was obtained, which seems to
have had the effect of restoring the men to health and
vigour.   But far more trying times were in store for
them.   It was resolved to attack the Portuguese town
of Santos, in the hope of filling up with fresh provisions.
The service was carelessly performed by Captain Cocke
of the *Roebuck.*   He took the boats up the river, surprised the settlers while they were hearing mass, and
captured the town.   But he afterwards allowed the
people to pass to and fro as they pleased, and in a few
days the place was left without inhabitants or provisions.   It ended by the expedition only getting a few

baskets of cassava meal, and by its having to leave the coast in great distress for want of fresh food.

Cavendish had few of the requisites for an efficient commander. He was personally brave, but without feeling or sympathy for his men, and his plans were wanting in judgment and forethought. He never gave directions to his captains with regard to the course they were to steer in the event of being separated, and he appears to have neglected the precautions which were usually taken by an officer leading a squadron of ships. Leaving Santos on the 22nd of January 1592, the fleet encountered a severe gale of wind on the 7th of February, probably a "pampero," off the River Plate, and on the 8th the ships were separated by the fury of the storm. Being without instructions, Davis consulted Mr. Pery, his master, as to the best course to take. He had frequently applied to Cavendish for a rendezvous in the event of parting company, but without being able to induce that commander to name one. During his former voyage Cavendish had anchored in a bay on the coast of Patagonia which he named Port Desire, and it was thought probable that he would now shape a course for this refuge. Captain Davis, therefore, resolved to go there on the chance of finding the *Leicester*, and on his way he fell in with the *Roebuck*, seriously shattered and disabled. The two vessels reached Port Desire on the 6th of March, and the *Black Pinnace* joined them two days afterwards.

But the crew of the *Dainty* had shamefully deserted. They steered homewards soon after the fleet left Santos, leaving their captain, who appears to have been dining on board the *Roebuck*, with nothing but the clothes on his back. Captain Randolph Cotton was an intimate

friend of Davis, and he was a guest on board the *Desire*
during the rest of the voyage. There is some reason to
believe that Cavendish was a party to this treachery.
One of his crew, named Knivet, says that the general
told the men of the *Dainty* that he wanted them to go
into the River Plate, but that afterwards "they might
return home with all his heart." Cavendish knew well
that this desertion would be the death-blow to Davis's
hopes of achieving discovery. It was indeed a great
calamity, for the *Dainty* was the ship in which the great
Arctic Navigator had intended to continue his northern
exploration.

The surmise of Davis and his master proved to be
correct. The *Leicester* arrived at Port Desire on the
18th, having lost two of her boats during the gale, and
Cavendish came on board the *Desire* in a very bad
temper, and related his grievances to Davis. He complained bitterly of the crew of the *Leicester*. He declared that he was "matched with the most abject-
minded and mutinous company that ever was carried out
of England by man living, who never ceased to practise
and mutiny against him." His accusations appear to
have been unfounded, for when Mr. Janes and other
officers of the *Desire*, who regretted to hear their friends
thus spoken of, had an opportunity of conversing with
the *Leicester's* officers, they were perfectly loyal in their
remarks, and resolute in proceeding on the voyage.
The conduct of Cavendish was deplored by his officers
and men. But he persisted in it, and took the extraordinary course of refusing to return to his ship,
declaring that he intended to remain on board the
Desire as the guest of Captain Davis.

So, with these seeds of failure on board, and with the

prospect of foul weather ahead, the three ships and the little pinnace sought refuge and rest in this wild Patagonian port. It was dreary enough. In the middle of the bay the coast consists of steep white cliffs nearly two miles long, the upper part streaked with black lines from water draining down it. On the south side the Tower Rock breaks the monotonous outline of the land. It is a mass of red claystone forty feet high, cleft in the upper part, so as to give it the appearance of the forked branch of an immense tree, covered with moss and lichens. Undulating plains extend inland, where the gravelly soil is so poor as only to produce a few tufts of grass, with here and there a straggling bush. In one direction an inlet runs some fifteen miles up the country, on the banks of which a few plover and waterfowl are met with, but fresh water is only found in pools, and the supply is precarious. In examining the country more closely, the sailors found some slight refreshment. In the valleys, between the rocks, there were wild pease, with green leaves and bluish blossoms, and herbs like sage, with very sweet-smelling leaves. The herbs and leaves of the pease made wholesome salads against scurvy, and abundance of very good mussels and limpets was found on the rocks. Nine miles S.S.E. of the harbour was Penguin Island, which was covered with seals and sea-lions.

Having obtained such refreshment as the place afforded, the expedition sailed for the Straits of Magellan on the 20th of March, Cavendish still remaining on board the *Desire* with Captain Davis. After encountering very severe weather, the famous Cape of Virgins was sighted on the 8th of April. This eastern end of the Straits is bare and without trees, presenting little to interest the voyager; but as he makes progress to the westward the scene entirely alters. Cape Virgins is a precipitous line of cliffs of a whitish colour. After passing it, the ships had to sail across what Sir John Narborough afterwards called "a little sea," for about sixty miles to the first Narrow, named by Sarmiento "La Angostura de la Esperanza." On the 16th the second Narrow was passed, called "La Angostura de San Simon," the distance between the two being ten leagues, according to Davis. Here great masses of sea-weed are seen drifting with the tide, which are rooted on the rocks, and rise to the surface even at consider-able depths, yet trailing for about fifty feet on the water. This weed shows the set of the tide or current, and indicates the positions of all the rocks, thus acting the part of a buoy or lightship in those wild and distant waters. Passing through both the Narrows with a fair wind, Davis entered the long reach, running nearly north and south for over a hundred miles, where the character of the scenery entirely changes. Thickly wooded hills rise from the shore to a height of a thousand feet, and at Port Famine, near the southern end of the reach, there are many fine trees along the banks of the river, which was named San Juan by Sarmiento. The prin-cipal trees are the Winter's bark and an evergreen beech, the latter growing to a great size. Byron mentioned one which was eight feet in diameter. These trees are thickly covered with moss and dripping with moisture, and there is dense undergrowth consisting of arbutus, berberis, and a thorny ribes. On the south side of the strait there are lofty mountains, and one peak, 6800 feet high, rises above the rest, its snowy mantle con-trasting with the dark threatening clouds. Sarmiento

described it as the snowy volcano, and FitzRoy has
very appropriately given it the name of Mount Sarmiento. It is probably the "Campana de Roldan" of
Magellan.

After a short stay at Port Famine, Davis continued
his course to Cape Froward, the southern extreme of the
American continent, in 53° 53' 43" S. Just before
reaching it he came to the port of San Antonio, and
was able to gaze upon the magnificent scenery which
has been so well described by FitzRoy. Here the vegetation is very luxurious. An undergrowth of holly-
leaved berberis, fuchsia, and veronica is sheltered by the
spreading foliage of evergreen beech and Winter's bark
trees. A small paraquet, which lives on the seeds of the
Winter's bark, is often seen, and, what is still more
wonderful, a humming-bird flutters among the fuchsias,
even when snow is falling. While the lower hills are
clothed with trees quite down to the water's edge, the
sharp peaks and ridges, which form the background, are
covered with eternal snow.

Soon after leaving Port San Antonio, the forbidding
mass of the Morro de Santa Agueda, which had been
re-named by Cavendish in his former voyage Cape
Froward, loomed ahead. It is a bold promontory of
dark-coloured slaty rock, with the outer face nearly
perpendicular, and higher land at the back. At Cape
Froward the course of the fleet was rudely checked.
The ships doubled it on the 18th of April, and were
immediately encountered by a wintry gale in their teeth,
blowing down the straits from the north-west. Fortunately Captain Tobias, in the pinnace, discovered a safe
anchorage on the south side, twelve miles from the cape,
where the ships took refuge. It was named Tobias Bay,

and is probably the Mazaredo Bay of later charts. There were continuous gales of wind and snow-storms, and Cavendish remained at anchor for more than a month. The men suffered from cold and exposure, and they had to live on mussels and limpets, eked out by a small allowance of meal from the ships' store. Anthony Knivet, one of the crew of the *Leicester*, gave a marvellous account of the effects of the cold, which must be received with a grain of salt. He says that, coming on board with wet feet and pulling off his stockings, the toes came with them, and that a shipmate named Harris lost his nose, "for going to blow it with his fingers, he cast it into the fire."

Cavendish consulted Davis respecting the possibility of continuing the voyage into the South Sea in such weather. The experienced Arctic navigator assured him that the snow would not continue, and urged him to persevere. But he had lost heart, and seems to have cooled in his friendship for Davis when he found that a retreat would not receive his concurrence; for he left the *Desire* and returned to his own ship. He then proposed to go back into the Atlantic and attempt a voyage round the Cape of Good Hope. Protests were made against this plan, and Cavendish was obliged to abandon it. He finally resolved to make for the Brazilian coast to obtain supplies, and then to return to the Straits of Magellan.

On the 15th of May the fleet set sail from Tobias Bay, and rounding Cape Froward, remained for two days at Port Famine. Here Cavendish was again guilty of that selfish inhumanity which, in his former voyage, had led him to abandon the unfortunate Spaniards to their fate. But in this case his conduct was worse.

He actually landed all the sick of the *Leicester*, left them
exposed to damp, cold, and starvation, and allowed them
to perish miserably.

On the 18th the ships passed Cape Virgins, and were
once more in the Atlantic, clear of the straits. In the
evening of the 20th, the ship of Cavendish was close-
hauled with the wind N.N.E., and the other ships shaped
the same course; but next morning the *Leicester* and
Roebuck were out of sight. Davis naturally supposed
that they had borne up for Port Desire to repair some
damage or to get refreshments. Next day the *Desire*
fell in with the *Black Pinnace*, and they both anchored
at Port Desire on the 26th.

Cavendish must have altered his course during the
night without making any signal, and he had given no
rendezvous. The *Leicester* proceeded to the coast of
Brazil, where Cavendish repeated his abominable cruelty
of putting all his sick on shore, on a hot beach under a
blazing sun, where he left them to perish. He then
made sail for England, and died on the passage home.
He left a will, with a covering letter to Sir Tristram
Gorges, in which he falsely accused Davis of having
intentionally deserted him. Davis acted loyally throughout, and did all in his power to rejoin his chief. He
supposed that he would make for Port Desire, and
afterwards that he would return to the straits, in ac-
cordance with his avowed intention. Burney, in his
"History of Voyages to the South Sea," remarks that,
even if the separation had been intentional, the case
would have been very different from any other. He
says, "Instances without number are to be met with of
ships deserting their commander-in-chief to escape the
perils of a long and dangerous undertaking; but the

case of Captain Davis is of a different character. It is
one of the few in which the separation, if contrived, was
for the purpose of persevering in a pursuit after it had
been abandoned by the chief commander as hopeless
and impracticable."

Davis found himself at Port Desire in want of almost
everything. He had lost boat and oars in the straits,
his single set of sails was nearly worn out, and his
rigging and cables were chafed and old. Having moored
his ship, he landed on the south side of the harbour,
near the Tower Rock, and discovered a standing pool of
fresh water. At low tides his men collected mussels in
great quantities, and there was an abundant supply of
fish, which were caught with bent pins for hooks. Thus
the crew lived on fresh food, and the ship's provisions
were saved during the stay at Port Desire.

After consulting with the master, Captain Davis determined to send the pinnace in search of Cavendish; but
there were two mutinous scoundrels on board the *Desire*
named Charles Parker and Edward Smith, who persuaded
the crew that their captain intended to abandon them,
and went so far as to plot the murder of Davis and his
friends. The conspiracy was betrayed by the boatswain,
and the villainy of the two mutineers was disclosed.
Davis always relied on conciliation and the power of
reasonable exhortation, rather than on the violent
measures which were usually adopted to quell disaffec-
tion. He forgave the treachery of Parker and Smith,
abandoned his intention of sending away the pinnace,
and made a speech to the men in which he fully explained the situation. But he required all those who
had been insubordinate or discontented to put their
hands to a document setting forth the reasons of their

separation from Cavendish, which he also signed, as
well as Captain Randolph Cotton and Mr. Pery, the
master. The document, which is dated June 2, 1592,
has forty signatures, including those of the mutineers
Parker and Smith. After recapitulating the events
of the voyage, it explains the cause of separation,
declares that it was unintentional, and sets forth the
straits to which the crew of the *Desire* is reduced from
the condition of spars and rigging and the insufficiency
of stores and provisions.

Having calmed the excitement and satisfied the crew,
at least for the time, by the conciliatory course he
adopted, Davis set to work with his accustomed energy
and skill to repair defects. He set up a smith's forge
on shore, prepared charcoal, and made bolts, nails, and
spikes. Fresh rigging was laid up by using one of the
cables, and the fore-shrouds, which had been carried
away in a heavy gale, were spliced. While part of the
crew were at work on these repairs, the rest were employed to fish and collect mussels and limpets on the
rocks. The pinnace went to and fro to Penguin Island,
and a sharp look-out was kept for the *Leicester*. Thus
the time passed until August, when Davis came to the
conclusion that Cavendish must have returned direct
to the straits from the Brazilian coast without touching
at Port Desire. He, therefore, proposed to return to
the straits, in the hope of at length finding the missing
vessels—a course to which the crew readily agreed.

After salting down twenty hogsheads of seal-flesh at
Penguin Island, the *Desire* made sail on the 6th of
August, "the poorest wretches that ever were created,"
says Mr. Janes. They had been two months and ten
days in Port Desire.

In a storm which was encountered on the 9th, Davis was obliged to lie-to, for his sails were so worn that he did not dare to expose them to the probable chance of being split by the force of the wind. On the 14th he was " driven in among certain islands, never before discovered by any known relation, lying 50° or better from the shore east and northerly of the straits." Thus was Davis the discoverer of the group which has since improperly been called the "Malouines" and the "Falkland Islands," in 51° to 53° S. latitude. Burney attempted to do justice to the memory of Davis by adopting the name of " Davis's Southern Islands," but he was not successful. Davis saw a succession of barren hills sloping towards low and broken ground and rocky surf-beaten shores, with quantities of drifting kelp on the surface of the sea, and great numbers of birds. Of this group Davis was undoubtedly the discoverer. On two Spanish charts dated 1527 and 1529, there are islands shown near the same position, and called " Ascension Islands," and they also appear on the map of Plancius. But there is no reason to doubt that we have the narratives of all the explorers who had been so far south up to 1592, and none of them mention any such discovery. The insertion of these "Ascension Islands" must, therefore, be referred to the error or imagination of some map-maker. The claim set up for Amerigo Vespuccius, who is said to have made a voyage into the South Atlantic in 1502, is equally baseless, for, by his own account, he never went south of the River Plate. In 1594 Richard Hawkins sailed along the northern shores of the group, and being ignorant of the discovery of Davis, he named it " Hawkins's Maiden Land," and in 1600 the north-western extreme was

sighted by the Dutch navigator Sebald de Weert, and
named the "Sebaldines." In 1690 Strong landed, and
gave the name of Falkland
Channel to the strait between
the east and west islands, and
this name got transferred from
the strait to the islands themselves. Davis was thus de-
prived of the honour which was
his due, of having his name attached to his discovery.

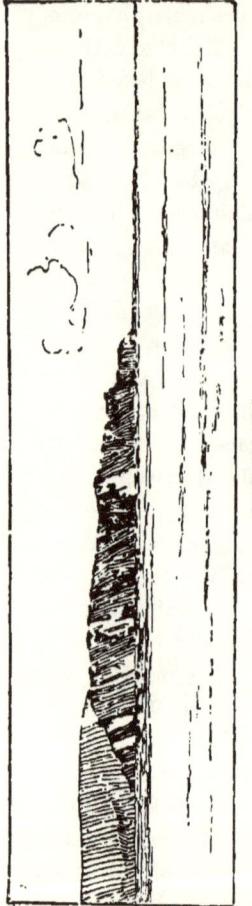

CAPE VIRGINS.

The wind shifted to the east
when the *Desire* was off the
newly discovered islands, and
on the 18th she sighted Cape
Virgins, passing through the
two narrows on the following
day, and doubling Cape Froward on the 21st. The voyage
through the straits had so far
been prosperous. Davis anchored in a port on the south
side of the Long Reach, probably the Abra of Sarmiento,
where he fell in with a number of the wretched natives of
Tierra del Fuego, and on the
24th he entered the "Sea
Reach" which opens on the
Pacific, anchoring within four-
teen leagues of the western entrance of the straits.
He was apparently in the "Puerto de Churruca" of later
charts, and here he proposed to wait for Cavendish. He

remained for a fortnight, but the sufferings of the men from the intense cold and want of food were terrible. They were insufficiently clad, and the seal-flesh having been badly cured, became uneatable. The master, who had become acquainted with the Chilian coast in the first voyage of Cavendish, advised that refuge should be taken at the island of Santa Maria near Concepcion, where the climate is temperate, and where fresh provisions could be obtained. He represented that Santa Maria would be equally well placed as a station for awaiting the arrival of Cavendish, as he would be sure to touch there. Davis adopted this advice, and entered the Pacific on the 13th of September, but was driven back by a westerly gale on the following day, taking refuge in the harbour of God's Merey, the "Misericordia" of Sarmiento, which is a few miles inside Cape Pillar. Another attempt was made a day or two afterwards; but again the *Desire* was driven back by a furious gale, and when they anchored in the Bay of Mercy one of the cables parted. As soon as the wind went down, Davis moored his ship to the trees, unrove his running rigging, and tried unsuccessfully to recover his anchor. He now only had one anchor with a broken fluke, a cable spliced in two places, and the remains of another old cable.

On the 1st of October the wind came fair. The ship was expeditiously rigged and got under weigh, and for the third time a course was shaped for the South Sea. But a mutinous spirit again began to appear among the crew, some wanting to return to Port Desire, while others sided with the officers in their wish to reach the coast of Chile. Davis, therefore, delivered the following speech to the master, to be repeated to the crew :—

I

"Master! you see the wonderful extremity of our estate, and the great doubts among our company of your reports as touching reliefe to be had in the South Sea. Some say in secret, as I am informed, that we undertake these desperate attempts through blind affection that we bear to the General. For mine own part, I plainly make known unto you that the love which I bear to the General caused me first to enter into this action, whereby I have not only heaped upon my head the bitter calamity now present, but also have in some sort procured the dislike of my best friends in England, as is not unknown to some in this company. Now being thus entangled by the providence of God, for my former offences (no doubt), I desire that it may please his Divine Majestie to show us such merciful favour that we may rather proceed than otherwise, or, if it be His will that our mortal being shall now take an end, I desire that it may rather be in proceeding than in returning. And because I see in reason that the limits of our time are now drawing to an end, I do in Christian charity entreat you, first, to forgive me in whatsoever I have been grievous unto you; secondly, that you will rather pray for our General than use hard speeches of him; and let us be fully persuaded that not for his cause and negligence, but for our own offences against the Divine Majesty, we are presently punished. Lastly, let us forgive one another, and be reconciled as children in love and charity, and not think upon the vanities of life; so shall we, in leaving this life, live with our glorious Redeemer, or, abiding in this life, find favour with God. And now, good master, forasmuch as you have been in this voyage once before with your master the General, satisfy the company of such truths as are to you best known ; and you and the rest of the General's men, which likewise have been with him in his first voyage, if you hear anything contrary to the truth, spare not to reprove it, I pray you. And so I beseech the Lord to bestow His mercy upon us."

The master, in reply, protested that the separation from Cavendish had been a source of anguish and sorrow to him, and again advised that a course should be shaped to the island of Santa Maria on the Chilian coast, where pork, corn, and roots could be obtained in abundance. He declared that if they returned, there was nothing but death to be hoped for.

On hearing these speeches, the crew unanimously agreed to continue the voyage, and by the 2nd of October the *Desire* was in the Pacific Ocean, and clear of the Straits. But that night the wind sprung up from the W.N.W., and soon increased to a gale. The *Desire* stood on under courses, while the fury of the storm increased and tremendous seas broke over her. On the 3rd the little *Black Pinnace* came under her consort's lee, and her captain hailed that she had taken in many grievous seas, and that he could not tell what shift to make. It was quite impossible to give her any assistance, and next day she suddenly broached to and went down with all hands. On the 5th the foresail of the *Desire* was split, and the fury of the gale continued with hail and snow, the seas breaking over her, so that it was doubtful every moment whether she might not share the fate of the pinnace.

On the 10th of October the weather was dark and stormy, and the reckoning made the ship very close to Cape Pillar—a dead lee-shore. The men were so tired that they could work no longer, and had thrown them-

selves down in despair. All hope seemed gone. Captain
Davis had yielded to despondency, and was sitting in
the stern-gallery immersed in his own melancholy
thoughts. He was so cold as scarcely to be able to
move a joint. At this juncture his old and tried friend,
Mr. Janes, brought him some "*Rosa solis,*" or, in plain
English, a good stiff glass of hot grog. After he had
drunk it, the weather-beaten navigator was comforted,
and offered up a prayer that their days might either be
speedily ended, or that they might be shown some
merciful sign of the divine love. Suddenly, even before
Mr. Janes had left him, the sun broke out from amongst
the threatening clouds, so that both Davis and the
master were able to get meridian altitudes and shape a
course for the straits. This so revived their spirits that
they made cheery speeches to the men, and every one
felt that the danger was passed. Next day they sighted
the famous headland which forms the southern portal
of the western entrance to the straits. The master was
very doubtful whether the ship could weather Cape
Pillar, but Davis said, "You see there is no remedy;
either we must double it, or before noon we must die;
therefore loose your sails and let us put it to God's Mercy."

So sail was made, and the *Desire*, close-hauled, made
for the terrible cape, with seas breaking over her
furiously. Hope and anxiety gradually gave way to
despair as it was seen that she continued to sag to
leeward more and more, and it seemed as if she could
not possibly weather the cape. The ship was now
within half a mile of the point, and so near the land
that the counter-surf rebounded against the ship's side.
They seemed to be at the very point of death, "the
wind and sea raging beyond measure," and the relent-

less cape frowning above them. At this critical moment the master eased off the main-sheet. He judged that it was too flat aft, and that the ship, instead of going through the water, was rapidly bagging to leeward. The sheet being eased, she gathered way and weathered the danger. They had escaped literally by a hair's-breath. Then, with no sail set; she flew before the gale, and in six hours was twenty-five leagues within

SCENE IN MAGELLAN STRAITS—MOUNT SARMIENTO.

the strait. She was brought into a cove and moored to the trees, that the exhausted men might get a little rest. · During his long sojourns in the Straits of Magellan, Captain Davis had surveyed the coast-lines and many of the harbours with great care, and had prepared an elaborate chart; so that he was enabled to pilot his ships through the numerous dangers with a sure and well-instructed eye, "even in the hell-darke night." Mr. Janes was struck with admiration at the diligence of Davis and his master in this respect. "I conclude," he wrote, "the world hath not any so skilful pilots for that place as they are, for otherwise we could never have passed in such sort as we did."

Leaving their first refuge, they went through the strait as far as the island near the western entrance of the second Narrow, which used to be called Penguin and now Elizabeth Island. Here the *Desire* was anchored, and a boat was sent on shore to collect birds. Misfortune continued to attend on this ill-fated expedition. A sudden squall half-filled the boat, the birds had to be abandoned, and it was with great difficulty that Captain Randolph Cotton and Mr. Janes succeeded in getting back to the ship. On the 27th of October the *Desire* passed Cape Virgins, and on the 30th she reached the other Penguin Island, nine miles south of Port Desire. Here they had better luck. The boats were sent on shore, and returned laden with birds and eggs; the penguins being so closely packed on the island that the men could not move without treading on them.

After the mutiny at Port Desire, Captain Davis said to the culprits Parker and Smith that God would judge between him and them. The time had now come for retribution. They were ordered, with some others, to remain on Penguin Island and collect birds, a boat being sent for them as soon as the ship had anchored in Port Desire. But their guilty consciences led them to suspect that they were going to be abandoned, and they refused to obey the order. Davis then made the following speech to them, in presence of the rest of the crew :—"I understand that you are doubtful of your security, through the perverseness of your own guilty consciences. It is an extreme grief to me that you should judge me bloodthirsty, in whom you have seen nothing but kind conversation. If you have found otherwise, speak boldly and accuse me of the wrongs that I have done; if not, why do you then measure me by your own uncharitable consciences? All the company knoweth, indeed, that in this place you practised to the utmost of your powers to murder me and the master causeless, as God knoweth, which evil in this place we did remit you; and now may conceive, without doing you wrong, that you again purpose some evil in bringing these matters to repetition. But God hath so shortened your confederacy as that I nothing doubt you. It is for your master's sake that I have forborne you in your unchristian practices; and here I protest, before God, that for His sake alone I will endure this injury, and you shall in no sort be prejudiced, nor in anything be by me commanded. When we come into England (if God so favours us) your master shall know your honesties. In the mean space be void of these suspicions; for I call God to witness that revenge is no part of my thought."

The *Desire* was moored in Port Desire on the last day of October, and on the 3rd of November the boat was sent to Penguin Island with as many men and as much wood and water as she would carry, to prepare penguins as provisions for the voyage. Parker and Smith preferred to go by land. They set out well armed with eight other men, but were never heard of again. Thus did God appear to judge between the mutineers and their captain.

Captain Davis, the master, and six men remained by the ship; and the opportunity was taken of exploring the river or creek, and making a careful survey of the anchorage. A large body of Patagonians came upon them suddenly, and set fire to bushes to windward of the ship, but they fled as soon as a gun was fired, and did not appear again. The health of the men was provided for by serving out fresh food in the shape of penguins, young seals, birds of several kinds, and eggs. The leaves of the herb resembling sage, which they called scurvy-grass, was fried with the eggs, and its effect appears to have been excellent in curing scurvy. The great difficulty was to secure a sufficient supply of salt to cure the birds. Captain Davis, with the help of the master and Mr. Janes, manufactured it by collecting salt water in shallow holes on the rocks above the reach of the tide. In six days it had evaporated, leaving salt in powder. Thus they were enabled to dry and salt 14,000 penguins.

On the 22nd of December the *Desire* weighed and commenced her voyage home to England. Captain Davis calculated the quantity of provisions, and drew up a scale by which they would be made to last for six months. It consisted of five ounces of meal a week, five penguins for four men, and six quarts of water daily, and three spoonfuls of oil for each man three days in the week. In this miserable condition the voyage home commenced. Davis was sorely in need of patience and high courage, for all his hopes were shattered and destroyed. He had lost at least £1100 in the venture, and returned a ruined and disappointed man.

On the 30th of January 1593 the ship arrived at the island of Placencia, off the coast of Brazil. Landing with a boat's crew, Davis found the settlement abandoned, but he got a supply of fruits and roots in the deserted gardens, and was able to pilot his ship into a sheltered creek, where there was fresh water near the beach. They worked very hard in making hoops for casks, collecting roots and vegetables, and getting water on board.

On the night of Monday the 5th of February, not only the captain, but several men had dreams which foreboded murder or worse calamities. The dream made so strong an impression on Davis that he gave strict orders for all the men to take their weapons with them when they landed next morning. Towards noon it became very hot, and the working party rested in their shirts, some bathing, and others lying in the shade. Suddenly a body of Portuguese and Indians surprised them, and killed all but two, who brought the news of this wretched massacre to the ship. Davis manned and armed his boat with all speed, but only found the dead bodies of his poor men, and saw two pinnaces pulling away towards Rio de Janeiro. Out of seventy-six souls who left England in the *Desire*, only twenty-seven now survived. The casks were still in a deplorable condition, and only eight tons of water could be taken on board. Yet there was danger of being attacked by an overwhelming force from Rio; and on the whole, Davis decided that it would be better "to fall into the hands of the Lord, rather than into the hands of men." On the 6th of February the *Desire* once more put to sea, and off Cape Frio a plentiful fall of rain enabled the long-suffering crew to refill their water-casks.

Now commenced a tale of horror such as is not surpassed in the annals of the sea. The penguins turned out to have been insufficiently cured. A loathsome and hideous worm began to form in the corrupting flesh, and multiplied prodigiously.—Then, after they had crossed the line, the scurvy broke out in a most malignant form. The burning sun poured its rays on the miserable men like a helmet of burnished steel. Their bodies began to swell, and they could scarcely breathe. Davis

exerted himself to the utmost. Though scarcely able to
speak for sorrow, he exhorted the poor stricken creatures
to have patience, and, like dutiful children, to accept the
chastisements of God. Some went raving mad and died
in frightful pain. The master fought it out bravely,
and was just able to crawl about. Captain Cotton and
Mr. Janes were in like case. Davis and a boy alone
remained in perfect health. These five had to work the
ship, for the eleven survivors of the crew were unable to
move. The captain and master took turns at the helm,
and managed to trim the spritsail with the help of the
other three. The rest of the sails were all blown away.
"Thus, as lost wanderers upon the sea, it pleased God
that we arrived at Bere-haven in Ireland on the 11th
of June 1593, and there ran the ship on shore." Thence
Davis proceeded in a fishing-boat to Padstow in Cornwall.

John Davis returned to his home at Sandridge need-
ing welcome and consolation as much as any man ever
did in this world. He found it desolate. A scoundrel
named Milburne had seduced his wife in his absence,
and, not content with that, had devised accusations
against the man he had injured in the hope of securing
his imprisonment, and so preventing him from prosecuting any plan of vengeance against the destroyer of his
peace. This was what Davis had to face after he landed
on his native shore. For several months he appears to
have been dazed with the weight of his misfortunes.
His friend Sir Walter Raleigh, in March 1594, wrote
from Sherborne to warn him that a warrant was out
against him, and to advise him to come up to London;
but he was intercepted by a pursuivant and brought
up in custody. The nature of the accusation does not
appear. It was investigated by the best gentlemen

in Devon, and proved to be false. Moreover, the diligence, fidelity, and intelligence of Davis in the Queen's service were shown to be very great. He was set at liberty, sureties being taken for his appearance, within twenty days after warning given, at Mr. Blackaller's house in Dartmouth; but it does not appear that he was ever molested again by the emissaries of the law. Milburne was a dissolute person, with nothing to lose, and Raleigh heard that he had coined money and was likely to be hanged at the assizes. It is to be hoped that this was the villain's end.

The disastrous voyage to the Straits of Magellan brought out some of the best traits in the character of the great Arctic navigator. He showed himself to be as resolute and persevering as in the Northern voyages. He was loyal to his chief under very trying circumstances. He missed no opportunity of surveying and collecting information that would be useful to future navigators. He was kind and considerate to his men, and took constant thought for their welfare; and if he was too conciliatory to mutineers, and strove to restore subordination by gentle rather than by strong measures, the fault was on the right side. He, finally, met crushing misfortune with the calm fortitude of a hero. The faults as well as the fine points of the character of Davis were brought out in this terrible voyage, and tried as by fire.

The narrative of the voyage of Davis to Magellan's Straits was written by his friend Mr. John Janes, and was published in Hakluyt's collection. Purchas gives a letter from Cavendish to Sir Tristram Gorges written shortly before his death, and the marvellous narrative of Anthony Knivet, one of the sick men who were so heartlessly abandoned by Cavendish on the coast of Brazil.

CHAPTER VIII.

THE failure of the expedition on which all the hopes of Davis had been set, and the heavy losses entailed on him, destroyed every chance of soon being able to renew an enterprise with similar objects. The money he had accumulated as the result of many years of work at sea was all lost. Yet he retained his patrimony at Sandridge, and thither he retired, with the intention of communicating to his countrymen the professional knowledge he had acquired, in the form which seemed most likely to be useful to them. His wife would never more welcome his return. She had deserted her husband and children, and appears to have died soon afterwards. But in the home of his own childhood he was surrounded by his three little boys. His energy was not weakened, his enthusiasm was not damped, by his sorrows and misfortunes; and, though living in strict retirement during the next two years, he was neither idle nor despondent. Busily engaged on hydrographical work of various kinds, and watching with deep interest the progress of maritime enterprise, his two published works were composed at Sandridge during the two years which followed his return from Magellan's Straits.

The rise of England's maritime power during the

reign of the great Queen naturally led to the cultivation of those mathematical and astronomical studies which are a necessary part of a sailor's profession. Although John Davis was not a profound classical scholar, he was acquainted with the works of the ancients as well as with the more recent discoveries of mediæval and Spanish labourers in the same field. For the erudition of such men as Hues and Wright was open to their sailor-friends, and the practical navigator was able to appreciate the position of nautical science in his own day by comparing it with the ideas and practices of his predecessors. If we would understand the place which the "Seaman's Secrets" of Davis takes in the history of navigation, we must pass in review, with the same object as he would have had in examining former labours, the progressive work of those who had brought nautical astronomy to the point it had reached in the days of Elizabeth; for the contemporaries of Davis still treated the work of the ancients with respect and discussed their methods, and the English had but recently begun to assume independence of foreign help, and to publish original treatises on navigation.

All students of the sixteenth century, while welcoming the advances and improvements of later times, looked upon the philosophers whose labours and discoveries are recorded in the "Almagest" and "Geography" of Ptolemy as the founders of nautical science. The lectures of Hood and the popular treatise of Hues instructed the Elizabethan seamen in the former history of their science, and the interest of young navigators was aroused by the stories of the earliest scientific discoveries, and by a review of subsequent progress. Aristarchus, Eratosthenes, and Hipparchus

were names more familiar to the young seamen of the
Elizabethan era than they are to us. Davis and his
fellows knew how the famous librarian of Alexandria
had calculated the obliquity of the ecliptic by means of
the *armillæ*, or great copper circles which were fixed in
the square porch of the Alexandrian Museum. They
were familiar with his method of determining the
circumference of the earth; and his learning and
ingenuity must have satisfied their reason, while it
excited their imaginations. Eratosthenes had heard
that deep wells at Syene were enlightened to the
bottom on the day of the summer solstice, and he
therefore knew that Syene must be on the tropic. He
had ascertained the latitude of Alexandria by observation, and he assumed that the two places were on the same
meridian. The arc thus measured enabled this original
thinker to calculate the proportion it bore to the whole
circumference of the earth, and his result was a fair
approximation to the truth. This story of the methods
by which the great Alexandrian made his discovery was
a useful and suggestive lesson. The work of Hipparchus,
though more complete and extensive, did not appeal so
directly to the imagination. But the catalogue of stars
and constellations, the system of mapping by degrees of
latitude and longitude, the theory of the precession of
the equinoxes, were all due to the genius of Hipparchus,
though the thanks of posterity for their preservation
belongs to Ptolemy. Hence the system of Ptolemy was
the text-book of the Middle Ages, and the study of his
great work, translated into Arabic under the name of
the "Almagest," was the foundation of astronomical
knowledge down almost to the time of Davis. It was
to learned Arabs, well versed in the "Almagest" of

Ptolemy, that King Alfonso the Wise committed the task of constructing the tables which bear his name; and the principal work of Purbach and Regiomontanus, the two most learned German astronomers of the fifteenth century, was their translation of Ptolemy. But Regiomontanus was not merely a translator. He constructed valuable instruments, and was the first to publish an almanac with tables of the sun's declination calculated for the years from 1475 to 1566.

The adaptation of instruments and calculations in use at the observatories of astronomers on shore, to the requirements of seamen, was the most important work to be accomplished in those days, and the development of maritime enterprise in the fifteenth and sixteenth centuries made it a matter of urgency to utilise the discoveries of students. Progress was first made in this direction by Martin Behaim of Nuremburg, a pupil of Regiomontanus. He first combined the theoretical knowledge of a student with the practice of a navigator. He had burnt the midnight oil while poring over the pages of the "Almagest," and he had accompanied Diogo Cam when that explorer reached the mouth of the Congo in 1484.[1]   This combination of theoretical and practical knowledge was calculated to effect changes which its absence had long delayed.   The astrolabe, which had been known for centuries as an astronomical instrument, was first applied by Martin Behaim for purposes of navigation.[2]   A graduated ring of metal, held so as to hang as a plummet, with a movable limb across it fitted with two perforated sights, enabled a sailor to observe the angle between the

---

[1] We learn this from an inscription on the globe of Behaim.
[2] This is stated by Barros (Dec. I. Lib. iv., cap. 2).

horizon and the sun at noon. The sun's declination on
each day was given in the almanac of Regiomontanus,
and with these elements the latitude was found by a
very simple calculation. But it is probable that if
Behaim had not himself made long voyages, his
theoretical knowledge would never have led him to
adapt the astrolabe for use at sea. Behaim also constructed a globe which is still preserved at Nuremburg, and which is the oldest now in existence.[1] It was
not long before another instrument of simpler construction, and better adapted for use at sea, was invented
to observe the sun's altitude. This was the cross-staff,

[1] I am glad to be able to add the following note on the globe of
Martin Behaim, which has been kindly furnished me by the
distinguished geographer, Baron Nordenskiöld. "The globe of
Behaim is, without comparison, the most important geographical
document that appeared between A.D. 150, the date of the com-
position of Ptolemy's Atlas, and A.D. 1507, when Ruysch's Map of
the World was published. This globe is not only the oldest known
to exist, but, from its size and its wealth of geographical detail, it
far surpassed all analogous *monuments de géographie*, until the
appearance of the globe of Mercator. It is the first geographical
document which, without any reserve, adopts the existence of
antipodes. It is the first which plainly shows the possibility of
a passage by sea to India and Cathay. It is the first on which
the discoveries of Marco Polo are clearly indicated. It is true that
the Behaim globe may be said to have been preceded, in some
respects, by some other earlier maps of the fifteenth century, for
instance the map in a codex of Pomponius Mela of 1427 in the
library of Rheims, and that of Fra Mauro. But if these are
impartially studied, it will be found that they are based on the
idea of Homer, that the earth is a large circular island encompassed
by the ocean, a conception totally incompatible with the new
geographical discoveries of the Spaniards. These and analogous
maps are, therefore, not in the slightest degree comparable with
the globe of Behaim ; which may be said to be an exact repre-
sentation of the geographical knowledge of the period immediately
preceding the first voyage of Columbus."

which was first described in 1514 by Werner of Nuremburg in his notes on Ptolemy's "Geography."

Longitude continued to be a difficulty, although
Werner had proposed the method of observing the
distance of the moon from the sun with simultaneous
altitudes, afterwards known as a "lunar;" and Gemma
Frisius, the learned professor at Louvain, had an idea,
which he published in 1530, that longitude might be
found by comparison of times kept by small clocks.

The first use of the mariner's compass at sea by

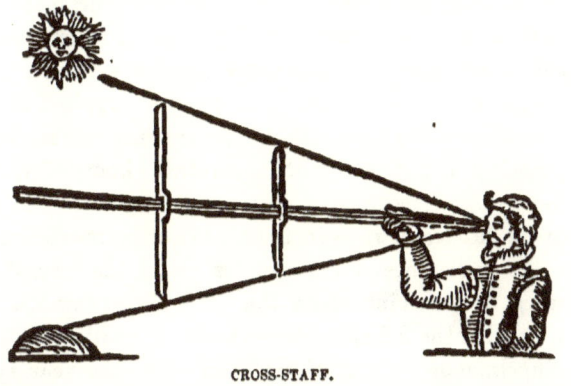

CROSS-STAFF.

European seamen is doubtfully attributed to Flavio
Gioja of Amalfi, who lived about the beginning of the
fourteenth century; and it was certainly in general use
when Prince Henry of Portugal dispatched his expeditions of discovery a century later. The variation of the
needle was first observed by Columbus on the 14th of
September 1492; it attracted the close and constant observation of Sebastian Cabot; but later Spanish writers
believed it to be due to inaccurate observation, and as late
as 1571 such a navigator as Sarmiento doubted its exist-

K

ence. It was not until the English seriously took up
the study of navigation that advances were made in the
science of terrestrial magnetism, or that any but the
roughest guesses were used for estimating a ship's run.

The use of the plane chart was a source of enormous
error and proportional danger to the early mariners.
By it the degrees of latitude and longitude were made
of equal length on a plane surface, so that the error
increased with the distance from the equator. Careful
navigators, like Davis, preferred the use of globes, which
for a long time formed part of the furniture of a
navigator. The discovery of a projection which obviated
the disadvantages of the plane chart was an era in the
progress of navigation. As it also supplies another
remarkable example of the importance of combining
practical experience with theoretical knowledge, it is
deserving of more than passing notice, while the story
of its discoverer is as instructive as it is interesting.

At a distance of eight miles above the city of Antwerp, at the point where the little Rupel forms a junction with the Scheldt, there stands a small town called
Rupelmonde. On a wintry evening of the year 1512 a
poor shoemaker, with his wife and six children, who had
travelled all the way from Germany on foot, entered this
Flemish town. The man, whose name was Hubert Cremer,
was in sore need; but his uncle was a clergyman in Rupelmonde, and he looked to him for help. The old canon,
Gisbert Cremer, received this forlorn party with kind-
ness and hospitality, and on the 5th of March 1512, a
few days after their arrival, the wife gave birth to a
boy, who received the name of Gerard, and was brought
up by his great-uncle. It was the custom in those days,
especially in Holland and Flanders, for clergymen and

other learned persons to adopt a Latin form of their name. "Cremer" and "Mercator" mean a trader or merchant in Flemish and Latin respectively, so the canon had taken the name of Mercator, his adopted nephew also being known as Gerard Mercator.

The uncle, Gisbert, was a poor man, but he contrived to send young Gerard to the great University of Louvain, where he was enrolled among what were called "the indigent students." Gerard had a genius for mathematics, and after he had taken his degree he earned his livelihood by drawing and engraving maps, at the same time receiving lessons in nautical astronomy from the learned Gemma Frisius. Mercator published his first map in 1537, and his great terrestrial globe, two feet in diameter, appeared in 1541. Owing to the persecutions of the Inquisition, he removed to the small town of Duisburg on the Rhine, in the dominions of the Duke of Cleves, in 1552, and he made that place his home for the remaining forty-two years of his long life.

It was in the year 1569 that Mercator completed and published his famous chart of the world on his new projection. There is only one copy in existence, in the National Library at Paris—a sheet 6 feet 6 inches long and 4 feet 4 inches broad. It is beautifully engraved, and dedicated to Mercator's friend and patron, the Duke of Cleves. In the centre there is a long Latin inscription, which is the only indication given by Mercator of the principle on which he constructed his chart. He there tells us that he had been led to give the degrees of latitude towards the two poles a slight increase beyond the proportion they present at the equator. The meridians are, as on the old plane charts, parallel to each other. The advantage of the new projection, as stated by Mercator, is that, although distances are distorted, the positions of places relatively to each other are correct.· But he nowhere describes in detail the principle on which the chart is constructed. It is, indeed, doubtful whether he had worked it out himself, for the chart is incorrectly drawn, only being approximately accurate up to 40°.[1] Mercator deserves the great praise of having conceived the idea of a most useful projection, but it was not enough to do this without enabling others to construct it by a fixed rule. This is a striking example of the necessity for combining practical knowledge with theory —a combination which was wanting in the case of Mercator and his chart. The diagram opposite shows the idea which had occurred to the illustrious cartographer.

Supposing the triangle A, B, C, to represent a section of the surface of the earth, C being the pole, and A, B, an arc of the equator, A, C, and B, C, two meridians,

[1] The meridional distance of 10° at the equator being $= \kappa$, the distances of the parallels, according to Mercator, were—

$$0° - 10° = \kappa \frac{1}{\text{cosine } 5°}$$

$$10° - 20° = \kappa \frac{1}{\text{cosine } 15°}$$

$$20° - 30° = \kappa \frac{1}{\text{cosine } 25°}$$

This distance from the equator to 80° of latitude would therefore be—

$$\kappa \left\{ \frac{1}{\cos 5} + \frac{1}{\cos 15} + \frac{1}{\cos 25} + \frac{1}{\cos 35} + \frac{1}{\cos 45} + \frac{1}{\cos 55} + \frac{1}{\cos 6 \ 5} + \frac{1}{\cos 75} \right. $$

The correct formula is *Mer. Parts* for $l° = \frac{180° \times 60°}{\pi}$ log. tan. $(45° + \frac{l°}{2})$.

the distance between the meridians a degree of longitude, and the distance between the parallels A, B, and D, E, a degree of latitude. Then let A be the point of departure of a ship, and E its port of destination. The line A, E, is the line which the ship will take, or its course. If the meridians are made parallel, they will be represented by the lines A, F, and B, G. The consequence is that the position of the port of destination is changed from E to I. This was the distortion caused by the old plane chart. The diagram shows that the line E, I, not only increased the distance, but altered the course. Mercator's object was to cure the distortion in direction, that is, to keep the course correct, even if he increased the distortion in distance. He effected this by pushing the port of destination farther north to H. In other words, he lengthened the degrees of latitude as they receded from the equator towards the pole in

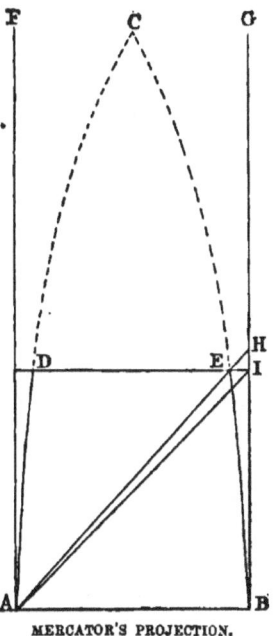

MERCATOR'S PROJECTION.

the same proportion in which the degrees of longitude are lengthened in consequence of the meridians being made parallel. The courses would always be correct, although the distances would be distorted.

But Mercator supplied no practical method of working out his principle. He died before any use had been made of it; and it was reserved for an Englishman, who combined practice with theory, to utilise his idea by supplying rules for constructing charts on his principle. Mercator breathed his last at Duisburg in the year that Davis wrote his "Seaman's Secrets." Tables of meridional parts, which supply the omission of Mercator, had already been prepared in England.

Germans and Flemings had thus made great advances in theory, but the nations which took part in the maritime discoveries of the fifteenth century felt the necessity for converting theory into practice. Portugal took the lead in this work, followed closely by the sister kingdom of the peninsula. Pedro Nunez, better known as Nonius, lived from 1497 to 1577. He taught mathematics at Coimbra for many years, and published his work on the art of navigation in 1530. Nonius gave the solution of several problems, including the determination of the latitude by the sun's double altitude. He introduced the use of rhumb lines on charts, and exposed the errors of plane charts, without, however, suggesting any improvement. The Spaniard Martin Fernandez Enciso was the contemporary of Nonius, but he was an explorer as well as an astronomical student. In his "Suma de Geografia," the second edition of which was published in 1530, he gives tables of declination and descriptions of the use of instruments. His work was the first practical navigation book for the use of sailors. Enciso was followed by Guevara, Zamorano, and Chaves; but the best known Spanish navigation books were those of Medina and Cortes. The "Rules of Navigation," by Pedro de Medina, first published at Seville in 1563, went through many editions, and was translated into Dutch with a supple-

ment by Michel Coignet of Antwerp.   It was the work
on which Dutch navigators mainly relied in their voyages during the earlier years of independence, and a copy
was found at the winter quarters of Barents in Novaya
Zemlya in 1871, which had endured the Arctic frosts
and snows for nearly three centuries.   But Martin
Cortes was the Spanish author best known in England.
His work covered more ground than that of Medina,

VARIOUS PROJECTIONS.

and was entitled "A Brief Compendium of the Sphere
and of the Art of Navigation, with New Instruments,
and Rules illustrated by very Subtle Demonstrations."
Cortes was the first to suggest the existence of a magnetic pole different from the pole of the earth.   Spanish
pilots had to pass a stiff examination before receiving
charge of a ship; and such care was taken in ascertaining positions and in navigating, that Spanish seamen

were constantly held up as examples to Englishmen by the writers of the day. Practice led, in some instances, to the introduction of improvements and to inventions; and it is probable that when Sarmiento tells us that he himself constructed a new cross-staff to subtend a larger angle than could be taken with any then in use, he was endeavouring to observe a lunar distance.

When England began to take a lead in maritime enterprise, her people were far behind the sailors of the Peninsula in knowledge of nautical astronomy and navigation. As Englishmen acquired skill in the art of war by studying the military system of the Spanish army in the Low Countries, so they took Spanish navigators as their masters and instructors in the seaman's art. In both they soon came up with and passed their guides. The first publications for the use of English sailors were the "Rutters of the Sea," the earliest having been written in the fifteenth century; but they were merely rough sailing directions for the English and adjacent coasts. It was to Stephen Borough, the Arctic navigator and countryman of Davis, that England owes her first navigation book. Feeling the want of such a manual very strongly, he induced Mr. Richard Eden, the publisher of the first collection of voyages and travels, to undertake a translation of the Spanish work of Martin Cortes. It appeared in 1561, and there were ten fresh additions between that date and 1615. The work of Guevara was published in a translated form by Edward Hellowes in 1578. Medina was also translated into English by John Frampton in 1581, but it never attained the same popularity as Eden's edition of Cortes.

Bourne's " Regiment of the Sea," published in 1573,

was the first original work on navigation by an Englishman, but even it was merely designed as a supplement
to Cortes. There was a considerable demand for it, and
an enlarged edition was brought out by Dr. Thomas
Hood in 1596, with new tables of the sun's declination.
A special interest attaches to the work of Bourne, because it is the first in which the existing method of
measuring the run of a ship is fully described. It has
scarcely been improved since. A "log-ship" is thrown
overboard in such a way that it remains in the water
where it falls, while the line attached to it is allowed to
run out during a fixed interval, timed either by counting
or by a minute-glass. Then the number of knots marked
on the line that have run out is to the time interval
shown by the glass as the number of miles equivalent
to the knots is to an hour. After the publication of
Bourne's "Regiment" the practice of heaving the log
is mentioned in narratives of voyages, especially by
Luke Fox in his voyage to Hudson's Bay.[1]

As the interest in maritime adventure increased in
England, and voyages became more numerous, the demand for navigation books and instruments became
greater. The attention of many of the ablest men in
both Universities was turned to the subject. · Dr. Dee
contributed several useful treatises from his richly-stored
brain; John Blagrave and Thomas Hood made improvements in the astrolabe and cross-staff, and Thomas
Blundeville wrote his "Exercises" in 1594, which was
very popular, and went through several editions. The
science of terrestrial magnetism was much advanced in

---

[1] Bourne in his "Inventions or Devices" (1578), No. 21, tells
us that the deviser of the log and line was Humphrey Cole of the
Mint in the Tower.

England during the same period. The subject of compass variation was first treated of in the "Discourse of the Magnet and Loadstone," by William Borough in 1581, and it was more closely investigated by Robert Norman. In a work called the "New Attractive," Norman described his discovery of the dip of the needle and his invention of the dipping-needle. A few years afterwards the series of observations for the variation of the compass at London was commenced, which has been continued uninterruptedly to the present day. But the greatest advance was made by Dr. Gilbert of Colchester, who, in his work published in 1600, propounded the theory that the earth itself was a magnet.

The learned cosmographers who had acquired practical experience by making sea-voyages did most valuable services to nautical science in England as elsewhere, and it is to one of these that we owe the complete utilisation of charts on Mercator's projection. Edward Wright was a native of Garveston, a village in Norfolk, and was born in 1560, being nine years of age when Mercator published his chart in 1569. He was entered of Gonville and Caius College at Cambridge, and before many years he became well known as a profound mathematician. He accompanied the Earl of Cumberland in his expedition to the Azores in 1590, and we have already seen how he met John Davis at Horta, in the island of Fayal. Wright then acquired that practical knowledge of navigation which completed his education. He applied the test of practice to his theories, and saw for himself of what sailors were most in need. From that time he gave much attention to the improvement of the charts then in use. He tells us how the chart of Mercator suggested the means. "By reason, he wrote, "of that map of Mercator, I first thought of correcting so many and grave errors and absurdities in common use on charts, by increasing distances of parallels from the equinoctial to the pole. *But the way how it should be done, I learnt neither of Mercator nor of any one else.*"

After his return from the voyage to the Azores, Wright resided at Cambridge as Fellow of his College, and it was there, in 1594, that he discovered the method of dividing the meridian, in the very year of Mercator's death.   He sent his discovery to his friend Thomas Blundeville, with a table of meridional parts, a specimen of a chart correctly divided, and an explanation of the principle.   All this was published in the same year in Blundeville's "Exercises."   Wright did not publish his own treatise, entitled "The Correction of Certain Errors in Navigation," until five years afterwards.   He then showed the principle of the division of meridians, the manner of constructing a table of meridional parts, and its uses in navigation.   So that it is to Wright, the practical navigator, and not to Mercator, the theoretical student, that the honour is due of being the first to demonstrate the true principle upon which sea-charts should be constructed, by means of tables of meridional parts.   Before Wright's publication of the tables Mercator's projection was practically useless.   Almost immediately after Wright's publication the charts on Mercator's projection came into general use; Hondius having produced his new chart of the world at Amsterdam, by the use of Wright's tables, in 1595.   Mercator was the inventor.   Wright completed the invention, and made it practically useful.

Wright was not the only learned university professor

who combined practical knowledge of life at sea with
theoretical study.   Robert Hues of Hereford, who was
born in the same year as John Davis, was an Oxford
graduate.   He was the friend of Sir Walter Raleigh
and his executor.   He accompanied Cavendish in his
second voyage, and had also been on the coast of North
America.   Hues and Davis must often have met at
Port Desire and in the Straits of Magellan, and have
exchanged ideas.   Davis would enjoy conversations
with one who was deeply versed in the history of
astronomical science, while Hues would benefit from
the great practical experience of the Arctic navigator.
The results of the learning and ripe knowledge of Hues
were given to the world in his "Tractatus de Globis
et eorum Usu," which was published in 1594.   While
reviewing all the knowledge of the ancient Greeks and
Arabians, he explained the uses of the globe, and propounded various problems in navigation, including that
famous one afterwards proposed by Halley.   The
"Tractatus" was much read, and was translated into
English and Dutch.   It included a valuable chapter on
the use of rhumbs by Thomas Heriot, another learned
scholar who had practical experience as a navigator.
Heriot accompanied Sir Richard Grenville in his
voyage to Virginia, and wrote the "Brief and True
Report of that New Found Land."   He was the
mathematical instructor of Raleigh, the correspondent
of Kepler, and the author of a great work on algebra.
Hues died at Oxford in 1632, at a good old age.   But
Heriot was a martyr to science.   His death, in 1621,
was due to a dreadful ulcer on his lip, caused by a
habit of holding instruments with verdigris on them
in his mouth.   Wright, Hues, and Heriot were all

examples of men whose most useful work in advancing nautical science was due to their having added experience derived from sea-voyages to the knowledge acquired in their studies.   John Davis, on the other hand, was a man who added knowledge derived from students and books as opportunity offered to profound and extensive experience as a seaman.

CHAPTER IX.

John Davis wrote his work on navigation at Sandridge, and dated the dedication to Lord Howard of Effingham on the 20th of August 1594. It is entitled, "The Seaman's Secrets, divided into Two Parts, wherein is taught the Three Kinds of Sailing, Horizontal, Paradoxal, and Sailing on a Great Circle; with many other most necessary Rules and Instruments not heretofore set forth by any." It was printed by Thomas Dawson, "dwelling near the Three Cranes in the Vinetree."

The object of Davis was to furnish his brother sailors with hints and suggestions derived from his own long experience, rather than to write a regular treatise on navigation. He described his book as "a brief account of such practices as, in my several voyages, I have from experience collected." His dedication to his old admiral recalled the glorious days when the Spanish Armada was repulsed, and he touchingly referred to the false accusation of treachery which had been made by Cavendish, but which his whole conduct refuted. He then makes some remarks on the importance of the art of navigation. "It is," he says, "the means whereby countries are discovered, and community drawn between nation and nation. By navigation commonweals, through mutual

158

THE
SEAMANS SE
CRETS.

Deuided into 2. partes, wherein is taught the
three kindes of Sayling, Horizontall, Paradoxall, and sayling vpon a
great Circle : also an Horizontall Tyde Table for the easie finding of
the ebbing and flowing of the Tydes, with a Regiment newly calcula-
ted for the finding of the Declination of the Sunne and many
other most necessary rules and instruments
ont heretofore set foorth
by any.

Newly corrected by the author *Iohn Dauis* of *Sandrudge,*
neere *Dartmouth*, in the Countie of *Deuon*. Gent.

❧ *Imprinted at London by* Thomas Dawſon,
dwelling neere the three Cranes in the Vinetree,
and are there to be folde. 1607

trade, are not only sustained but mightily enriched;"
and he therefore claims that the "painful seaman ought
to be held in great esteem, by whose hard adventures
such excellent benefits are achieved; for by his exceed-
ing great hazards the form of the earth, the quantities
of countries, the diversity of nations, the natures of
climates, countries, and people, are made known to us."
He takes Spain as an example, pointing out that the
greatness of that nation is caused by "the painful industry of the Spaniards in navigation."

The momentous character of the subject makes it the
duty of every man who has a knowledge of it to impart
that knowledge to the best of his abilities, "among whom,
as the most unmeet of all, yet wishing all good to the
painful traveller, I have published this short treatise,
naming it the 'Seaman's Secrets,' because by certain
questions demanded and answered I have not omitted
anything that appertaineth to the secret of navigation,
whereby if there may grow any increase of knowledge
or ease in practice, it is the thing which I chiefly desire."
The work was intended for sailors. It was a book of
wrinkles. Omitting "cunning conclusions" and problems only suited for scholars to study on shore, it
dwelt exclusively on "those things that are needfully
required in a sufficient seaman." He thus explained
his intention to the Lord Admiral, but, in addressing
his own brethren of the sea, he appealed with confidence
to their sympathy. "I distrust not but all honest-
minded seamen and pilots of reputation will gratefully
accept this book—only in regard of my friendly good-
will towards them, for it is not only in respect of my
pains, but of my love that I would receive favourable
courtesy."

. Davis divides the art of navigation into three parts. Horizontal navigation is the same as what is now called plane sailing, or problems which require the use of plane trigonometry only. By paradoxal sailing Davis means sailing on the spiral a ship would describe if she continued sailing round the world on any course except east and west, north and south. He defines it also as the gathering together of many courses into one, or what is now called " working a traverse." A " traverse table " is now used to obviate the necessity for computation which existed in the time of Davis. The third part is " great circle navigation," which Davis defines as the one shortest way between place and place, the ship keeping on the great circle which passes through the place of departure and the place of destination.

Having defined the three kinds of navigation, Davis proceeds to describe the instruments which, in his time, " were necessary for the execution of this excellent skill." These were a sea-compass, a cross-staff and astrolabe for measuring the altitudes of heavenly bodies, an azimuth compass, a chart, and a paradoxal compass. This last instrument was probably designed to show how the line of the course cuts the several meridians, these meridians being drawn upon their proper inclination.   .

After explaining the use of these necessary instruments, the author treats of the moon's motion and of the tides, describing an instrument which he invented, called a " horizontal tide-table," for finding the time of high and low water. The diagram referred to in the text is not to be found in the copy of the " Seaman's Secrets " at the British Museum ; but it is fully explained, with several examples, and appears to have been a useful contrivance for assisting a navigator to ascertain the tides at various places.

The rules for ascertaining the latitude are then given. Old writers almost invariably speak of the latitude as the pole's altitude, or the height of the pole. Davis begins by demonstrating the simple problem that the height of the pole above the horizon is equal to the latitude, and he then explains the methods of finding the latitude by observing the meridian altitude of the sun or of a fixed star. He describes the cross-staff, and the way to observe with it, and gives some necessary hints respecting corrections for declination, derived from his experience both in the Northern Seas and in Magellan's Straits. Davis used the "Ephemeris" of Stadius in preparing tables of the sun's declination, a work which was in general use in this country. Johannes Stadius was professor of mathematics at Paris, and afterwards at Louvain. He published his first almanac at Cologne in 1545.

. The sections devoted by Davis to the sea-chart and its uses are very complete. He clearly explains the errors of the plane chart then in use, and shows that it is almost worthless for a long voyage ; although for short courses, and for plans of coast-lines and anchorages, it is "to very good purpose for the pilot's use." Davis lays down three rules which ought to be observed with special care by a good pilot. The first is to obtain a reliable observation for latitude, the second to ascertain the variation of his compass, and the third to note down the rate the ship is going every hour. The method of finding what a ship is going by the log and line, which was explained by Bourne in 1573, appears to have been in such general use in Davis's time that he

did not think it necessary to refer to it.   He, however,
makes a number of practical suggestions, confessing at
the same time that "these things are better learnt by
practice than taught by pen," and he concludes this
section of his subject with an admirable passage :—"It
is not possible that any man can be a good and sufficient pilot or skilful seaman but by painful and diligent
practice, with the assistance of art, whereby the famous
pilot may be esteemed worthy of his profession, as a
member meete for the common weal." Captain Bed-
ford, in his "Sailor's Pocket-Book," impressed the same
truth on his readers, nearly three centuries after Davis
had written.   "The mastery of the ocean cannot be
learnt upon the shore, and can only be acquired by
incessant practice on shipboard, and at sea."   Davis
illustrated his section on charts with a special chart
of the British Channel, usually called "the Sleeve" in
those days.   It contained soundings as well as the outlines of the coast, and was drawn partly from his own
surveys, and partly from the work of other reliable
pilots.   He justly valued this carefully prepared chart,
for it had never failed to give him the true position of
his ship when he had got what he calls "the altitude
and depth," in other words, the latitude and soundings.
"Therefore," he says, "have it not in light regard, for
it will give you great evidence, and is worthy to be kept
as a special jewel for the seaman's use, be he never
so expert."   Unfortunately Davis's chart of the British
Channel is neither in the copy of the "Seaman's Secrets"
at the British Museum nor in that in the Pepys Library
at Cambridge.

Davis concludes his first book by giving the form
in which a log should be kept, adding a page from the

log of the *Desire* in March 1593. The first column gives the date, the second the observed latitude, the third the courses, the fourth the distances run, the fifth the wind, and the sixth the variation of the compass.

The second book of the " Seaman's Secrets " is devoted to a description of the globe, its uses, and the solution of numerous problems by its means. Davis thought most highly of the globe as an instrument for use in navigation. " The use of the globe is of so great ease, certainty, and pleasure as that the commendations thereof cannot sufficiently be expressed ; for of all instruments it is the most rare and excellent." Considering the errors of a plane chart, it is no wonder that a careful and scientific seaman, like Davis, should turn to the globe for the solution of his problems. Unacquainted with the tables by which Wright was about to utilise Mercator's projection, Davis had given much thought to some means of improving the sea-chart then in use. He announced his intention of publishing what he called a " paradoxal chart," serving the purpose of a globe. It was probably a scheme for representing the globe on a flat surface with due regard to the convergence of the meridians. But the publication of Wright was on the eve of bringing Mercator's projection into general use.

At the close of his little volume, Davis gives an indication that he had discovered a method of solving problems in navigation by arithmetical calculation. He speaks of "that sweet skill of sailing which may well be called navigation arithmetical, because it wholly consisteth of calculations comprehended within the limits of numbers. For there can be nothing that by

this heavenly harmony of numbers shall not be most
copiously manifested, to the seaman's admiration and
great content, the orderly practice whereof, to the best
of my poor capacity, I purpose to make known." He
never found an opportunity of fulfilling this promise,
but he had evidently made some discovery of a means of

THE CROSS STAFF.

handling figures analogous to that which Napier gave
to the world a few years later. It was reserved for
Henry Briggs to improve upon the discovery of Napier,
and to bring logarithms into general use, by the publication of his "Arithmetica Logarithmica" in 1624.
Davis was probably on the verge of a similar discovery.

This remarkable man was·an enthusiast. His pat- ⌐
riotism, and his love for his noble profession led him to
concentrate all the energies of his mind on the means
of improving the art of navigation and facilitating the
work of seamen. "It was not in respect of his pains,   ⌐

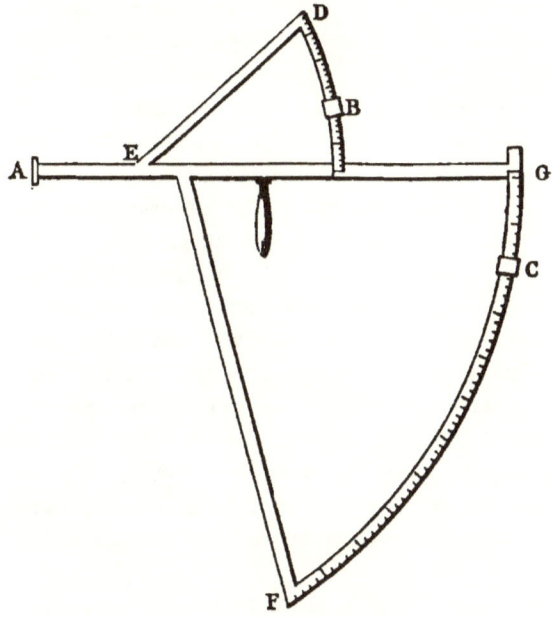

THE BACK-STAFF, OR DAVIS QUADRANT.

but of his love," that he desired to be judged. Not
only did he promote the safety of British ships by his
surveys and charts, and assist their navigation by the
publication of his secrets; he also invented a great
improvement in the instruments for observing for
latitude. The "back-staff" or "Davis quadrant" was

the offspring of his brain, and was perfected at about
this time. It consisted of two concentric arcs of box
wood, G, F, and E, D, and of three vanes, A, B, and C,
with the necessary frame, the arc of one radius being
60°, and of the other 30°. A vane was set on each arc,
that on the longer arc, C, being called the sight vane,
and on the shorter, B, the shade-vane. At the end of
the long radius was the horizon-vane, A. The shade-
vane upon the arc of 60° was set an even degree with
some latitude less by 10° or 15° than the complement of
the sun's altitude was judged to be. The observer then
turned his back to the sun and looked through the sight-
vane on the longer arc, raising or lowering the instrument until the shadow of the upper edge of the
shade-vane fell on the upper edge of the slit in the
horizon-vane. Then, if he could see the horizon through
the slit, the observation was exact and the vanes were
rightly adjusted. If the sea or sky, and not the
horizon, appeared, the sight-vane was moved upwards
or downwards until the horizon was on. The degrees
and minutes cut by the edge of the sight-vane, added to
the degrees cut by the edge of the shade-vane, were
equal to the complement of the latitude or zenith distance.

This instrument was a great improvement on the
cross-staff, and came into general use. It was improved
by Flamsteed, and was the forerunner of the discovery
of the plan of taking angles by reflection. Davis's
quadrant was the received instrument until Hadley's
reflecting quadrant superseded it in 1731.

It is to be regretted that the charts constructed by
Davis have been lost, including those of his Arctic discoveries, of the Scilly Islands, of the British Channel,

and of the Straits of Magellan. But his labours were
not in vain, for his work was embodied in subsequent
maps, and was useful alike to his own generation and
to posterity. For instance, the Northern discoveries
of Davis are given on that famous globe "which Mr
Sanderson, to his very great charge, hath published, for
the which he deserveth great favour and commendations." The expenses of constructing this globe were
defrayed by Mr. Sanderson, the old patron of Davis, and
the construction of the two globes was intrusted to
Emery Molyneux, an able mathematician and drafts-
man. The celestial and terrestrial globes are two feet
in diameter, beautifully executed and well mounted.
They were completed in 1592, but received additions
up to 1603. The terrestrial globe not only shows the
discoveries of Davis, but the tracks of Drake and
Cavendish round the world, and the later northern
discoveries of Barents. The Molyneux globes were the
first ever constructed in this country, and they are still
preserved in the library of the Middle Temple. Such
was the importance attached to them, that they formed
the subject of special treatises by Hues and Hood, and
were elaborately described by Blundeville. It is
evident that Davis assisted in their preparation, for
there are several names on the northern coasts which
he explored, that do not occur elsewhere; and it is
probable that the employment of Molyneux by Mr.
Sanderson was due to the recommendation of the Arctic
navigator. The globe of Molyneux has preserved the
northern labours of Davis, although his original work is
lost; and the other charts which gave the results of his
varied labours served a useful purpose during many
years, and until they were superseded by later surveys

The "New Map" of the world on Mercator's projection, which was intended to illustrate Hakluyt's great work, but which was not published until 1599, also contains the discoveries of Davis. It is attributed to Wright, but there is evidence that Davis assisted in its construction. Both the Molyneux globe and the "New Map" of 1599 have the "*Furious Overfall*" at the entrance of Hudson's Strait.

It was in these years of sorrowful retirement, when he turned to study and literary labour for some alleviation to his grief, that Davis probably achieved his most permanently useful work for mankind. His charts proved invaluable guides to British pilots for a long course of years, his treatise on navigation was equally serviceable, and his "back-staff" facilitated observations, increased their accuracy, and was the direct forerunner of reflecting quadrants and of the sextants of the present day. Columbus, Behaim, and Enciso, Hues, Wright, and Heriot have been referred to as examples of men who advanced the science of navigation through a combination of practical experience at sea with the theoretical knowledge of the student. But Davis is perhaps the most remarkable instance of the importance of such combination. His discoveries would not have been made, his hydrographical work would not have been executed, his hints and suggestions for improvements in navigation would not have had the same value, if he had not combined scientific knowledge acquired by deep study, with unrivalled experience as a practical seaman. Above all, he possessed and cultivated the power of hard work, and he was inspired by the patriotic desire to perform useful service to his country. "What made John Davis so

famous for navigation but his learning, which was confirmed by experience," wrote Sir William Monson in
one of his "Naval Tracts."

The dream of Davis's life was the discovery of the
North-West Passage, for the increase of the wealth and
prosperity of his country. For this he undertook three
dangerous voyages to the Arctic Regions; for this he
risked life and fortune in the Straits of Magellan; and
now, in his retirement, he took up his pen to make a
final effort, with the hope of arousing in the Government
and the country a sense of the importance of achieving
this great undertaking. Sir Francis Walsingham, the
powerful and enlightened patron of Arctic discovery,
had died on the 6th of April 1590. But surely some
of his patriotic spirit must linger with his colleagues.
In the hope that zeal for exploration was not quite dead
at the Council Board, but only sleeping, Davis addressed
an appeal to the Lords of Her Majesty's Most Honourable Privy Council on the 27th of May 1595, just ten
years after his departure on his first Arctic voyage.

The appeal is entitled "The Worlde's Hydrographical
Description, wherein is proved, not onely by aucthoritie
of Writers, but also by late experience of Travellers and
reasons of substantial probabilitie, that the World in
all his zones, climates, and places is habitable, and the
sea likewise universally navigable without any natural
annoyance to hinder the same; whereby appeares that
from England there is a short and speedie passage to
India by northerly navigation; to the renown, honour,
and benefit of Her Majesty's State and Commonalty."
It was published by "J. Davis of Sandridge by Dartmouth, in the county of Devon, Gentleman," and printed
at London by "Thomas Dawson, dwelling at the Three

Cranes in the Vinetree, and are there to be sold," in
1595.

Davis opens his argument by stating the objections
of adverse critics.   It was urged that America and
Asia were joined, so as to make a passage impossible,
as was shown by the fact that the passage had been
often attempted and never achieved.   Another objection
was, that even if the continents were not joined, the
cold is so extreme that no mortal creature can endure
it.   The quantities of ice carried down to Newfoundland, by which fishermen are " so noisomely pestered,"
proves that the sea to the northward is congealed into
one mass of ice.   " When in these temperate parts of
the world the shod of that frozen sea breedeth such
noisome pester as the poor fishermen do continually
sustain, what hope remains in 60° to 80° ? "   Finally, it
was argued that no ordinary sea-chart can describe
those regions, either in the parts geographical or hydrographical, where the meridians do so speedily gather
themselves together, and where quick and uncertain
variation of the compass may greatly hinder or overthrow the attempt.

The replies, as is natural, are set forth much more
fully than the objections.   The connection of Asia and
America is disproved both by the evidence of ancient
writers and modern explorers.   America must needs
be an island, seeing that we know Europe, Asia, and
Africa to be an island, on the authority of Homer,
Strabo, Pomponius Mela, Higinus, and Solinus.   But
we need not rely on any early authorities, seeing that
we have the evidence of later discoveries.   From the
North Cape to the Cape of Good Hope the navigation
is continuous, the nearest part of the American conti-

nent being 500 leagues distant. On the other hand, from the North Cape to Novaya Zemlya there is passable sailing, and the north parts of Tartary to the Cape Tabin of Pliny are known to be bounded by the Scythian Sea. It is apparent, therefore, that America must be far removed from the Old World. In like manner, the south side, from the Cape of Good Hope, by Sofala, Mozambique, Arabia, India, Malacca, and China to Cape Tabin, the coasts are all bounded by a great ocean. From California to the Philippines the distance is 2100 leagues, so that it is clearly manifest that Europe, Asia, and Africa form an island far distant from America.

These premises, as Davis next proceeded to show, had been established by the attempts of explorers. Sir Hugh Willoughby, Stephen Borough, and Anthony Jenkinson made voyages to the north-east which proved that the north parts of Europe were not joined to any other continent. The voyages of the Portuguese and Spaniards show that America is far from India and the other southern coasts of Asia. It is true that the Spaniards take pains to conceal their knowledge, but they trade from Mexico to China and Japan, and they have information that the east coast of Asia lies due north and south as high as Cape Tabin, where the Scythian Sea and the main ocean of China are conjoined.

Davis then turns with pride to the achievements of his own countrymen. "John Hawkins," he says, "was the first to attempt a voyage to the West Indies, for before he made the attempt it was a matter doubtful, and reported the extremest limit of danger, to sail upon those coasts. So that it was generally in dread among

us, such is the slowness of our nation,.for.the most part
of us rather joy at home like epicures, to sit and carp
at other men's hazard, ourselves not daring to give
any attempt.   How then may Sir John Hawkins be
esteemed, who being a man of good account in his
country, of wealth and great employment, did notwithstanding, for the good of his country to procure trade,
give that notable and resolute attempt.   Whose steps
many hundreds following since, have made themselves
men of good esteem, and fit for the service of Her
sacred Majesty. . . . Then succeeded Sir Francis
Drake in his famous and ever-renowned voyage round
the world, who passed the dangers of the Straits of
Magellan, coasted all the west coast of America to 48°
N., and found that the Moluccas were 200 leagues from
the American continent."

Davis then turns to the evidence derivable from his
own Arctic voyages. "There resteth only the north
parts of America, upon which coast myself have had
most experience of any in our age; for thrice I was
that way employed, for the discovery of this notable
passage.   But when his Honour (Sir Francis Walsingham) died, the voyage was friendless, and men's minds
alienated from adventuring therein."   He proceeds to
describe the results of his three Arctic voyages, and
concludes his review with the expression of a decided
opinion that the passage was to be found northwards
from Hope Sanderson.   "But," he adds, "by reason of
the Spanish fleet and unfortunate time of Mr. Secretary's death, the voyage was omitted and never sithins
attempted."   The interesting digression in which Davis
explains the objects and results of his own voyages was
made to stay the cavils of those who might say, "Why

hath not Davis discovered the passage, being thrice that
ways employed ?"

Having established the fact of the insularity of
America, and of the consequent existence of a North-
West Passage, Davis proceeds to deal with the objections
based on the physical condition of the country.   Those
who sail from the North Cape to St. Nicholas in the
White Sea, find that the seas are free from the pester
of ice; the farther from the shore the clearer from ice.
He did not deny that he had himself seen in some parts
of those seas two sorts of ice in great quantity—icebergs
breaking off from the glacier, and flake-ice bordering
close on the shore.   But he had found navigation free
from ice up to 72° N., and he maintained that the open
sea was never frozen over.

With regard to the intense cold, he appeals to the
facts that the people of Lapland and Russia travel in
mid-winter in sledges over the snow, having the use of
reindeer to draw them; that in Greenland the country
is inhabited by people of tractable conditions, and by
divers kinds of birds and beasts, while in summer there
are such quantities of mosquitos that he and his people
were stung by them, and unable to have quiet while
they were on shore; and that Iceland is also inhabited.

He puts forward the opinion that the pole is the
place of greatest dignity on this earth, by reason of the
long presence of the sun, and a place most worthy to
be discovered.   The author of the "Seaman's Secrets"
easily disposes of the objection based on want of
astronomical knowledge on the part of his brother
sailors, and he enumerates some of the advantages to
be derived from polar exploration.

Davis tells the Lords of the Council that he is always

DAVIS'S HANDWRITING.

ready " with his person and his poor ability " to undertake the service whensoever he may be called upon, and
he concludes with an eloquent and enthusiastic appeal
in favour of his project.   " All the premises considered,
there remaineth no more doubting but that there is a
passage by the north-west, of God for us alone ordained
to our infinite happiness, and for the glory of Her
Majesty.   Then will her stately seat of London be the
storehouse of Europe, the nurse of the world, and the renown of nations; and all this by reason of the excellent
commodity of her position, the mightiness of her trade
by force of shipping thereby arising, and most abundant

DAVIS'S AUTOGRAPH.

access and intercourse from all the kingdoms of the
world.   Then shall the idle hand be scorned, and plenty
by industry in all this land shall be proclaimed.   Therefore the passage proved and the benefits to all most
apparent, let us no longer neglect our happiness, but
like Christians, with willing and voluntary spirits, labour
without fainting for this so excellent a benefit."

For a time the gallant sailor entertained a hope that
his stirring appeal would not be without effect upon the
minds of the Lords of the Council.   He thought that
his clarion blast would revive the spirit of enterprise,
and rouse men from their lethargy.   Once more he

fancied himself sailing out of that lovely harbour of
Dartmouth, and steering towards his beloved polar seas
with the cry of "Northward ho!" Once more his pulse
beat high with enthusiasm, and all the hopes of his
youth were renewed. But the time slipped past, and
no favourable reply arrived. Slowly and unwillingly
he told himself that the prize was not for him. He
had worked hard, he had nobly borne the heat and
burden of the day. But the fruition was for other
men, for later generations. Yet there was work for
him to do elsewhere. He could no longer remain idle,
and before the year 1595 was ended it would appear
that John Davis was again at sea.

During the following two years there is nothing from
the great seaman's own hand, and only faint though
tolerably certain indications of the services on which
he was employed. He received command of a ship
belonging to Mr. Honeyman, a merchant of London,
who traded with Rochelle and the south of France, and
often supplied Mr. Secretary Cecil with valuable information. Davis's vessel was captured by some French
ships of the League sent out of the ports of Brittany
by the Duc de Mercœur; but they only took the cargo,
allowing the ship and crew to go free. On his return
from this unlucky venture, he found the English ports
busy with preparation; for the Queen had resolved to
carry the war into the enemy's territory and to attack
the important city of Cadiz.

Davis had many old friends in the fleet destined for
the service of delivering a crushing blow to Spanish
commerce. His old admiral of the Armada days
commanded the fleet in the same stout ship, the *Ark
Royal*, and he naturally took with him his nephew, Lord

Thomas Howard, in the *Mere-Honour*, and his son-in-law, Sir Robert Southwell, in the *Lion;* while the gallant Sir Ames Preston, who had served with Davis in the Azores under the Earl of Cumberland, was flag-captain.   The chivalrous young Earl of Essex commanded the land forces, with Sir Francis Vere as his marshal and chief adviser.   Essex was on board the *Repulse*, with Sir William Monson as his captain, and Vere was in the *Rainbow*.   Sir Walter Raleigh was rear-admiral in the *Warspite*, and for him were all the naval glories of the campaign; while Essex and Vere shared the credit of capturing Cadiz with the land forces.   Leaving Plymouth on the 1st of June 1596, the operations of this well-planned and successful expedition were completed by the 5th of July, and the fleet returned on the 8th of August.   In the following year the expedition to the Azores was dispatched, under the command of the Earl of Essex, which is known in history as the "Island Voyage."   This time Essex was again on board the *Repulse*, with Middleton as his flag-captain, the same officer who had cruised with Davis in 1590, and who had brought the news of the approach of the Spanish fleet to the heroic Grenville in 1591.   Raleigh again commanded the *Warspite*.   Sir Ames Preston was with Lord Mountjoy in the *Defiance*.   Vere was in the *Mary Rose*, with Winter, the companion of Drake and discoverer of Winter's bark in Magellan's Straits, as his captain.   Monson commanded a ship of his own, the *Rainbow*.   The *Moon* was commanded by Sir Edward Michelborne, a brave seaman, whose name is connected with the last days of John Davis.   Sailing from Plymouth in August 1597, this expedition cruised among

the Azores, for which islands Davis was an excellent
pilot, and returned in November.

It is certain that Davis served under Essex in one or
both of these expeditions; for in a letter to the Earl
written after his return from India, he says that he
ordered his men "after that excellent method which we
have seen in your Lordship's most honourable actions."
Collateral evidence is also furnished by Sir William
Monson in his "Naval Tracts," who says that he often
had conversations with Davis during these expeditions;
and immediately afterwards we find Davis under the
patronage of the Earl of Essex. In all probability he
was pilot of the *Repulse* at Cadiz and in the Azores.
The expedition to the Azores returned in November
1597, at the very time when the Zeelanders were
fitting out an expedition for the East Indies. The
voyage of Lancaster had drawn the attention of English statesmen to the East, and it was considered very
important that further information should be obtained
respecting the various routes and centres of commerce.
The Earl of Essex, therefore, suggested to Davis that if
he could arrange to accompany the Dutch expedition to
India, he would have an opportunity of doing good and
acceptable service to his Queen and country. Particulars
respecting the equipment of ships destined for India
by a wealthy mercantile house in Zeeland had been
reported by Sir Francis Vere.

CHAPTER X.

THE DUTCH VOYAGE.

The quaint little town of Veere is built along the banks of a canal which runs through the island of Walcheren in Zeeland. At the south entrance of this canal is the port of Flushing, then (in 1598) in the hands of an English garrison under the command of Sir Robert Sydney as a cautionary town. Half-way down the canal is Middelburg, the capital of Zeeland, with its stately town hall, containing niches with statues of the Counts of Holland, and its vast monastery, with hall and cloisters, converted to secular purposes. Hard by the cloister gate stood the house of Zacharias Jansen, who constructed the first telescope in 1608. At the north end of the canal was the thriving port of Veere, famous in English history as the place where our King Edward IV. embarked on his triumphal return in 1470. Now Veere is a forlorn little town, with grass-grown streets, and many houses for sale. But the scene was very different in the sixteenth century. The canal, opening on the "Room-pot" or "cream-jug," as the sea was called between the islands of Walcheren and Schouwen, was crowded with shipping. The quay was busy with the working of cranes and windlasses, and the carrying to and fro of merchandise. The houses,

with their curiously carved gables, were inhabited by
wealthy merchants. High above them rose the great
church and the handsome town hall, rich in pictures and
valuable plate. Here is the exquisitely chased silver
flagon representing the passage of the Rhine by Maximilian of Burgundy ; and the walls are hung with curious
representations of sea-fights between Hooks and Kabel-
jaws, which took place in sight of the port of Veere.

A rapid and marvellous change had come over the
face of this island of Walcheren. Only a quarter of a
century before 1598, when Davis landed on its shores,
the country was in the hands of a cruel enemy, the
fields were devastated, and Middelburg was held by a
Spanish garrison. In 1572 Sir Humphrey Gilbert, the
neighbour and early companion of John Davis, had
landed with a feeble force of inexperienced recruits to
help the Dutch patriots against the matchless infantry
of Spain. It was a life and death struggle for many
years, but the right prevailed at last. In 1598 there
was no longer any danger from the terrible enemy of
liberty. He was gone like an evil dream. Peace and
prosperity reigned in Walcheren. Flushing was
occupied by friendly allies. Middelburg was the busy
capital of a free State. Veere was a thriving seaport.
Not a little of this prosperity was due to the short-
sighted bigotry of the Spaniards. Their Inquisition had
obliged large numbers of the most active and industrious
citizens of Antwerp and other cities of Flanders to
take refuge with their free neighbours, and these exiles
gave an additional impulse to the commercial enterprise
of the Dutch.

Balthazar de Moucheron was one of the most illustrious of the Antwerp fugitives. He established a great

commercial house at Middelburg, whence he removed to
Veere in 1597. It is very striking, and proves what
a stimulating effect the love of liberty has on a people
under its influence, that the Dutch should have pushed
forward voyages of discovery and commercial enterprise at the very time that they were grappling with
Spain in a struggle for bare life. But so it was.
Moucheron opened a trade with Russia, and sent his
brother Melchior to reside on the river Dvina and
form a commercial establishment in the White Sea.
Melchior is said to have been the founder of Archangel.
The attention of the Dutch merchants was turned to the
possibility of opening a direct trade with India and the
Spice Islands by the reports of Linschoten, and it was
not long before the great merchant-prince of Veere
took the lead in those new ventures.

Jan Huygen van Linschoten was born at Haarlem in
1563, but his parents moved to Enkhuizen on the
Zuyder Zee when he was a child, and he was brought
up there. Of a roving disposition, young Linschoten
joined his brothers, who were engaged in commercial
pursuits in Spain, and he went thence to Lisbon, where
he was allowed to embark on board a fleet which was
taking out a new Archbishop to Goa in 1583. He
remained in India for five years, chiefly at Goa, where
he diligently collected information. On his way home,
he was at the Azores when Sir Richard Grenville in the
Revenge fought the whole Spanish fleet, and his narrative usefully supplements the report of Sir Walter
Raleigh. Returning home in 1592, Linschoten proceeded to give his countrymen the valuable results of
his travels. His "Nautical Directory" appeared in
1595, and his "Itineraris" in the following year. The

merchants of Amsterdam were incited by the information of Linschoten to attempt voyages to the East
by two different routes, even before his books were
published. An expedition was sent by the Cape of
Good Hope in 1594 to make a voyage to the East
Indies, under the command of Cornelis de Houtman;
but it returned without any very lucrative result, and
the Amsterdam merchants were not particularly satisfied with the way in which it had been conducted. In
the same year the first of three memorable attempts
was made by the Dutch to discover a route to China and
the Indies by the north-east. The expedition consisted
of three vessels, the *Swan* of Veere, the *Mercury* of
Enkhuysen, with Linschoten on board as supercargo,
and another *Mercury* of Amsterdam, commanded by
William Barents, the most illustrious of Dutch Arctic
navigators. While Linschoten examined the ice in the
Kara Sea, Barents discovered the whole of the west
coast of Novaya Zemlya, struggling persistently with
the ice, constantly observing for latitude and variation,
and making an accurate survey. The ships returned in
September, and Linschoten made such an encouraging
report that the Dutch merchants resolved to send out a
fleet of several vessels in the ensuing year to achieve
the North-East Passage. Two vessels were fitted out in
Zeeland under the auspices of the house of Moucheron,
the *Griffin* and *Swan*. Enkhuysen furnished two ships,
and Amsterdam sent the *Greyhound* under Barents as
chief pilot. But they were unable to get through the
ice in the Waigat, and returned unsuccessful.

The efforts of Barents and of the eminent geographer
Plancius induced the Amsterdam merchants to make
one more attempt. Barents sailed in May 1596, dis-

covered the north-western coast of Spitzbergen, rounded
the northern extremity of Novaya Zemlya, and passed
his memorable winter in the haven on the north-eastern
coast. The ship was abandoned, and the crew escaped
in boats, Barents himself dying in the midst of his
discoveries. The survivors reached Amsterdam in November 1597, and the Arctic attempts of the Dutch came
to an end, although in the succeeding century their
whalers did much to complete the discovery of the
Spitzbergen coasts.

Linschoten continued to live at Enkhuysen, in the
society of accomplished geographers and seamen, chief
among whom was his neighbour Lucas Jansz Wagenaar,
author of the "Mariner's Mirror," the first marine
atlas ever published. Four editions appeared between
1584 and 1596, and it was translated into English by
Anthony Ashley in 1588. The fourth edition contains
a chart of Norway by Barents, and observations on his
expeditions to the north. While his friend Wagenaar
was engaged in the preparation of valuable charts,
Linschoten supervised the publication of his eastern
travels, and translated the valuable history of the
Western Indies by Acosta from Spanish into Dutch.
Linschoten died at Enkhuysen at the age of forty-eight,
in 1611. His "Itinerario" had been published in English in 1598.

It was the valuable and detailed information collected by Linschoten which induced Balthazar de Moucheron to turn his attention to the East Indies, and on
the failure of the three attempts of the Dutch under
Barents to discover a passage by the north-east, he
resolved to dispatch an expedition by way of the Cape
of Good Hope. He informed the States-General of his

intention, and requested that his ships might be supplied with guns and ammunition.   Every encouragement was given to him, and an order was issued that an
armament from the Zeeland arsenal should be furnished
to his ships. The news of his undertaking was received
with interest in Holland and in England.   Sir Francis
Vere, the general in command of the English troops in
the Low Countries, reported the details to the Queen's
Government.   It was probably in consequence of this
report that the Earl of Essex suggested to Davis that
he should accompany the expedition.   Two ships were
fitted out at Middelburg, *De Leeuw* (the *Lion*) and *De
Leeuwin* (the *Lioness*), the former commanded by Cornelius de Houtman, who had charge of the Amsterdam
voyage to India in 1595, and the latter by his brother,
Frederik de Houtman.   Cornelius de Houtman was
the *Baas* or commander-in-chief, with Pieter Stockman
as captain, and Guyon Lefort as treasurer of the *Lion*.

In the winter of 1598 John Davis came over to
Walcheren to offer his services to the merchant-prince
of Veere. The friend of Raleigh, of Walsingham, and of
Essex would have been welcomed by many friends. The
governor of Flushing was a brother-in-law of Walsingham's daughter; and young Arthur Randolph, a captain
in Vere's army, and son of Walsingham's intimate friend
and relative, was married to the daughter of Jacques
Gellert, the wealthy burgomaster of Flushing. Through
these friends Davis would have had no difficulty in
making the acquaintance of the leading merchants of
Middelburg and Veere. But their assistance would have
been superfluous. The fame of John Davis as a discoverer and as a scientific seaman had spread to Holland.
He needed no introduction when he presented himself

at the house of Balthazar Moucheron at Veere. The offer of his services was readily accepted, and he was appointed chief pilot of the expedition on board the *Lion*. A few other Englishmen joined, including a Mr. Hopkins, who was an acceptable messmate to the chief pilot, a countryman and friend in the midst of jealous and suspicious foreigners.

The *Lion* and *Lioness* sailed from Flushing on the 15th of March 1598. The *Lion* was 400 tons, with a crew of 123 persons, and the *Lioness* 250 tons, with 100 souls on board. Houtman had the title of General, with a commission from Prince Maurice of Orange, but he was usually called the Baas. The two ships were at anchor in Tor Bay for more than a fortnight, and Davis had the opportunity of paying a last visit to his little boys at Sandridge. On the 7th of April the wind was at last fair, and the *Lion* and *Lioness* made sail, sighting Porto Santo on the 20th, Palma on the 23rd, and anchoring at St. Nicholas, one of the Cape Verds, on the 30th.

After watering at St. Nicholas, the long voyage across the equator was commenced—a voyage of which Davis had already had experience—and the coast of Brazil was sighted on the 9th of June; but refreshment was obtained at the lonely island of Fernando Noronha. This solitary spot in the South Atlantic had already been occupied by the Portuguese. Davis found that it was inhabited by twelve negro slaves, who had been left there to cultivate Indian-corn. They had not been visited by a ship for three years, but were well off, the island abounding in pigs and poultry, goats and cattle. There was plenty of fish in the surrounding ocean and multitudes of sea-birds.

Leaving Fernando Noronha on the 26th of July, the
two ships doubled Cape San Agustin on the Brazilian
coast, and passed the Abrolhos rocks in 17° S., and
forty miles from the coast, about which Davis felt some
anxiety. In celebration of the event, the Dutch commander indulged in and permitted disorderly_festivities
of which the honest English pilot_highly disapproved.
The Baas chose a master of misrule, who was called the
"Kaiser," and passed three days in drunken orgies.
"After dinner the Baas could neither salute his friends
nor understand the laws of reason, and those that ought
to have been most respectable were both lawless and
witless." Having recovered from the effects of their
drunken bout, a course was shaped for the Cape of
Good Hope, and on the 11th of November the *Lion*
and *Lioness* were anchored in Saldanha Bay, the
modern Table Bay. The Saldanha Bay of modern geographers, on the west coast of Africa, and about fifty
miles to the northward of the present Cape Town, is a
misnomer.

The conduct of the Dutch officers and crew was very
different from anything that Captain Davis had been
accustomed to on board the ships he had commanded.
The discipline was lax, and there was a want of order
and system. Houtman appears to have been an unfortunate selection, and his intemperate habits did not
conduce to subordination among his men. The Caffres
at Table Bay brought oxen and sheep to exchange for
old iron. Davis observed the appearance and habits of
these Caffres with care and attention. He describes
them as a strong and active race, with olive-black skins
and curly heads; speaking a language of most peculiar
sound. An idea of the pronunciation could not be con-

veyed better than in the words of Davis. He says, "In speaking they cluck with the tongue like a brood-hen, which clucking and the word are pronounced together very strongly." He understood them to be subjects of the King of Monomotapa, a region behind the seaboard of Mozambique.

It was not long before misunderstandings arose between the insubordinate Dutch seamen and the natives. Having received some rough usage, the Caffres departed, and for three days there were fires blazing on the surrounding hills. They then came back and began bartering their cattle, but they were only watching an opportunity for retaliation. They suddenly attacked the Europeans, and killed thirteen with their darts at close quarters. The Dutchmen fell into a panic, threw away their arms, and ran to the shore. Houtman prudently remained on board. He sent corslets, mus-kets, swords, and pikes to the men on shore, but no one to lead them. They remained at their tents with-out taking the offensive, and were surrounded by the Caffres and their cows. "We were in muster giants with great armed bodies," says Davis, "but in action babes with wren's hearts." Then the English pilot, with his mate Hopkins, came forward, and undertook to marshal them and lead them against the enemy. But although some consented, several ran to the pottage-pot, swearing it was dinner-time, and at night they all went on board. The great mastiff belonging to the Baas was left behind. "He by no means would come to us, for I think he was ashamed of our company."

The year was coming to a close before the expedition rounded the Cape, and on the 3rd of February 1599 the two ships anchored in the Bay of St. Augustine, on the

south-west coast of Madagascar. Houtman had visited
this place during his first voyage, and had cruelly ill-
treated the natives. The consequence was that they all
fled into the interior, and would have no intercourse
with the strangers. No supplies could be obtained, and
after a fortnight the Dutchmen made sail for the Comoro
Islands, naming the place "Hungry Bay." In the
Comoro group they were more fortunate, and obtained
fresh provisions at the island of Mayotta, where they
anchored. All the care of Davis was required for the
eastern navigation from the Seychelles. After visiting
Mayotta and Johanna in the Comoro group, he navigated the ships past the Amirante shoals to the Mal-
dives, where they again anchored, and obtained a native
pilot who took them through the difficult channel
between the coral islands. Thence the voyage was continued to Sumatra, and on the 21st of June the ships
were anchored in the Bay of Achen.

During the whole voyage Davis made hydrographical
notes with great diligence, observed the appearance,
manners, and customs of the natives; and collected information respecting the trade of each place, both as
regards the exports and the kind of goods that are
most in demand. While his skill as a pilot and
navigator was most acceptable to his employers, he was
acquiring knowledge and experience which would be
useful to his own country.

Achen, the most northern kingdom in the island of
Sumatra, has great historical interest, owing to its
having been so much frequented by the early Dutch
and English voyagers. The name is properly Acheh;
and Colonel Yule suggests that we got our form of the
word from the Arabs. The King of Achen at that time

was a usurper named Allah-u-dín Shah, who had murdered the former king, Mansur Shah, and his family in 1585. He is said to have been originally a fisherman, whose courage and prudence raised him to the position of commander of the forces, and he eventually became King of Achen. He sent his officers on board the *Lion* and *Lioness* to measure their length and breadth, and take the number of men and guns. Two men were sent back with them to take presents on shore, and they returned with news that there would be peace and plenty of trade. In the harbour there were three small vessels from Arabia, one from Pegu, and a Portuguese named Dom Alfónso Vicenté, who had come from Malacca with four vessels, with the object of thwarting the Dutch in their efforts to trade. The Baas Houtman was, however, received by the King in a friendly manner, and presented with a *kris* of honour. He came back with a cargo of pepper in his boat, and boasted loudly of his influence with the King. The Dutch merchants then landed with their goods, and the King proposed that if Houtman would help him in his war against Johore, he would give him a lading of pepper in return.

Houtman had shown a foolish jealousy of the Englishmen who were serving in his ship. The native officers had reported to the King that there were some men on board who appeared to be different from the others. The King rightly conjectured that they must be English, and asked Houtman if he had any Englishmen on board. At first the Baas declared that there were none, but on being hard pressed, he admitted that the chief pilot and a few others were Englishmen who had been brought up in Flanders. He would not let Davis or Hopkins go on shore until the King insisted upon seeing them, and then he allowed them to land very reluctantly. On the 22nd of August Captain Davis had an audience with the King, who was very friendly. Davis was robed in a dress of honour, and allowed to sit and feast with his Majesty, who made him answer numerous questions about England and the great Queen, and about her war with the Spaniards. In a second interview Davis rode to court on an elephant, and he was so fortunate as to meet a Chinese merchant who spoke Spanish, a language known to Davis, from whom he received much valuable information respecting the trade of China. This again excited the jealousy of Houtman, who ordered Davis to return on board.

Great preparations were being made for the expedition against Johore. The harbour was full of armed *prahus* and boats. On the 1st of September an officer of rank, named Abdalla, with a secretary, and a party of soldiers armed to the teeth, came on board the ship with provisions and liquor, and made show of friendship. But their conduct excited suspicion in the mind of Davis, who advised the crew to fill the tops with stones, secure the gratings, and get their arms ready. Houtman was very angry at this interference, and ordered his men to desist from their hostile preparations; but they refused to obey his orders and remained on the defensive.

There was indeed treachery. The food and liquor were drugged, and the intention was to make all the Europeans insensible or incapable, and then to seize the ships. Abdalla and the secretary had completely deceived the unfortunate Houtman, who became a helpless prisoner without knowing it. They then sent for Davis and Hopkins, pressed them to partake of their hospi-

tality, and used all their art to secure compliance.
Suddenly these treacherous Malays threw off the mask.
Houtman was quickly murdered; but Davis, aided by
Hopkins and the Treasurer Lefort, secured the approach
to the poop with great presence of mind, and repulsed
the savage onslaughts of the enemy.   If their defence of
the poop had failed, the ship would have been lost, as
the Malays had secured the cabin and the gun-deck.
Pieter Stockman, the captain, and several others, jumped
overboard in despair, but eventually got back again.
The precaution of placing stones in the tops was most
fortunate, for the Dutch sent volleys among the Malays,
who were vigorously attacked in front by Davis and his
little band from the poop.   The enemy began to give
ground, and the gallant pilot came down from the poop
to follow up his success.   As Hopkins jumped down
after him, he was badly wounded by a Turk who rushed
out of the cabin, and they both rolled on the deck
together.   Davis turned round quickly and ran the Turk
through with his rapier, and Stockman, the skipper, who
had scrambled on board again, thrust a pike down the
poor wretch's throat.   Meanwhile a similar scene of
treachery had been enacted on board the *Lioness.*   All the
officers but Frederik Houtman were murdered.   The
Lion then cut her cable, bore down on her consort, and
recovered her.   The Malays fled, jumping overboard
and swimming away.   The King of Achen was on
the beach watching the event, and when he saw that
his villainous *ruse* had failed, he caused all the Europeans who were on shore, except eight, to be murdered.   The Dutch loss amounted to sixty-eight men
killed, including Captain Stockman, and three boats
destroyed.   The two ships made sail the same day,

and anchored off the town of Pedir, on the north coast
of Sumatra.

Frederik de Houtman, the captain of the *Lioness*,
although he escaped death, remained a prisoner at Achen
for two years, during which time he compiled a dictionary of the Malay language, and took several observations of stars in the southern hemisphere, which, with
his dictionary, were published after his return to Holland. Three sealed letters were on board the *Lion*,
marked A, B, and C, which were to be opened in
the event of Houtman's death. In A, an ófficer was
appointed to succeed who had been killed at Achen.
B named a Frenchman, Guy Lefort, who had been
treasurer; and he was accordingly accepted as Baas or
commander of the expedition. The letter marked C
was not opened.

From Pedir the two ships went to Pulo Lotum,[1] in the
territory of Queda, on the west side of the Malacca
peninsula, where water and fresh provisions were obtained.
Lefort then resolved to return to Achen, to obtain tidings
of the men who had been left on shore, and to rescue
them if possible. Arriving in Achen Bay on the 12th
of October, the *Lion* fired some shots at a galley which
was sent out to oppose her, but no communication
appears to have been held with the shore, and a few
days afterwards Lefort shaped a course to Tennasserim,
and thence to the Nicobar Islands. Here they obtained
fruit and vegetables, but they were in great want of
grain and other provisions necessary for a long voyage.
From the Nicobars they sailed for Ceylon, and on the
passage were so fortunate as to meet a vessel from
Negapatam in India, laden with rice. Trade was

[1] This is probably a misprint. It may be Pulo Buton.

opened, the greater part of the cargo of rice being sold to the Dutchmen, and regularly paid for.   But the *Lion* and *Lioness* were never able to reach Ceylon, and in January 1600 it was resolved to shape a course homewards.

The two ships doubled the Cape of Good Hope on the 26th of March, and reached the island of St. Helena on the 13th of April.   They got fresh water and fruit, but at sunset on the second day of their stay a large Spanish caravel arrived, and anchored a musket-shot to windward of the Dutchmen.   Her guns were dismounted, so the *Lion* and *Lioness* kept up a steady fire on her during the first part of the night without a single shot being returned.   By midnight the Spaniards had mounted some of their guns, and began to use them with effect, hitting the *Lion* several times and killing two men. Lefort then thought it prudent to retreat, and the two ships sailed from St. Helena on the 16th of April, and proceeded to Ascension, with many sick men on board. But there they were again disappointed, finding nothing but a fruitless green rock, without wood or water.   Then Davis advised that a course should be shaped for Fernando Noronha, the lonely island in Mid-Atlantic, which they had visited during the voyage out, and where they knew that fresh provisions could be obtained.   Refreshment was thus secured for the sick and enfeebled crew before commencing the long voyage northwards, and on the 29th of July 1600 the second Dutch voyage to the East Indies was concluded, the two ships arriving safely at Middelburg.

There is no narrative of this voyage in Dutch, and the only one extant is that written by John Davis as an enclosure to a letter addressed to the Earl of Essex.

Davis describes the kingdom of Achen, its inhabitants and commodities, besides narrating the events of the voyage. He himself was a heavy loser, for all his European goods were seized before he had received any merchandise in exchange for them. A vein of pleasant humour runs through his narrative, and he even jokes over his own losses. " I do most grieve over the losses of poor John Davis," he says, " for I may conclude that although India did not receive me very rich, yet she hath sent me away reasonable poor."

The letter from Davis to the Earl of Essex is dated at Middelburg on the 1st of August 1600. The object of his voyage is here stated to have been " the discovery of these eastern parts of the world, to the service of Her Majesty and the good of our country." The employment of such a man as Davis was a benefit to both countries; and there is evidence that the Dutch merchants fully appreciated his services. When W. Walker translated the Dutch voyage of Jacob Neck in 1601, he sent a covering letter to Sir Thomas Smith, the Governor of the East India Company, in which he wrote :—" The Dutch had special assistance in their late navigations by the means of Master John Davis and other skilful pilots of our nation ; and in return the Dutch do in ample manner requite us, acquainting us with their voyages, discoveries, and dangers, both outward and homeward."

Davis returned exactly at the right moment. The English East India Company was fitting out its first fleet, and the services of the illustrious pilot would be needed by his own countrymen.

CHAPTER XI.

THE FIRST VOYAGE OF THE EAST INDIA COMPANY.

Two important events at the close of the great Queen's life were among the most momentous in her reign as they affected future history—namely, the foundation of the East India Company and her noble reply to the Commons on the question of monopolies. Several circumstances had conduced to a determination on the part of the leading merchants of London to undertake commercial voyages to India by way of the Cape of Good Hope. The court of the Emperor Akbar at Agra had been reached by Ralph Fitch and two companions, travelling by land, in 1585; and Fitch, after visiting Bengal, returned and wrote an interesting narrative, which was published in Hakluyt's Collection. In 1599 Dr. Thorne, who had long resided at Seville, sent home a full report on the advantages of a trade with India; but the most direct information was derived from Captain James Lancaster. This admirable seaman was a native of Basingstoke, and in his early years he had been in Portugal in the capacity of a soldier, and afterwards of a merchant. In 1591 he sailed on his first voyage to India as rear-admiral of the *Edward Bonaventure*, in a fleet of three ships com-

manded by Captain Raymond, an old servant of Lord
Howard of Effingham, who is mentioned with com-
mendation · by John Davis in his preface to the "Seaman's Secrets." Raymond's ship was lost with all
hands off the Cape, but Lancaster was more fortunate. His vessel was the first commanded by an
Englishman to round the Cape and visit the Eastern
islands, and Lancaster brought back much valuable information, although he lost his ship in the West Indies,
and went through many adventures before he reached
England again in 1594. In the following year he commanded a fleet of three ships fitted out by the merchants
of London, with which he made a successful attack on
the town of Pernambuco in Brazil.

From these various sources the merchant-princes of
London collected information sufficient to justify the
formation of a company. The life and soul of English
commercial enterprise at this time was Sir Thomas
Smith. This enlightened and liberal merchant inherited an estate called Brooke Place in the Kentish
parish of Sutton-at-Hone from his father, as well as
considerable wealth, which he largely increased. He
built a house at Brooke Place, while his town-houses
in Philpot Lane and in Gracechurch Street were the
centres of hospitality. It was his great merit to have
encouraged maritime enterprise and discovery throughout a long life, not mainly for the sake of gain, but for
the honour of his country. He was an active member
of the Muscovy Company, and may be considered as the
chief founder of the East India Company. He strove
to promote the efficiency and welfare of seamen, and
engaged Dr. Hood to deliver lectures on navigation at
his house in Philpot Lane.

Under the auspices of Sir Thomas Smith, the merchants of London subscribed £72,000 with the object of establishing a direct trade with the East Indies, and several noblemen joined in the venture. On October 16, 1599, the Queen's gracious acceptance of the voyage was announced, and preparations were energetically pushed forward all through the autumn. On the 10th of December Captain James Lancaster was nominated general of the fleet, with a commission of martial law from the Queen; and Captain Middleton received the appointment of vice-admiral. On December 31, 1599, the charter of incorporation of the East India Company was granted, being a privilege for fifteen years to certain adventurers for the discovery of trade with the East Indies, the list of adventurers being appended. It is headed by the name of George Clifford, Earl of Cumberland, followed by those of 215 knights, aldermen, and merchants. Sir Thomas Smith was chosen first governor of the Company, and there were twenty-four directors, including James Lancaster and John Middleton, the leaders of the expedition.

A ship of 600 tons belonging to the Earl of Cumberland was bought for £3700. Her name was the *Malice Scourge*, which was altered to that of the *Red Dragon*, and she underwent a thorough refit. She was selected as the admiral, and Captain Lancaster was on board her with a crew of 202 men. Captain Middleton had the *Hector* of 300 tons with 108 men; the *Ascension* was under William Brand, a ship of 260 tons, with 82 men, and the *Susan* of 240 tons with 88 men was commanded by John Heywood. There was also a store-ship of 13 tons called the *Guest*, to accompany the fleet with additional supplies and enable the ships to fill up on the voyage.

Besides the General, which was the title given to
Lancaster, there was in each ship a master, who was
responsible for the goods brought on board; a master's
mate, who kept the keys of the hatches; a pilot, who
navigated the ship from port to port; a purser, a surgeon,
and a rummager, who superintended the stowage of the
hold.   There were also merchants to establish factories
in the East and to arrange the commercial affairs of the
Company.   Sir Thomas Smith was most careful in issu-
ing regulations for the health and comfort of the men,
and he was well seconded by Captain Lancaster, who
was a seaman of great experience, a good organiser and
administrator, and a commander who sympathised with
his men while he maintained strict discipline.   The
ordinary provisions were bread, meal, oatmeal, salt beef,
pickled beef and pork, peas, beans, salt fish, beer, cider,
and wine, with smaller allowances of cheese, butter, oil,
vinegar, honey, and rice.   Great attention was paid to
the quality of the meat, the beasts being purchased alive
after inspection, and slaughtered in the Company's yard
at Blackwall.   The ordnance provided for the ships
consisted of cannon, demi-cannon throwing a ball of 36
pounds, culverins with 20-pound and demi-culverins with
12-pound balls.   There was a large supply of small-
arms, and each ship was provided with twelve streamers,
two flags, and one ensign.   Nearly the whole sum subscribed was expended on the ships, and on the merchandise to be exchanged for spices and other products
of the East.

John Davis returned from his Dutch voyage when
the preparations for the English expedition were well
advanced and all the captains appointed.   But Sir
Thomas Smith was anxious to secure his valuable ser-

vices, and he was nominated chief pilot of the fleet, to embark on board the *Red Dragon.* His remuneration was to be according to results, and he received a " bill of adventure" upon the gains of the voyage. He was to receive £500 if the voyage yielded two for one, £1000 if three for one, and £2000 if five for one. The knowledge acquired by Davis while serving with the Dutch was a very useful guide to the Directors in selecting

THE RED DRAGON.

their merchandise for the Eastern markets, and his recent navigation of the Indian Ocean enabled him to furnish most valuable advice.

On the 13th of February 1601 the expedition sailed from Woolwich for the Downs, the General having been supplied with letters from the Queen to the King of Achen and other Eastern potentates, and with rich gifts for them from the Company. The ships were detained by westerly winds, and it was Easter Day before they

arrived in Tor Bay harbour. At length Davis was able
to visit his home, and to arrange about the care of
his children during his long absence. The faithless wife
appears to have been dead, and a lady named Judith
Havard appears upon the scene, who kept house at
Sandridge and attended to the education of the mother-
less children. A dark shadow now rested upon the once
happy home. Davis was a struggling man, striving to
retrieve his fortunes. Unequalled as a navigator and
pilot, with almost every qualification for high command,
famous as a discoverer even in his own generation, he
had not been fortunate. His home was darkened by
sorrow, and his ventures had been uniformly unlucky
since his ill-starred engagement with Cavendish. But
now his appointment as chief pilot of the first fleet sent
forth by the East India Company opened a brighter
prospect and gave ground for renewed hope.

On the 2nd of April 1601, the wind being fair, the
fleet sailed from Tor Bay and commenced that memorable voyage which was destined to be the foundation-
stone of the glorious edifice of British empire in the
East. After obtaining water at Grand Canary, the
ships were steered southerly until the region of equatorial
calms was reached, where they were detained from the
20th of May to the 12th of June. Then there were light
breezes, generally from the south, and one day a sail was
seen on the horizon. The *Dragon* immediately went in
chase, and captured the stranger by two in the same
afternoon. She was a Portuguese ship laden with wine,
oil, and grain, and her valuable cargo was a great assistance to the English. Lancaster divided it equally among
the four ships. On the 30th of June they crossed the
equator; and for the third time Davis rounded that

Cape-San Agustin on the Brazilian coast, which has so prominent a place in the history of all the early voyages to India. All the stores were taken out of the *Guest* when the fleet was about 1200 miles south of the line, her bulwarks were broken down for fuel, and she was turned adrift. It was the 9th of September before the welcome refuge of Table Bay was reached, and life-saving vegetables and fresh meat could be procured for the scurvy-stricken crews.

This dreadful disease, which was so fatal to sailors who undertook long voyages in the sixteenth and seventeenth centuries, broke out with exceptional virulence among the crews of Captain Lancaster's fleet, commencing when the men were exposed for weeks to the burning heat of the tropics.

The *Dragon* suffered least, for in the other three ships nearly all hands were prostrated by scurvy. The weakness of the men was so great that the merchants were obliged to take their turns at the helm, and go aloft to lay out on the yards and reef the topsails. The *Dragon* anchored first in Table Bay, and Captain Lancaster sent parties of men to the other ships to help them in bringing-to and getting the boats out. The reason why the crew of the *Dragon* suffered less was that Lancaster had taken the precaution of having a supply of lime-juice on board. So long as it lasted, he gave three spoonfuls to each man every morning; and to this specific, combined with closer attention to cleanliness and other requisites for health, the comparative exemption of the *Dragon* was due.

As soon as the ships were at anchor and the boats out, the General went on shore to see about arrangements for obtaining supplies of fresh provisions, and the Caffres soon made their appearance with their sheep and oxen. Davis had been witness of the consequences resulting from the ill-usage of the Caffres by the Dutch sailors in the previous voyage. He had warned Lancaster of what had taken place, and that able commander took special precautions to prevent any misunderstanding with the natives. Only a few selected men were allowed to come near the market, and no one else was permitted to interfere. Then tents were made out of the sails, and all the sick were landed. The disease had carried off 105 men before the ships arrived in Table Bay; but, with the aid of wholesome food and fresh air, the survivors rapidly recovered, and when the expedition sailed they were as strong and well as when they left England.

On the 29th of October Captain Lancaster put to sea, passing by Robben Island with its seals and penguins, and observing the peculiar shape of the Table Mountain. The passage northwards was rough and tedious, symptoms of scurvy again began to appear, and it was thought advisable once more to seek for refreshment in some haven. This was found at St. Mary's, a long narrow island off the east coast of Madagascar, lying parallel to the shore, and about four miles from it. Here the ships were anchored on the 18th of December, and a good supply of oranges and lemons was obtained for the sick. Thence they moved to the Bay of Antongil in Madagascar, where Lancaster opened a market for traffic with the natives, under the same carefully thought-out rules as he established in Table Bay, which were strictly enforced. There was no misunderstanding of any kind, and the English bought 15 tons of rice, 40 bushels of beans, many fowls, 8 oxen, and a quantity of oranges, lemons, and bananas. They also put a pinnace together, which had been brought out in pieces. There was, however, a heavy list of deaths from sickness, including the chaplain, surgeon, master's mate, and ten men of the *Dragon*, and the master and two men of the *Hector*.   An unfortunate accident also happened at the funeral of the master's mate.   The captain of the *Ascension* was going on shore to attend it, when the gunner fired the usual salute from the *Dragon*. By a sad mischance the guns had been loaded with shot.   The *Ascension's* boat was struck, and the captain and boatswain were both killed, meeting their own deaths on their way to attend the funeral of a comrade.

The fleet left the Bay of Antongil on the 6th of March 1602, and commenced the intricate navigation to India, among the Coral Islands.   Here the scientific knowledge and experience of John Davis were invaluable.   Steering northwards, he fell in with the low, sandy island of Roquerez on the tenth day, a danger the existence of which is considered doubtful in modern times.   But our early voyagers could feel no doubt, for they saw its groves of coco-nut trees, and there came to them such a pleasant smell from the land that they were reminded of a garden of flowers.   On the 13th they came upon ledges of rocks, with deep water close to them, and other low islands in sight.   Davis, with clear head and vigilant eye, was threading his way through the Chagos archipelago, with rocks and hidden dangers in all directions.   The pinnace was constantly kept ahead sounding, and, thanks to the watchful care of the pilot, the perils of this intricate navigation were overcome. On the 9th of May the four ships were safely anchored off the Nicobar Islands, where the crews were refreshed for ten days, the guns mounted, and all things got in readiness for defence in case of need.

On the sands of the Nicobar Islands a curious growth was observed. The narrative describes it as a small twig growing up to a young tree. But when they tried to pull it up it sank down into the ground and disappeared, unless it was held very tight. When plucked up, the root proved to be a great worm. As the tree grows the worm diminishes, and when the worm is wholly turned into a tree, the tree becomes rooted in the ground. The voyagers looked upon this transformation as one of the strangest wonders they had seen, and they gathered many of the twigs to take home. They are, in reality, coralliferous polyps (*Virgularia mirabilis*), which protrude from their holes as the tide rises, and disappear almost completely when touched, unless they are very firmly clutched. The leaves on them are supposed to be seaweed or fungus parasites. The part projecting above the surface does branch out like a small tree, and they vary in colour, length, and shape. When pulled up they have a large fleshy root, which is really the intestines of the animal, and not a separate worm. But on the whole the description of these curious creatures is correct, and shows what careful observers were John Davis and his companions.

On the 5th of June the English fleet cast anchor in the Bay of Achen, where a number of vessels from various ports of India were lying. Soon a boat came alongside with Frederik de Houtman and another survivor from among those who were captured from the Dutch ships in 1600. They reported that Ala-u-din Shah, the King of Achen, would welcome the English traders, and that he had heard much of the Queen of England, who was very famous in those parts, owing to her victories over the Spaniards. Captain Middleton was then sent on shore, to inform the King that the general had a letter for him from the great Queen. He was very well received, and on the third day Lancaster came on shore with a suitable escort. Six elephants were sent to convey the envoy to court, the Queen's letter being carried on one, while Lancaster mounted another. At the audience the Queen's letter was delivered with great ceremony, as well as the valuable presents from the Company. The most important request in the letter was that licence should be given for certain merchants to have a settled factory in Achen, and to remain there, learning the language and collecting merchandise, until the arrival of another fleet. After several conversations between Lancaster and the King, two native commissioners were appointed to arrange the heads of a treaty with the English envoy. Lancaster had brought out with him a Jew interpreter, who spoke Arabic fluently, so that there was no difficulty in carrying on the negotiations. A treaty was finally agreed upon, by which free trade was granted to the English.

As soon as the treaty with Achen was ratified, the merchants began to collect pepper for the return voyage. The *Susan*, under Henry Middleton, was sent to Priaman, on the west coast of Sumatra, where it was reported that there was a better market for pepper and spices than at Achen. Meanwhile a Portuguese envoy was busily engaged at Achen in fruitless attempts to undermine and counteract the influence of Lancaster. Two merchants were left behind to form a factory, and on the 11th of September the English ships weighed, and

shaped a course for the Straits of Malacca, where some
richly-laden prizes were captured.

Returning to the Bay of Achen in the end of October,
Captain Lancaster found that the King had faithfully
observed the terms of the treaty, and that the merchants
were well satisfied with their treatment. The King
then delivered his reply to Queen Elizabeth, and a rich
present to Lancaster. All the pepper and spices collected
by the merchants were shipped on board the *Ascension*,
leave was taken of the King, and the three ships sailed
from Achen with the intention of touching at Bantam
in Java. The *Ascension* was sent off to England with
her cargo. The *Dragon* and *Hector* proceeded southward along the coast of Sumatra to Priaman, where the
Susan was filling up with pepper and cloves. She also
was despatched to England, while the two larger ships
remained at Priaman for a few days to refresh the
crews. Davis found the navigation somewhat difficult
between Achen and Priaman, and for some time the
ships were in danger among rocks and islets off the
coast. Priaman is an open roadstead, sheltered by coral
islets, forty miles south of the equator, and in those
days Priaman, and the neighbouring port of Tiku, were
the principal marts for pepper in Sumatra.

Lancaster arrived at Bantam, in Java, on the 16th of
December, and delivered a letter from Queen Elizabeth,
with some presents, to the infant king of the place.
The merchants then landed, and were very successful
in obtaining full cargoes of pepper. By the 10th of
February 1603 the two ships were fully laden, and ready
to depart on their return voyage to England. Captain
Middleton of the *Hector* died suddenly at Bantam, to
the great sorrow of all the members of the expedition,

for he was popular, and had worked hard to secure the success of the venture. Lancaster sent the pinnace to the Moluccas to settle a factory, and three merchants were left on shore at Bantam. He then received a letter from the King of Bantam to the Queen, with presents, took his leave, and made sail for England on the 20th of February.

For some days the ships were becalmed in the Strait of Sunda, but on the 26th they were clear of all land, steering S.W. The voyage was satisfactory until the 28th of April 1603, when a furious storm burst upon them. They were obliged to scud under bare poles in a tremendous sea for two days, but eventually the wind became less violent, and they were able to repair damages. Another gale was encountered on the 3rd of May, continuing all night, the seas breaking with such fury on the quarter that they loosened the iron-work of the rudder. Next morning the rudder broke clean away and sank. The ship broached to, and drifted about helplessly, at one time being carried far south among sleet and snow, and at others being borne by the current into the neighbourhood of the Cape of Good Hope. Through all this trying time of peril and anxiety the *Hector* kept close to her consort very loyally. At last it was resolved to unstep the mizen-mast and place it over the stern, as a substitute for a rudder. But the seas were so heavy that the mizen-mast was dashed about and shook the stern to such an extent that they were glad when they had hauled it back into the ship again. The carpenter was then ordered to convert the mizen-mast into a rudder, and after much trouble it was fixed. This success, however, was of short duration, for within a few hours the seas unshipped it again, while

all but two of the rudder-irons were lost. The men
began to be anxious to abandon the ship and take refuge
in the *Hector*, but the General said, " Nay. I despair
not to save ourselves, the ship and the goods, by one
means or other, as God shall appoint us." He then
went down into his cabin and wrote a letter to his
employers, in which he declared his intention of standing
by the ship to the last. He delivered it to the *Hector*,
and ordered her to part company and make the best
of her way to England. But the captain of the *Hector*
was too loyal a man to obey such an order. He would
not leave his consort in her distress, but remained by
her.

At length the sea began to be comparatively smooth,
and the carpenter repaired the damage done to the
temporary rudder. The *Hector* sent men to assist, and
the rudder was hung on the two hooks that were left.
They were enabled to proceed on their course, and on
the 16th of June they arrived at the island of St.
Helena.

The storm-tossed mariners thus reached a haven of
rest and refreshment. St. Helena afforded fresh water
and some wild goats, but the latter called for the
exercise of cunning in procuring them. Lancaster
appointed four of his best shots to go into the interior
of the island, with four men attending upon each gun,
who at once carried the dead goats to a rendezvous.* A
party from the ships was sent daily to the rendezvous
to bring down the precious day's shooting, and in this
way a plentiful supply of fresh meat was quickly obtained. The sick men all recovered, the *Dragon's* new
rudder was carefully secured, and the two ships were
refitted.

They sailed from St. Helena on the 5th of July, and crossed the line on their homeward voyage on the 25th. On the 23rd of August they sighted St. Mary's, the easternmost island of the Azores, and on the 7th of September they had soundings in the channel. The return of the expedition, with good ladings of pepper and spices on board all the ships, was a splendid success. The perils and hardships of the undertaking can scarcely be appreciated now any more than the momentous character of the enterprise, in the consequences it led to, could be fully understood then. Sir Thomas Smith, and a few others, may have felt some presentiment of the glorious future in their most enthusiastic moments, but the great majority only saw in the return of the East India Company's fleet from its first venture a successful voyage which encouraged them to persevere. Lancaster was knighted, and was for many years a worthy director of the Company. He had certainly commanded the expedition with distinguished ability.

The second voyage of the East India Company, which sailed from Gravesend in March 1604, was commanded by Henry Middleton, who had brought home the *Susan* in Lancaster's expedition. He had the same four ships, and was almost as successful as his predecessor. Other voyages followed year by year, and the sixth, commanded by Sir Henry Middleton, who had been knighted, was on a large scale. Middleton's ship, the *Trade's Increase*, of 1100 tons, was the largest merchant vessel ever built in England, and there were two other ships which sailed with her in April 1610. In the eighth voyage Captain Saris established an English factory in Japan; and from 1612, when the tenth voyage under Captain Best was undertaken, dates the establishment

o

of permanent English factories on the coast of India.
A regular firman for trade was procured from the
Great Mogul, and the East India Company secured its
first footing on the continent of India. From these
small beginnings the British Empire of India arose,
and the services of the earliest pioneers, whose work
was the most hazardous and difficult, should never be
forgotten.

To Sir James Lancaster the first place is due, as the
efficient and courageous leader of the first voyage. But
John Davis stands second to him alone. In his voyage
with the Zealanders, Davis collected much needed commercial information, acquired experience as a pilot and
navigator of the Indian Ocean, and by his gallantry
and presence of mind he saved the *Lion* and all on board
when treacherously attacked by the Achenese. In his
capacity of chief pilot to the first voyage of the East
India Company he brought all the knowledge and
experience acquired with the Dutch to bear for the
service of his own country. In seconding Lancaster he
played no unimportant part. Among the worthies who
laid the foundations of our Indian Empire, an honourable place is due to the great Arctic navigator and
discoverer—John Davis.

CHAPTER XII.

THE LAST VOYAGE.

John Davis was at home for one year and three months before he sailed on his last voyage. It had been a sad home-coming. The great Queen was dead. Adrian Gilbert, his more than brother, had also passed away. Sir Walter Raleigh, his true and constant friend, had fallen on evil days. The learned scholar, the gallant sailor, the patriot statesman, the brilliant courtier was about to be subjected to years of persecution and imprisonment by the shambling pedant who desecrated the throne of Elizabeth. Davis, and the half brothers of Greenway, were spared the knowledge of Raleigh's sufferings. They went before him. But it was the sight of Raleigh's execution which first kindled the patriotic ardour of Eliot, and the cruel death of Eliot gave that stern and unswerving resolution to the action of the Long Parliament, which led to the erection of a scaffold at Whitehall. Retribution, though slow in coming, was certain; and there was no link missing in the chain connecting the execution in Palace Yard and the Tower dungeons with the scene before the window of the Banqueting House.

Davis only saw the beginning of these things. The wretched change in public affairs was visible at once.

At court drunkenness and folly were substituted for
decency and public spirit. The ship of the State, with
Elizabeth at the helm, was like Lancaster's *Red Dragon*,
orderly, decent, and well-disciplined. The *régime* of
James would remind Davis of the lord of misrule and of
the orgies he saw on board the *Lion*, with Houtman in
command.

The chief pilot received his due share of the profits of
the successful voyage, and he still owned the little estate
at Sandridge. Few men had seen more service afloat.
He might well have sought rest and retirement in his
declining years. But Davis was not a man to take his
hand from the plough, while there was a furrow left to
turn. He was destined to die in harness. Like the old
Roman he felt that he should work to the last :—

"Oportet Imperatorem stantem mori."

Yet there were a few last months of home life in Sandridge, during which he might set his affairs in order,
before he set sail on his final voyage.

At this time he prepared the second edition of his
"Seaman's Secrets" for the press, which was published
in 1607. He became engaged to Judith Havard, but
the marriage was deferred until his return from the
next voyage. His boys were growing up. Two months
before he sailed to return no more, John Davis made his
will as follows :—

"In the name of God Amen. Being nowe bounde
to the seas for the coaste of China in the *Tiger* of
London, and uncertaine of my returne, I doe committ my
bodye to God's favourable direction and my sowle to his
everlastinge mercie, and for my worldly goods, whatsoever lands, leases, merchandizes or money, either in my

possession or in due commynge unto me, as by speciali-
ties or otherwise shall appeare, my will is that it shall be
devided and parted into fower equall parts or porc'ons;
that is to say I give and bequeath th' one foureth „parte
thereof to Judith Havard, unto whom I have given my
faithe in matrimony, to be solempnized at my returne.
The other foureth parte I give to Gilbert Davis, my
eldest sonne. The third foureth parte I give to Arthur
Davis, my second sonne; and the last foureth parte to
Phillip Davis, my thirde youngest sonne now living.
Soe my will is that my goods be equally divided between
my three sonnes and Judith Havard, my espowsed love,
and to be delivered after my deathe ys manifestlie
knowne. But if any of them shall dye before they receive their parte, then it shall be equally divided
betweene those that live. If they all die before it be
devided, then I give th' one haulf to the poore, and th'
other haulf to my brother Edward Davis and to his
children : and soe, commyting my soule to God, I desire
that this my wyll may be faithfully p'formed, and to
testifie that this is my deede and desire, I doe hereunto
sett my hande and seale this 12th of October 1604. By
me, John Davis."

The East India Company did not have the advantage
of the services of Davis during their second voyage.
It was unfortunate that he did not continue in their
employment. The great fault in his character was a
facility of disposition which led him to comply with the
wishes of friends, or even the requests of mere acquaintances if strongly urged, and that when the line of
conduct they proposed was opposed to the interests of
enterprises, the welfare of which he had most at heart.
It was this weakness which led him to join the ill-con-

ducted expedition of Cavendish. He now left the service of the Company, in compliance with the desire of an old friend with whom he had probably served in the *Island Voyage.* Sir Edward Michelborne was a seaman of some· distinction, and he had strong interest at court. His friends urged his claims to command the first voyage of the East India Company. The Lord Treasurer used much persuasion with the Company to accept of his employment as principal commander, but the merchants announced that they were resolved not to employ any gentleman in any place of charge in the voyage, desiring " to sort their business with men of their own quality." Michelborne's name appears third in the list of subscribers, but in July 1601 a minute records that Sir Edward, with two others, "was disfranchised out of the freedom and privileges of this fellowship, and utterly disabled from taking any benefit or profit thereby." No reason is given for this expulsion. Perhaps the subscription was not paid. Michelborne became a gentleman pensioner to James I., and in 1604 he began to prepare for a voyage to the East Indies on his own account. On June 25th, 1604, King James, regardless of the Charter giving exclusive rights to the East India Company, granted a license to Sir Edward Michelborne to discover and trade with China and Japan, notwithstanding any grant or charter to the contrary.

Michelborne equipped a vessel of 240 tons called the *Tiger*, with a pinnace named the *Tiger's Whelp*, and John Davis accepted the appointment of pilot. Purchas calls this the second voyage of John Davis into the East Indies. It was his second voyage thither in an English ship, but his third including the Dutch expedition.

The *Tiger* and her whelp set sail from Cowes on the

˙5th of December 1604, and arrived in the insecure
anchorage of Oratava, on the north-west side of the
Island of Teneriffe, on the 23rd.   Crossing the line on
the 16th of January, Davis shaped a course for Fernando
Noronha, where he found the number of inhabitants
reduced to six, and the live stock not so plentiful as
at the time of his former visit.   There were, however,
plenty of wild gourds and water-melons.   They observed
also trees of *Jatropha gossypifolia*, which is abundant
on the island, and which they called "rotten trees,"
because when they were there it was the dry season
and the trees were devoid of leaves.   A climbing
asclepiad, with large pods full of a silky fibre, was seen
growing on the leafless *Jatrophas*, just as Mr. Moseley
observed them during the visit of H.M.S. *Challenger*
270 years afterwards.   A very pleasant sight must this
bright vegetation have been to men who had been several
weeks at sea, and they gladly landed to fill their water-
casks and get in supplies of fresh provisions.

During the voyage from Fernando Noronha to the
Cape, the *Tiger* sighted Ascension, and on the 3rd of April
a small island was seen which Davis reported as Dassen,
or Coney Island, about eight leagues south of the present
Saldanha Bay.   Sir Edward Michelborne went in a boat
to land on it.   In his absence the ship was driven out to
sea by a gale of wind, and the General did not get on
board again for two days.   On the 8th, the anchor was
let go in Table Bay.   Here, as usual, there were abundant supplies of fresh beef and mutton, and the shooting parties got great quantities of birds.   Their stay of
three weeks quite revived the spirits of the men, and
when they sailed, on the 3rd of May, they were in as
good health as at the time of their departure from

England.   Rounding the Cape of Good Hope on the 7th,
they encountered a furious gale of wind on the 9th, which
lasted for two days with rain and thunder.   In the full
fury of the storm, flickering flames, like candles, appeared
on the *Tiger's* mast-heads.   Spanish mariners would
have believed that these St. Elmo lights were indications
of the presence of their guardian saint.   Protestant
Englishmen could not believe a Popish fable.   Nevertheless the fact remained that the weather improved
from that time, and that the sea went down.

Stretching boldly across the Indian Ocean, the able
pilot of the *Tiger* made the northernmost island of the
Chagos Archipelago, and a supply of coco-nuts was
obtained.   But Michelborne altered his plans.   Diego
Garcia, at the southern end of the group, was sighted,
the line was again crossed, and on the 26th of July the
ship was near the coast of Sumatra.   She was anchored
off the little island of Batu, and the crew set to work to
put together a small shallop which had been brought
out from England in pieces.   This addition to Michelborne's force was named the *Bat*, in honour of the
flying squirrels which were found hanging from the
trees, on the well-wooded island.   From thence the
Tiger proceeded to Priaman, the pepper mart on the
west coast of Sumatra, anchoring there on the 13th of
August.   The *Tiger's Whelp* had been separated from her
consort during the gale of wind off the Cape of Good
Hope ; she had made the voyage alone and had reached
Priaman, where she was once more united with the
Tiger, amidst great rejoicings.   The captain of the
whelp came out in his boat, when her dam was still
half a league from the anchorage, and Michelborne
welcomed him with a peal of great ordnance.

At Priaman it was found that the King of Achen had been dethroned by his sons, that there was a civil war between the brothers, and that little trade could be done. Michelborne therefore resolved to proceed southwards to Bantam. On the 23rd of October the *Tiger* and her whelp anchored off an inhabited island called Pulo Marra, in the Straits of Sunda, near the southern extremity of Sumatra, where plentiful supplies of fresh provisions were obtained. While he was on the west coast of Sumatra, Davis devoted his attention to the execution of careful surveys, and to the preparation of sailing directions for the use of his countrymen. In this last year of his life he was as zealous and diligent as in the days of his prime. One result of his meritorious labours is preserved in the Sloane collection of manuscripts at the British Museum. It consists of minute and carefully prepared sailing directions from Achen to the pepper marts of Priaman and Tiku; with latitude and variation of the compass for each port, descriptions of watering-places, and some account of the trade at various points along the west coast of Sumatra. He gives excellent advice to keep the lead going when near the land, and notes the bearings of conspicuous marks from the different anchorages. It is touching to note how, in seeking for a comparison, his thoughts revert to home scenes. Thus, in describing a gutt or break in a line of high land, he compares it to the entrance of Dartmouth, that beloved haven on which his eyes were never destined to rest again.

Leaving Pulo Marra, the *Tiger* proceeded to Bantam, where Michelborne communicated with the factors of the East India Company residing there. He then shaped a course to Patani, the most northern state

on the eastern side of the Malay Peninsula. For a
long time they beat up against a northerly wind; and,
having captured a junk belonging to Pahang, they took
some rice out of her, for which Sir Edward Michelborne
paid in full, and engaged the services of a native who
was acquainted with the pilotage of the Patani coast.
Davis then shaped a course for Pulo Tioman, the largest
of a chain of islands on the east coast of the Malay
Peninsula. Still baffled by the northerly winds which
prevail on this coast in November, they were for many
days off Pahang, a native state which extends for eighty
miles along the coast, bounded on the south by Johore,
and on the north by Tringano. This eastern coast is
very beautiful, with mountains inland rising to a height
of 3000 feet above the sea.

Then the end came. As the *Tiger* was beating against
a head wind on the Pahang coast, she fell in with a
junk, on the 24th of December. It was full of Japanese
who had been committing piracies along the coasts of
China and Cambodia. Their pilot being dead, they
had wrecked their ship on a shoal off the coast of
Borneo. Taking to their boats they boarded a junk
belonging to Patani, massacred the crew, and took
possession. She was laden with rice, and having taken
their arms out of the wreck, they shaped a course for
Japan. But their ignorance, and the contrary winds,
were the causes for their being so far out of their
reckoning; and so, by an evil chance, the *Tiger* fell in
with this shipload of Japanese ruffians off the coast
of Pahang. There were ninety men crowded into a
junk of seventy tons. They at once submitted to the
orders of Sir Edward Michelborne, with much show of
humility, and told their story with apparent frankness.

The current had drifted them to the south, and the *Tiger* anchored under a small island to the east of Singapore, one of a cluster at the eastern extremity of the Strait of Malacca, with the junk nearly alongside. Michelborne entertained the ruffians and used them well, in the expectation of obtaining valuable information respecting the trade routes to China. The Japanese, on the other hand, being hopeless of ever reaching their own country in the leaky junk, had secretly resolved to seize the *Tiger* or lose their lives in the attempt.

Meanwhile there were mutual courtesies and entertainments passing between the English and Japanese, sometimes there being as many as twenty-five or twenty-six of the pirates on board the *Tiger* at one time. For some reason which is not explained, probably owing to a rumour of concealed treasure, Michelborne ordered the cargo of rice to be searched, and while this work was being done, he desired Captain Davis to disarm the Japanese and send them before the mast. Davis, being deceived by the pretended humility of the desperadoes, did not take away their weapons, although Michelborne appears to have sent two messages to him on the subject. This went on all day, the English crew searching in the rice, and the Japanese looking on, some before the mast in the junk, and others on board the *Tiger*. While they were passing the time in apparent idleness, the villains were agreeing upon a plan of action. At a preconcerted signal, they were suddenly to attack the English in both ships.

Towards sunset the storm burst. Taking the captors completely by surprise, the Japanese killed or drove overboard all the Englishmen that were in the junk. A certain number of Japanese had been confined in the

Tiger's cabin during the search. On the signal being
given, they rushed out and met Captain Davis coming

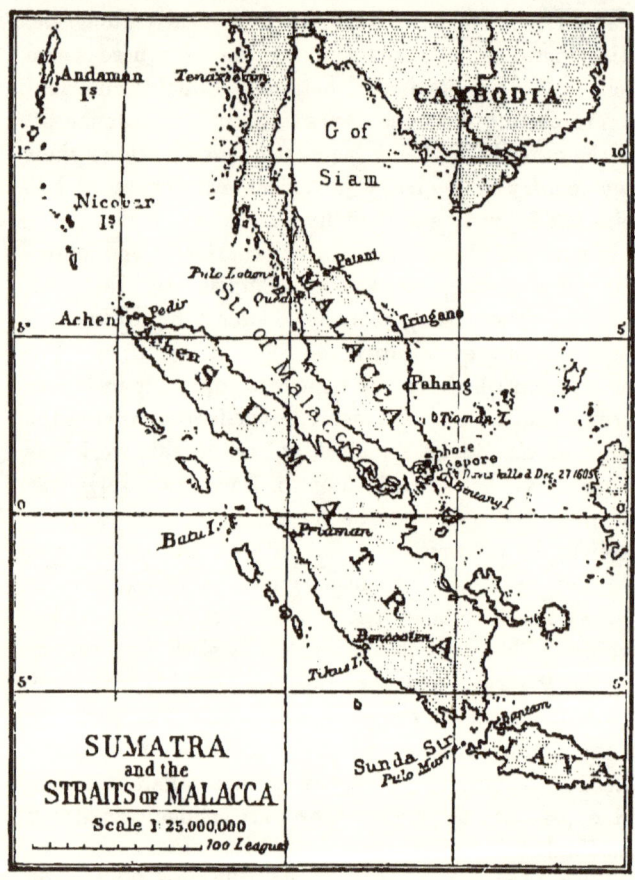

SUMATRA
and the
STRAITS of MALACCA
Scale 1 25,000,000
100 Leagues

out of the gun-room. They pulled him inside the cabin,
gave him six or seven mortal wounds, and then thrust
his body out into the waist. He was dead before he

reached the deck. Michelborne was on the poop. He
rallied the boatswain, carpenter, and a few men round
him, and leapt into the waist, where the pirates were
kept at bay. They fought with desperate tenacity, dis-
puting the ground inch by inch, as they were gradually
driven from the waist back into the cabin. Here they
held out for upwards of four hours, making several
attempts to set the ship on fire. At last Michelborne
got two demi-culverins to bear on the cabin bulk-head,
loaded them with cross-bars, bullets, and case shot, and
let fly into the midst of the enemy, blowing the survivors
to pieces. Not one asked for life. All fought to the
bitter end. Thus did John Davis close his eventful
life, on the 27th of December 1605. He found a watery
grave at the eastern end of the Strait of Malacca, within
sight of the lofty Island of Bintang.

Michelborne, after the loss of his illustrious pilot,
hesitated for some time, but eventually resolved to
return home, and made sail on the 5th of February
1606. On the 17th of April he reached St. Helena and
refreshed his crew, and on the 27th of June he arrived
at Milford Haven. Finally the *Tiger* came to an anchor
at Portsmouth on the 9th of July, where the crew was
dismissed, having been a year and a half on the voyage.
They brought home the sad news of the death of John
Davis—the discoverer, surveyor, and true-hearted sailor ;
one bright star out of many in the glorious Elizabethan
constellation. He had just reached his fifty-sixth year.

Of the four boys who had been companions on the
banks of the Dart, and had together listened to the
yarns of sailors on Dartmouth quay, three had run their
course and passed away. Humphrey Gilbert, in the
prime of life, had sunk beneath the Atlantic waves,

with words upon his lips that have become immortal.
The more peaceful, though not less useful, career of
Adrian Gilbert ended quietly at home. John Davis,
after a long series of valuable services to his country
and to science, met with a violent death outside the
Straits of Malacca. Walter Raleigh was destined to
outlive them all, and to endure a long drawn-out
martyrdom before his brilliant career was closed in
Palace Yard. He was not found wanting when tried
in the furnace of adversity. Its fruit was the " History
of the World."

Davis was distinguished in every branch of a sailor's
profession. After losing sight of him at the home of
his boyhood, when he went to sea, we first encounter
him again in the companionship of Adrian Gilbert,
planning the details of an important expedition of
discovery. His conduct of the three successive Arctic
expeditions was able and judicious. He was a thorough
seaman, a scientific observer, with attainments which
were unusual in those days, and an admirable organiser.
Above all, he had that love of enterprise, that fervent
enthusiasm without which mere attainments cannot
secure success. He made the subject of a North-West
Passage his own, and he never lost sight of it during a
long life of hard and almost constant service. As a
scientific explorer and discoverer he was certainly the
first man of his age and country.

The practically useful labours of John Davis were
valuable to his own and to succeeding generations. His
charts of the English Channel and the Scilly Islands,
of the Arctic coasts, and of Magellan's Straits ; and his
sailing directions, especially for the Eastern Seas, are
a few among the numerous results of his observations.

His opportunities were great, he was always diligently on the look-out to record anything that could be useful to his countrymen, and the skill acquired by years of practice rendered the work of his hands as accurate as it was justly prized. He did not work for fame or for money, but for the love he felt for his brother sailors. It was this love that conquered difficulties, and inspired him to work unceasingly. From the same source came the "Seaman's Secrets," and the invention of the back-staff. "It was not in respect of his pains but of his love" that he desired to be judged. No nobler motive ever influenced a man in the execution of difficult and laborious work.

For war services Davis had no special aptitude; yet he was prompt and ready, when opportunities offered, to fight for his Queen and country. In the repulse of the Spanish Armada, he commanded a tender, and acted as pilot to the Lord Admiral. In the campaign with the Earl of Cumberland at the Azores, he was active and enterprising. He served in the brilliant attack on Cadiz; and in the arduous cruise among the Azores in 1597. His personal gallantry and presence of mind saved the *Lion*, when treacherously attacked by the Malays. But no part of his fame rests on his war services. He was essentially a man of peace. It was by the calm and collected way in which he faced, and encouraged others to face, the most terrible hardships and sufferings; by his ever ready presence of mind and consummate seamanship in moments of danger, that he showed the stuff he was made of. The enemies against which he made war were the ice of the frigid zone, the storms of the far south, the pestilences of the tropics, and the evil designs of false companions. It was the mission of his life to study the forces of nature, and to mould and direct them, so far as the knowledge of his times rendered it possible, for the good of his Queen and his countrymen. If, as regards worldly success and his own fortunes, the life of Davis was, in some sort, a failure, in all that is worth living for, in valuable public services well performed, and in the acquisition of immortal fame, it was a success.

Davis was a God-fearing and loyal man from his youth upwards. He was a true and constant friend, and warmly sympathised with those who served under him. Raleigh and Adrian Gilbert never faltered in their life-long friendship, and never failed him in his need. Mr. Janes, after serving under him in two Arctic expeditions, embarked with him for Magellan's Strait, solely actuated by the love he bore him. For Davis was a genial companion as well as a true friend. He was imaginative and enthusiastic, and he had a strong sense of humour, as is shown in his narrative of the Dutch voyage. He bore the grievous misfortune at home with manly fortitude, neither abandoning his duties nor altering his mode of life when on shore. He lived on at his beloved Sandridge, for the sake of his children.

The faults in the character of Davis were of a nature which made it unlikely that he would be fortunate in a worldly sense. Although he was resolute and determined in facing the elements and in prosecuting his designs, he was often lamentably weak when appealed to by companions or acquaintances, and in quelling insubordination. He was apt to acquiesce when he should have resisted, and to yield rather than oppose. He was too good-natured. His disposition was too facile; and from this fault most of his misfortunes originated. He

preferred expostulation to force at times when force alone
was needed.

With all his faults, John Davis, the great discoverer,
the scientific seaman, the consummate pilot, takes rank
among the foremost sea-worthies of the glorious reign
of Queen Elizabeth.

Much that Davis wrote has been lost. We have his
letters to Secretary Walsingham and to Master Sanderson
after his return from the Arctic voyages, his narrative
of the second, and his log of the third voyage. The
speeches he made to the master and crew of the *Desire*
are given *verbatim* by Janes. His separate published
works are the "Seaman's Secrets," with the preface
addressed to the Lord High Admiral, and the "World's
Hydrographical Discovery." His narrative of the Dutch
voyage of Houtman is the only one in existence, and is
valuable as a specimen of the humorous side of Davis's
mind. It is accompanied by a covering letter to the
Earl of Essex. The Sailing Directions for the west
coast of Sumatra furnish an example of his method in
preparing the valuable guides for the use of his sea-
faring countrymen. Next to his own writings we are
most indebted to the pen of his devoted friend, John
Janes, in tracing the life-story of Davis. Two of the
Arctic narratives and the thrilling tale of adventures
in Magellan's Strait are from his pen.

CHAPTER XIII.

THE FOLLOWING UP OF THE WORK OF DAVIS.

I.

By the "Furious Overfall."

Davis, in completing his own discovery of the Strait, and its adjacent shores, set up two leading marks for future exploration. One pointed west by the "Furious Overfall," the other pointed north by "Sanderson his Hope." Each was followed up by worthy successors a few years after the death of the illustrious pioneer. Henry Hudson made his way by the "Furious Overfall" into Hudson's Bay. William Baffin, passing beyond "Sanderson his Hope," reached and explored the great bay which bears his name. The discoveries of Hudson and Baffin are the direct consequences of the work of Davis, and form the sequel of his life-story. A life of Davis would therefore be incomplete unless it included an account of the work achieved by those who followed up his leading marks.

When John Davis made his speech on Arctic discovery to the merchants of London in the house of Mr. Thomas Hudson at Mortlake, it is more than possible that the nephew of that merchant may have been present. Thus we may believe that the two great

226

discoverers may have been personally known to each other. But from that time we entirely lose sight of Henry Hudson, until we find him employed by the Muscovy Company to discover a shorter route to Cathaye by sailing over the North Pole.

On the 19th of April 1607 eleven men and a boy partook of the holy communion at the little church of St. Ethelburga, in Bishopsgate Street Within. They then returned to the river-side at Ratcliffe, and went

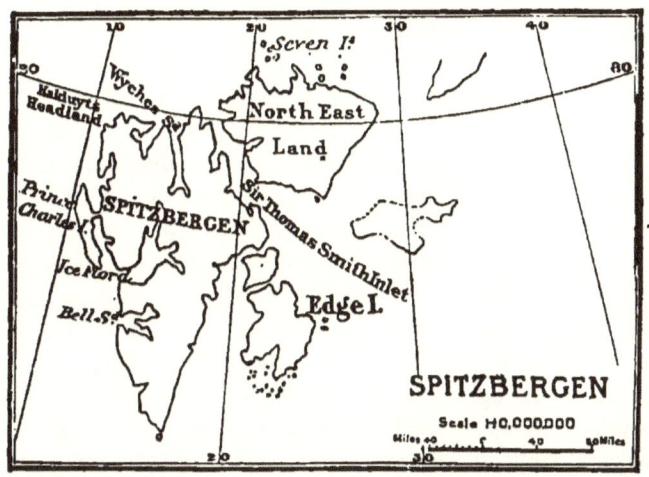

on board the *Hopewell*, a little vessel of 80 tons. Ten days afterwards Hudson commenced his first adventurous voyage. His little son Jack shared his cabin, William Collins and James Young were the mates, and the crew consisted of eight men. On the 13th of June he came in sight of the east coast of Greenland. He then shaped a north-easterly course until he sighted the famous Hakluyt Head of Spitzbergen, but he could find no opening whereby he might force his way northwards.

He returned in September, and in the following year
the Muscovy Company despatched him on a similar
service. This time he intended to attempt a passage
between Spitzbergen and Novaya Zemlya. His son
was again with him as a companion. On reaching the
edge of the ice he carefully examined it for an opening,
but again without success, and he returned to Gravesend
in August 1608. These voyages had useful scientific
as well as commercial results. Hudson was the first
sea-captain who took observations for the dip of the
magnetic needle, and his voyages led directly to the
establishment of a lucrative whale fishery in the Spitzbergen seas. Hudson's third voyage was undertaken
from Amsterdam, in a yacht called the *Half Moon*, with
a crew composed half of Dutch and half of Englishmen.
On this occasion he attempted discoveries on the coast
of North America. Crossing the Atlantic in the spring
of 1609, he explored the Bay of Chesapeake, rounded
Sandy Hook, discovered the river which bears his name,
and sighted the Catskill Mountains. Hudson landed
on the Island of Manhattan, the site of New York, and
returned to England in November, anchoring in Dartmouth Harbour. He there received orders not to go
back to Holland, but remain and give his services to
his own country.

Sir Thomas Smith, with two other eminent patrons of
discovery, had resolved to fit out another expedition for
the discovery of a North-West Passage. The previous
three voyages of Hudson had been his preparation for
following the beacon lighted by Davis, and completing
the examination of the route, the way to which was
pointed out by the great navigator—the way by the
" Furious Overfall." The *Discovery*, of 55 tons, was

provided, and ·Hudson received the command. Once more his young son Jack, who had reached the age of seventeen years, was his companion. His mate was Robert Juet, a treacherous old man, who had served with Hudson in his second and third voyages. Thomas Woodhouse, a mathematical student; Habakkuk Prickett, a servant of Sir Dudley Digges; Robert Bylot, an experienced old sailor; Arnold Ludlow, and Michael Pierce, were the leading men on board. Henry Green, a good-for-nothing young spendthrift, befriended by Hudson because he wrote a good hand, was taken on board at the last moment. Sailing from Greenhithe on the 22nd of April 1610, the *Discovery* made a prosperous voyage to Iceland, and thence across the Atlantic. In June, Hudson navigated his ship past the "Furious Overfall," and down the strait which bears his name and leads to the great bay or inland sea, the Mediterranean of America, as it has been called, which was ever afterwards to be known as Hudson's Bay. Hudson sailed through the strait, with little or no obstruction from ice, until the entrance to the bay was reached. The island on the south side of the entrance was named Cape Digges, and it was observed that myriads of birds were breeding there. Hudson's own journal unfortunately comes to an end on reaching Cape Digges. The story is continued by Habakkuk Prickett, whose narrative is open to some suspicion, and whose account is confused and unsatisfactory. Hudson's journal ends on the 3rd of August, and during the three following months it is not at all clear what he was doing, and what course he took. But on the 1st of November the *Discovery* was in a bay at the extreme south of Hudson's Bay, now called James Bay. She was frozen in and compelled to winter there.

A spirit of mutiny and discontent began to show itself during the long and dreary nights, which was increased by privation and hardship, and fostered by two or three designing villains. Hudson had felt obliged to supersede his old shipmate Juet in his rating of mate, and to appoint Robert Bylot in his place, owing to some misconduct. Henry Green was an unprincipled scoundrel, whose enmity against his benefactor arose from the refusal of some trifle for which he had asked. He formed a conspiracy with the boatswain, named William Wilson, and three men, named John Thomas, Michael Pierce, and Andrew Moter. They watched their opportunity. The provisions had run very low, but Hudson hoped to replenish them and to obtain a sufficient supply for the return voyage by salting down birds at Cape Digges. On the 18th of June 1611 the *Discovery* broke out of her winter quarters, and a course was shaped for the entrance of Hudson's Strait.

The mutineers thought that there would not be sufficient food to enable them to reach England, and they conceived the diabolical scheme of turning the sick and weak adrift in order to reduce the number of mouths. As they knew that Hudson would never consent to this villainy, and as they hated their commander because he had enforced discipline and had punished two or more of them, they included him and his son in the number of their intended victims, as well as all who remained loyal. Habakkuk Prickett and five others were in bed with scurvy when the ship broke out of the ice, and a course was shaped northwards for Cape Digges.

Prickett tells the story of what took place. He says that Green and Wilson came to his bunk after the ship had been three days at sea, and divulged their plot to him, assuring him that the course they proposed to take was unavoidable, because there were only fourteen days' provisions left in the ship. He declares that he entreated them to desist, at least for a few days, and that he appealed to the old scoundrel Juet, the disrated mate, but in vain. Prickett was probably spared because he was a servant of Sir Dudley Digges, one of the owners. The conspirators trusted that he would give a plausible account of the affair on his return home. He never attempted to warn the captain of his danger, and he was evidently a time-serving rascal, upon whom no reliance could be placed.

The day was fixed, and Prickett tell us that the villains passed the greater part of the previous night in whispered talk. At that time of the year, the night was as light as the day. In the morning they stood round the cabin door, waiting for the captain to come out. Hudson was entirely without suspicion. He got up as usual, and on stepping on to the deck he was seized by Thomas and Bennet the cook, while Wilson, the boatswain, tied his hands behind his back. The unfortunate captain must have struggled and called for help, for the carpenter and two other loyal men ran to his assistance. They were overpowered by the mutineers, who got possession of the ship. The shallop was then hauled up alongside. The sick men, including Mr. Woodhouse the mathematician, were pulled out of their berths and forced into the boat. Hudson, as a last hope, as soon as he saw what was intended, called to Prickett to remonstrate with the mutineers. But the time-server kept close in his cabin, and said not a word. The carpenter would have been allowed to remain, but he declared that he would rather die with true men than live as the associate of cowards.   He, and the two other loyal men, were forced into the boat with the four sick. Then young Jack Hudson, who had been his father's companion in all his voyages, and was now in his eighteenth year, was taken out of the cabin and driven into the boat.   Hudson followed.   The shallop was cast adrift, with nine men crowded into her, one fowling-piece, some powder and shot, an iron pot, and a little meal.

The ship stood clear of the ice, and then hove to, while the murderers ransacked the captain's cabin. This aroused a hope in the minds of the forlorn people in the boat that the villains had relented.   They pulled with all their might, and soon came close to the ship again.   But they were doomed to cruel disappointment.   As they came up alongside, the mainsail was let run, the topsails were hoisted, and the cowardly rascals fled as if from an enemy.   Hudson and his doomed companions were never heard of more.

Eleven men remained on board.   Robert Bylot, the mate, was, it is to be hoped, an unwilling spectator of the crime that was perpetrated before his eyes.   Juet, the disrated mate, the young scoundrel Green, Moter, Pierce, Thomas, and Wilson were the ringleaders.   The cook was an accomplice, as was Francis Clements, a friend of Thomas.   Simmes seems merely to have acquiesced, and Prickett was a time-server.   On the 29th of July 1611 the *Discovery* was hove to off Cape Digges, where the birds breed.   The five ringleaders of the mutiny went on shore in a boat, to communicate with a party of Eskimos.   They were unarmed.   Two were bartering for venison, two were gathering sorrel, and there was a boat keeper.   They were suddenly

attacked by the savages, and all were mortally wounded.
Tumbling into the boat together she was shoved off.
The Eskimos then began shooting at them with bows
and arrows, and Green was killed outright. The rest
got back to the ship, but they all died within a few days.
Seldom has retribution followed so quickly on the per-
petration of crime. They barely survived their victims.
Old Juet, who was not on shore with them, died on the
passage home.

The survivors were Bylot the mate, who took command, Bennet the cook, Clements, Simmes, and Prickett.
They shot about 300 birds at Cape Digges, and put
themselves on an allowance of half a bird a day, with a
little meal. They returned through Hudson's Strait
and shaped a course for Ireland. Soon the meal was
exhausted. Bennet the cook kept the birds' bones, and
fried them in candle grease. The last bird was in the
steep tub when they sighted Dursey Island, and anchored
in Berehaven, where a crew was hired to take the ship
round to the Thames. Bylot and Prickett hurried up to
London, and told the best story they could invent to
their employers. No one was punished. Prickett wrote
a narrative of the catastrophe. Bylot continued to
receive appointments from Sir Thomas Smith and his
colleagues. A younger son of Henry Hudson received
employment from the East India Company, on the
ground that "the father had perished in the service of
his country!"

Thus had bold Henry Hudson followed up the beacon
light of Davis, reached the strait and bay which im-
mortalise his name, and found a grave in the midst of
his discoveries. His labours were appreciated, and it
was resolved that an expedition should be despatched to

complete his work in the spring of the following year.
Two vessels were fitted out, the *Resolution* and *Discovery*. The command of the expedition was entrusted
to Thomas Button, an officer of tried valour and experience; and it was under the special patronage of
Prince Henry, who signed the instructions.

Thomas Button was the son of Miles Button of
Duffryn in Glamorganshire, whose family had been
seated there for seven generations. Young Thomas,
who was born at Duffryn, was sent to sea in 1592. He
was in the West Indies with Captain Newport in 1603,
and commanded a king's ship in 1609. In 1612 he
was appointed to lead the new expedition to Hudson's
Bay on board the *Resolution*, the *Discovery* being commanded by Captain Ingram. A relation named Gibbons
and a friend named Hawkridge accompanied him, while
Bylot and Prickett, the survivors of Hudson's fatal
voyage, were on board. The ships were supplied with
provisions for eighteen months, and in May 1612 they
left the Thames.

The expedition reached Cape Digges without encountering any difficulties from ice in Hudson's Strait,
and remained there three weeks in order to put a
pinnace together that had been taken out in pieces.
Button then entered Hudson's Bay, and proceeded westward, discovering the southern coast of Southampton
Island and off-lying islets, to one of which Button gave
the name of Mansell Island, after his relation Admiral
Sir Edward Mansell; to another "Cary's Swan's Nest;"
to a third, "Hopes Check'd," because there his expectations of making progress received a check. Bad weather
came on, and late in August Button sought refuge in
a small creek on the western side of Hudson's Bay,

which was named Port Nelson, after the master of the
Resolution, who died and was buried there. He was
thus the discoverer of the west coast of Hudson's Bay,
Hudson himself having only sailed down its east coast
to the southern extremity.

Button determined to winter at Port Nelson, and at
once set his people to work to procure as much game
as possible. They obtained a large supply of ptarmigan,
but the winter was very severe, and, although they had
fresh food, the health of the men suffered from the
intense cold. Button kept their minds employed by
requiring them to answer questions relating to the
voyage and its objects, and by thus interesting them
in the work upon which they were engaged. In June
1613 the ice broke up, and the ships left their winter
quarters and reached Cape Digges. In returning by
Hudson's Strait, Button discovered that the land on
which Cape Chidley is situated is an island, and he
took his ships through the strait which is thus formed.
On old maps the island is called Button's Island, a
name which ought to have been retained. He returned
to England in the autumn of 1613, but his journal was
never published. We are indebted to Luke Fox, a
later explorer, for all the information that has reached
us respecting Button's voyage. He became Admiral
Sir Thomas Button, and was in command on the coast
of Ireland in 1618. He was Rear-Admiral in the fleet
of Sir Edward Mansell, which was sent against the
Algerine pirates in 1620, and in 1623 was again employed in suppressing piracy in the Irish Sea. Sir
Thomas married Mary, daughter of Sir Walter Rice of
Dynevor, and, dying in April 1634, he left a son who
succeeded him at Duffryn. The expedition of Sir

Thomas Button to Hudson's Bay was ably conducted. It resulted in considerable additions to geographical knowledge as regards the southern shores of Southampton Island, and in the discovery of the western side of the bay. Button's relation, Captain Gibbons, received command of the *Discovery* in 1614 to follow up the discoveries of his predecessor. But he was unable to enter Hudson's Strait, and was driven by the ice into a bay on the coast of Labrador, where he remained for twenty weeks. His crew named the place " Gibbons his Hole ; " and on being released from the ice, he returned home.

The persevering adventurers of London were not discouraged by one or two failures. In 1615 they sent out another expedition, consisting of the *Discovery*, of 55 tons, commanded by Robert Bylot, who had served in the three previous expeditions under Hudson, Button, and Gibbons in the same ship. William Baffin was his " mate and associate," and the crew consisted of fourteen men and two boys. Sailing in April 1615, they sighted Cape Farewell on the 6th of May. Crossing Davis Strait, the *Discovery* was safely anchored in a good harbour on the west side of Resolution Island, which is at the northern entrance of Hudson's Strait, on the 1st of June. Bylot was an experienced seaman, and Baffin was a scientific navigator, who lost no opportunity of noting everything that would be useful to his brother sailors, like Davis before him. They had some difficulty with the ice at the entrance of the strait; but eventually sailed along the northern side until they reached a group, which Baffin named the Savage Islands, because they met with a party of Eskimos on the shore. Continuing a course westward along the northern coast,

the *Discovery* was closely beset by the ice off some land
which Baffin named "Broken Point." The ship was
immovable for several days; and the men amused themselves on the ice by firing at butts with bows and arrows
and playing at football.

Baffin was very differently employed. He was, like
his great predecessor Davis, a seaman who closely
studied the scientific branch of his profession, and
strove to improve the methods of observing. He was particularly anxious to test the various theoretical methods
of finding longitude. While beset in the ice off Broken
Point he took a complete lunar observation, and it is
the first ever recorded to have been taken at sea, with
the doubtful exception of one referred to by Sarmiento.
Baffin took altitudes of the sun and moon, and measured
the distance between them by the difference of azimuth.
He probably adopted this method because he possessed
no instrument with which he could measure so large an
angle.

On the 27th of June the ice opened out, and the
Discovery was able to proceed on her voyage, sighting
Salisbury Island on the 1st of July. Advancing across
the channel they reached a point on the north-west side
of Southampton Island, which Baffin named Cape Comfort. Here the ice was packed so close that the attempt
to proceed further was abandoned. Moreover, the water
began to shoal, and land was seen ahead, which led
Baffin to suppose that he was at the mouth of a large
bay. When Sir Edward Parry was exploring the same
region in 1824, he named the furthest land seen from
the *Discovery* Cape Bylot, and an island on the opposite
shore, Baffin Island. They are on either side of the
entrance to Frozen Strait, the former on Southampton

Island. Passing between Salisbury and Nottingham Islands, which are at the western end of Hudson's Strait, the *Discovery* came to an anchor at Cape Digges on the 29th of July.

The number of guillemots breeding at Cape Digges is almost incredible to those who have not seen it. The crew of the *Discovery* killed about seventy of these birds, but they could easily have shot several hundred if they had been wanted. Bylot and Baffin then shaped a course for England, on their return. Passing down Hudson's Strait without any trouble from ice, they crossed the Atlantic, sighted Cape Clear, and anchored in Plymouth Sound on the 8th of September 1615 without the loss of a single soul. The conclusion arrived at by Baffin respecting a north-west passage, after his return from this voyage, was that if there were any passage up Hudson's Strait it was by some narrow inlet, but that the main passage would be up Davis Strait. He was perfectly correct.

The completion of the examination of Davis's route by way of the "Furious Overfall" was steadily progressing, but after the return of Baffin in 1615 there was a pause for sixteen years. At last two voyages were planned, one vessel to sail from the port of Bristol and the other from London. The *Maria*, of seventy tons, under the command of Captain Thomas James, left Bristol on the 3rd of May 1631. James had made no study of previous voyages to the north, entered no seamen acquainted with ice navigation, and when he encountered drifting ice-floes in Hudson's Strait he was quite helpless. At length he reached Cape Digges on the 15th of July.

Luke Fox was a man of a very different stamp. He

was a Yorkshireman, clear-headed, intelligent, and full
of enthusiasm to advance the cause of Arctic discovery.
He made a special and most diligent study of previous
voyages, especially of the enterprises of John Davis. It
is to Fox that we owe a knowledge of the important
expedition of Sir Thomas Button, and of other voyages
which would otherwise have been lost to us. Besides
being a thorough seaman and an ardent explorer, he
was a quaint and very entertaining writer. If he had
a fault it was that he possibly had too good an opinion
of himself. He had been zealously urging the despatch
of a new expedition for several years. At length he
succeeded in interesting Mr. Henry Briggs in northern
discovery, and the great mathematician not only wrote
an able treatise on the subject, but also induced Sir
John Brooke to join in the venture. A vessel named the
Charles, of 80 tons, was fitted out, provisioned for eighteen
months, and manned with twenty sailors and two boys.
Old Mr. Briggs died while the ship was being prepared
for sea. As the introducer of the use of logarithms
he was one of the greatest benefactors the navy has
ever had. His place was taken by Sir Thomas Roe, the
eminent traveller and diplomatist, who entered heartily
into the project, and, with Sir John Wolstenholme,
superintended the fitting out of the ship. The Master
and Brethren of the Trinity House also gave their
help.

Captain Fox was perfectly satisfied with his stores
and provisions. He tells us that he had "excellent fat
beef, strong beer, good wheaten bread, Iceland ling,
butter and cheese of the best, admirable sack and aqua
vitæ, pease, oat meal, wheat meal, oil, balsams, gums,
unguents, plasters, potions, and purging pills. My

carpenter was fitted from the thickest bolt to the tin
tack, my gunner from the sabre to the pistol, my boatswain from the cable to the sail twine, my cook from
the caldron to the spoon."

Never was a commander so perfectly satisfied with
himself, his crew, and everything on board. It is quite
pleasant to read his journal. All was right that had
anything to do with him, and his geese were all swans.
On the 3rd of May 1631 this ablest of commanders,
with the best of ships, and the most excellent provisions, sailed from Deptford. He dropped his name
of Luke, and called himself North West Fox. But if
he was conceited, he had something to be conceited of,
and he was an able and accomplished man.

On the 18th of June the *Charles* was nearing her
work. Those "overfalls and races of tide," so fully
described by Davis, were encountered in the right
latitude, and Cape Chidley was sighted on the 20th.
Fox was now about to try his turn at following up the
beacon-light of John Davis. He found a good deal of
ice in Hudson's Strait, as is usual at that time of year,
but it was in small pieces floating apart, and was no
hindrance to navigation. On the 25th of June the sea
was calm, the sky clear, and pieces of spotless ice were
floating on the water; a lovely scene when the sun was
seen to touch the horizon. Fox was a classical scholar,
a careful observer, and he appreciated the beauties of
nature. "The sun kist Thetis in our sight," he wrote;
" the same greeting was 5° west from the north, and at
the same instant the rainbow was in appearance I think
to canopy them a bed." Next morning the sun rose
clear; "and so continued all this cold virgin day; but
now the frost takes care that there shall no more pitch

run from off the sunny side of the ship." The *Charles* was beset in the strait for several days, but Fox judged, from the appearance of the sky, that the northern side was clear of ice. On the 15th of July, the passage of Hudson's Strait was achieved, and the ship was in sight of the islands at its western entrance, named Digges, Salisbury, Nottingham, Mansell, and Southampton. "They were so named," says Fox, "as a small remembrance of the charge, countenance, and instruction given to the enterprise, and which, though small, neither time nor fame ought to suffer oblivion to bury. For whensoever it shall please God to ripen those seeds, and make them ready for his sickle; he whom he hath appointed to be the happier reaper of this crop, must remember to acknowledge that those honourable and worthy personages were the first advancers." Most true! neither the advancers and liberal merchants who supplied the means, nor the illustrious seamen who made the discoveries, should be forgotten by posterity. It is to them that we owe those solid foundations of national enterprise, and of love for the common weal, upon which the superstructure of the British Empire has been erected by their descendants.

On the 21st of July the *Charles* was off the island named "Cary's Swan's Nest" by Button; and on the 27th another island was discovered and named "Sir Thomas Roe's Welcome," in 64° 10' N. This designation has since been transferred to the channel in which the island is situated, and as such it often occurs in the narratives of more recent northern voyages.

Coasting round the western shore, he gave the names of "Brooke Cobham" and "Briggs his Mathematics" to two other islands, and he then proceeded along the

western shore of Hudson's Bay as far south as Port
Nelson, where Button's expedition wintered. No sign
of any opening to the westward appeared, and Fox was
making his way across Hudson's Bay again when he fell
in with the *Maria*, commanded by Captain James, of·
Bristol, on the 1st of August. Next day Captain Fox
dined on board the *Maria*, and had a cordial reception.
He found the ship ill found, and came to the conclusion
that the captain was no seaman. The cabin was so
small that they were obliged to dine between decks, and
though the ship was only under courses, she took in
such seas that "sauce would not have been wanting if
there had been roast mutton." "Their ship took its
liquor as kindly as themselves, for her nose was no
sooner out of the pitcher but her neb, like the duck's,
was in it again." Fox doubted whether it would be
better for the *Maria* to be beset in the ice, where the
crew would be kept from putrefaction by the piercing
air, or to be left in the open sea, where they would be
kept sweet by being thus daily pickled. He was very
facetious in his remarks on the Bristol ship and her
crew, which he thus encountered in that solitary sea,
and after being with them for seventeen hours, he
parted company with his rival and stood southward
along the land. He established the fact that there was
no opening along the western coast of Hudson's Bay
from 65° 30′ to 55° 10′ N., a distance of 620 miles.

Having completed this examination, Fox steered
northwards, and was in sight of "Cary's Swan's Nest"
again by the 7th of September. He then proceeded up
the eastern side of the coast-line, which trends northwards from the western entrance of Hudson's Strait, the
whole of which was a new discovery. Passing a head-

land, to which he gave the name of "Lord Weston's Foreland," Fox reached a point in 66° 47′ N., where the land began to trend to the south-east, and this he christened "Fox his Farthest." In after years Sir Edward Parry gave the name of Fox's Channel to the great opening leading to "Fox his Farthest;" and our gallant Yorkshireman has this credit down to the present day, that his *Farthest* is still an *Ultima Thule*, and that it has never since been visited by any later explorer.

Fox was sent out because Sir Thomas Button had reported that the tide off Nottingham Island came from the north-west, and that consequently there was probability of a passage in that direction. But by careful observations Fox had ascertained that the tide came from the south-east in that locality, and he therefore concluded that he ought to return to England. Parry, in 1824, observed that the tides were rapid and very irregular, and he had little doubt that this irregularity was caused by a meeting of the tides. The flood comes from the northward down Fox's Channel, and meets the rapid stream which sets in from Hudson's Strait.

On the 21st of September, after having well weighed all considerations which might make it advisable to winter, and the strong reasons against that course, North-West Fox decided upon returning home, and he made sail for England. That morning there was a brilliant sunrise, which gave rise to the following strange conceit from the pen of the old seaman : "This morning Aurora blusht as though she had ushered her master from some unchaste lodging, and the air so silent as though all those handmaids had promised secresy." With a fair wind the *Charles* ran down Hudson's Strait without any hindrance from the ice, sighting Resolution Island, on the north side of the eastern entrance, on the 27th. She arrived safely in the Downs, without losing a single soul, and with all the crew sound and well. Fox truly claimed that he had "proceeded in these discoveries farther than any of his predecessors, in less time and at less charge; that he cleared up all the expected hopes from the west side of Hudson's Bay;" and, he could now add, he discovered a coast-line on the east side of the channel bearing his name, which has never since been explored or visited.

The cruise of the *Maria* was not so fortunate. After parting company with Captain Fox in Hudson's Bay, she struck on a rock when Captain James was in a deep sleep. The ship seems to have been badly handled. The sails were thrown aback, but without effect. They were then furled and an anchor was laid out astern. All the water was started and the coal was thrown overboard. Then all hands went to the capstan and hove round with such good will that the cable parted. Eventually the ship floated off; and Captain James controlled his passion, and checked some bad counsel that was given him to revenge himself on the officer of the watch. The fault was his own. He ought not to have been in bed and asleep when the ship was so near the land. He found a secure harbour in the extreme south of Hudson's Bay, protected by an island afterwards named Charlton Island, and there he determined to winter. During October and November it was intensely cold and much snow fell. Yet the country was by no means Arctic in character. There were woods of fir-trees, and the crew was able to cut plenty of fuel. A hut was built on shore for the sick, in which a large fire was kept burning. The first man to succumb to the miseries of the situation was the gunner, who sank gradually in spite of being allowed to drink nothing but sack. The ship was driven on shore, and Captain James caused the provisions to be landed. But the cold increased, they could cut vinegar and wine with hatchets, and were in a condition of extreme misery. They were now all collected in a house they had built, in the shelter of a wood which they named "Winter's Forest" in honour of Sir John Winter. The house was under a clump of trees, and at a short distance from the beach where the ship was on shore. It was about twenty feet square, built of upright posts with the sides wattled with boughs, and about six feet high. The roof was of rafters and boughs, the whole covered over with the mainsail. In the inside the bonnet sails formed the walls, and bed places were built round three sides. The hearth was in the centre. A second house was built with the foresail for a roof. A store-house was also constructed, to receive all the provisions and stores from the ship. Before Christmas the houses were covered deep with snow.

In February the scurvy began to show itself, and before long two-thirds of the crew were down with it. Thus the miserable winter passed on, and by the end of April the snow had ceased, and rain began to fall. They obtained very few ptarmigan or game of any kind, and lived on the salt beef and oatmeal they had brought from England, with pork, fish, and boiled pease. All the men who were able to move were obliged to work on board, pumping and digging the ice out of the ship. On the 6th of May, John Warden, the master's mate, died, and was buried on the summit of a bleak rising ground, which was named Brandon Hill. A few days afterwards the carpenter died, and was interred beside the master's mate. The gunner's body, which had been buried at sea, was found imbedded in the ice under the gun-room ports. It was dug out and placed in the earth, by the side of his shipmates on Brandon Hill. As the weather got warmer the work of refitting the ship advanced. Captain James became more hopeful; he hoisted the ensign on the birthday of the Prince of Wales, and called the place Charlestown, which, by contraction, became Charlton Island. By the 8th of June the water was pumped out of the ship, but she was aground in the sand, and it was necessary to lighten her by taking out all the ballast, in order to get her afloat. This operation was successfully performed, the ship was rigged, and the stores were brought on board. As the snow disappeared, vetches and scurvy-grass were found in considerable quantities, which conduced to the recovery of the sick.

On the 1st of July 1632, Captain James took a last look at the graves of his companions, and, returning to the ship, made sail for Bristol, where he arrived safely in September.

By these successive voyages, the discoveries were completed in the direction pointed out by Davis, within a quarter of a century of the death of that great navigator. Hudson and Button, Gibbon and Bylot, Baffin, Fox, and James were the men who followed up the route which Davis had pointed out. They discovered Hudson's Bay, with its islands and coast lines. They opened up a vast region for development, and as a field for future enterprise. They thus increased geographical knowledge, and prepared the way for more complete modern research.

The results of their labours were valuable and important. A great commercial company was formed which carried on a lucrative trade by way of Hudson's Bay and Strait for two centuries; and it is probable that, in the near future, a still more important route for commerce will be established by Hudson's Strait, which will carry the harvests of the far west to the markets of Europe. Such are the far-reaching consequences arising from the discovery of the " Furious Overfall," and of the opening near Cape Chidley, by John Davis.

CHAPTER XIV.

THE FOLLOWING UP OF THE WORK OF DAVIS.

II.

BY "SANDERSON HIS HOPE."

"No ice towards the north, but a great sea, free, large, very salt and blue, and of an unsearchable depth." This was what John Davis saw from the base of that mighty cliff which he named "Sanderson his Hope." The cliff was his beacon, pointing to the route which filled him with most hope. The strait at whose entrance he described the "Furious Overfall," was his alternative route. It was followed up to important discoveries by Hudson and his successors. But the fairest promise came from the blue sea of unsearchable depth which stretched northward from Hope Sanderson. It was to this route that Davis referred in his last appeal to the Lords of the Council, for a renewal of Arctic enterprise. Ten years after his death, a worthy successor was found who passed onwards beyond Davis Strait, and completed the work of John Davis by his route of Hope Sanderson.

William Baffin resembled his illustrious predecessor, in character and disposition, more closely than any other navigator of the seventeenth century. He had the same enthusiastic zeal, the same mildness and geniality, and

the same devotion to the scientific branch of his profession.   Unfortunately we know nothing of Baffin
until we are introduced to him as an experienced seaman in the prime of life.   There is some slight reason
for the belief that he was a native of London or West-
minster, of Welsh extraction, and that he lived with
his wife in the parish of St. Thomas Apostle in the city,
near Queenhithe.   Here his daughter Susan appears to
have been born in October 1609.   But Baffin himself
must have been constantly at sea, and he probably raised
himself, by his good conduct and talent, from a very
humble position.   Purchas speaks of him as "that
learned unlearned mariner and mathematician, wanting
art of words."   No doubt he was self-educated, which
very much enhanced the merit of his valuable observations and discoveries.

Baffin's first recorded voyage was with Captain Hall
to Greenland in 1609.   James Hall was a Yorkshireman, and almost certainly a native of Hull.   His first
recorded voyage was as chief pilot of an expedition despatched from Denmark, by King Christian IV., in 1605,
to discover the lost colony of Greenland.   It reached
the western coast of that little known land, near the
site of the modern Danish settlement of Holsteinborg,
and Hall, having had much communication with the
Eskimos, wrote a very interesting account of them.   The
King of Denmark fitted out a second expedition under
Admiral Lindenov in 1606, and Hall was again employed as pilot.   They visited the same part of Greenland, and in their intercourse with the natives they
killed several, and carried off others, with their *kayaks*.
This conduct led to fatal retaliation when Hall appeared
among the Eskimos in a subsequent voyage.   In 1607

King Christian gave up his attempts to find the lost colony, and James Hall returned to England, eager to embark once more on discoveries in the direction of Greenland. His faithful follower, William Huntriss, a Scarborough lad, who had accompanied him in all his voyages, and had become so proficient as a navigator that King Christian had granted him a special allowance, returned with Hall.

In 1612 Hall induced four great merchant princes, Sir Thomas Smith, Sir James Lancaster, who commanded the first voyage of the East India Company, Sir William Cockayne, and Mr. Ball to join with him in an expedition to Greenland, to search for mineral ores. Two vessels, called the *Patience* and *Heart's Ease*, were fitted out at Hull, and William Baffin was pilot of Hall's ship, the *Patience*. Andrew Barker commanded the *Heart's Ease*, with William Huntriss as his mate, and John Gatonby, who kept a journal which has been published in Churchill's Collection, was quarter-master. The narrative of Baffin himself commences on July 8, 1612; when the expedition had already arrived in Cockin (correctly Cockayne) Sound, on the west coast of Greenland, where the Danish settlement of Sukkertoppen is now situated.

Baffin is first introduced to us, on this bleak Greenland coast, making preparations to take an observation for finding the longitude. He is thus brought to our notice as an ingenious and accomplished nautical astronomer. The first part of the observation he describes, is that for finding the time and place from the altitude of a heavenly body, the latitude and declination being known. But his method of finding the longitude by lunar culmination is unsuited to purposes of naviga-

tion, although his record of it is an interesting proof of
his zeal and ingenuity as an observer. He says of it,
"This finding of the longitude, I confess, is somewhat
difficult and troublesome; but if it be carefully looked
unto, and exactly wrought, there would be no great
error, if your ephemerides be true."

On the 21st of July the two ships anchored in
Rommel's Fiord, the present Holsteinborg; and about
forty Eskimos came to trade. When they saw Captain
Hall in one of the boats, an Eskimo gave him a fatal
wound with a dart from a distance of four yards. There
can be no doubt that this was an act of vengeance by
one whose relation had been killed or kidnapped by
Hall during his Danish voyage; for the Eskimos made
no attempt to harm any one else. Hall lingered for a
day, his last wish being that Andrew Barker should
succeed him, and that young Huntriss should be master
of the *Heart's Ease*. There were some objections raised
against Barker by the men, but the officers supported
him. He was an old and experienced seaman, was
three times Warden of the Trinity House at Hull, and
presented that institution with an Eskimo *kayak*, which
still hangs from the ceiling of one of the rooms. After
Hall's death some search was made for the mines
reported by the Danes, but it became evident that they
had mistaken the mica, often found in shining masses
in clefts of the gneiss, for silver ore. It was clearly a
fruitless quest, and the ships therefore returned home,
the *Patience* arriving at Hull in September 1612. Baffin
concludes his journal with some account of Greenland,
its physical aspect, plants and animals, and of the
manners and customs of the Eskimos. He mentions
having seen, some forty miles up the fiord he named

Ball's River, a small coppice of trees six or seven feet high. The tallest tree ever seen by Dr. Rink in Greenland was a birch fourteen feet high in 60° N. (*Betula alpestris*), but it is not found north of 62° N. Baffin also mentions the dwarf willow, the small berry (*Impetrum nigrum*), and the angelica, which he found in many places, and observed in the boats of the natives, showing that it was used by them. The young stalks, being brittle and sweet, are eaten raw, and the name *quan*, which is Norse, points to its introduction into Greenland by the Normans. Baffin mentions having seen reindeer, although they are generally far inland, near the foot of the glaciers, and he adds that white foxes and hares are common. He gives a graphic description of the Eskimo *kayaks* and *umenaks*, of their winter *iglus* and summer tents, of their rites and customs respecting burials, and of their superstitions.

The next voyage in which Baffin was employed was in the service of the Muscovy Company. A fleet of seven ships was fitted out in 1613, under the command of Captain Benjamin Joseph, who had the *Tiger*, of 260 tons, with Baffin as pilot. They left the Medway on the 13th of May, and sighted Spitzbergen on the 30th, the object being to catch whales in the Spitzbergen waters. Twenty-four Biscayans, who were in those days the most expert whale-fishers in Europe, had been engaged to serve in the fleet, and on the 4th of June the first whale was killed. It seems that the Biscayans, natives of villages on the coasts of Guipuzcoa and Biscay, went away in boats to look out for whales in the offing, and were called "our whale-stickers," while the English part of the crew took the casks and coppers on shore for melting blubber. The English commander took possession of the land in the name of his king, and claimed the right of ordering the ships of all other countries to leave the Spitzbergen seas. Several Spanish vessels were met with, and ships from Bordeaux, St. Jean de Luz, and Holland. They meekly obeyed as a rule, and Captain Joseph succeeded in carrying things with a high hand, either sending them away or allowing them to remain on such conditions as he proposed to them. They were to kill eight whales for the Muscovy Company, and after that as many as they could get for themselves. On this plan Captain Joseph got full ladings of whale oil for his ships. They returned to the Thames on the 6th of September.

While Baffin was on the west coast of Spitzbergen he made regular and very careful observations for latitude with a quadrant four feet in semidiameter, as well as observations for variation and dip of the magnetic needle. He also adopted an ingenious method of observing the refraction of the sun. He first obtained the latitude, and then took the difference between the co-latitude and the declination, corrected for the instant when he observed the sun on meridian below the pole to have one-fifth of its diameter above the horizon. Then dividing the whole diameter of the sun into fifths, he calculated that the sun's centre was three-tenths of its whole diameter below the horizon. Subtracting three-tenths of the difference between the co-latitude and the declination from that difference, he got the approximate refraction. It was in these special observations, made in addition to the regular navigating work of the ship, that Baffin showed his inventive talent, and his untiring zeal for the cause of science. Baffin himself wrote the narrative of Joseph's voyage.

In 1614 Baffin undertook a second voyage to the west coast of Spitzbergen as pilot, on board the *Thomasine*, forming one of a fleet of ten ships, again commanded by Captain Joseph. Leaving the Thames on the 4th of May, the ships were beset in the ice from the 28th to the 2nd of June, when the *Thomasine* got into the open sea, and reached the Foreland, the northern end of Prince Charles Island, on the west coast of Spitzbergen, which was the usual place of rendezvous. Baffin was sent in a shallop as far as Hakluyt Headland, the north-western point of Spitzbergen, to examine the state of the ice, but he found it close pressed on the land, so that it would not be possible for the ships to pass along the northern coast.

In July it was resolved that two shallops should be despatched to explore the northern coast, one under the command of Baffin, and the other under Robert Fotherby, the master's mate. The ship was left in a harbour, the two shallops were provisioned for several days, and they succeeded in advancing along the northern coast of Spitzbergen, as far as Wyche's Sound (the Wijde Bay of modern maps), where they landed, and walked several miles over the hills. From this point of vantage the Seven Islands, and the northern point of North East Land, would have been visible. Returning to the ship they proceeded with the fishery until near the end of the season, when another bold attempt was made to explore the northern coast. The weather became unusually warm in August. On the 27th there was a gale from the S.S.W., and the *Thomasine*, in company with the *Heart's-ease*—her chummy ship—made sail round Hakluyt Headland, and along the north coast of Spitzbergen, and got as far as the mouth of Sir Thomas Smith's Inlet, which is improperly called Hinlopen Strait on modern charts. The wind then shifted to the east and they were obliged to return, but not before having examined the whole northern coast of the main island. In the afternoon of the 29th Hakluyt Head bore S.E. The weather was calm and comparatively warm, as they shaped a southerly course, being homeward bound. A gale was encountered in mid ocean, which increased to a storm, and the men were not consoled by the sight of St. Elmo's light, or the *Corpo Santo*, as they called it, which the master saw upon the fore bonnet. English seamen believed that it always presaged a coming storm; and the omen was verified by the foul weather continuing, and the sea rising so that they were obliged to lie to under their foresail; and afterwards under no canvas for five hours, "lying a hull," as it was called. But the voyage at length came to an end, and on the 4th of October the *Thomasine* arrived off Wapping, with all her men in perfect health. Her journal was written by Robert Fotherby, the master's mate, and published in Purchas.

Baffin had now made three voyages to the Arctic Regions. He had visited the coast of Greenland, and passed two summers on the west and north coasts of Spitzbergen. When, therefore, the company for the discovery of the North-West Passage resolved to send out the *Discovery* under the command of Robert Bylot in 1615, William Baffin was selected to accompany him, and received the appointment of pilot. This voyage has already been noticed in the previous chapter. Its whole history was written by Baffin himself, together with a tabulated log-book, and a coloured chart of Hudson's Strait. This is the only one of Baffin's numerous charts that has been preserved, and it is now among the manuscripts in the British Museum. The coasts are coloured and shaded, and the track of the *Discovery* is shown by a red dotted line. When Sir Edward Parry went over the same ground he bore testimony to the accuracy of his predecessor, confirmed his tidal observations, and named the most distant land visible from the point where the *Discovery* turned back, in honour of Bylot and Baffin.

On the return of the *Discovery*, in the autumn of 1615, preparations were made for Baffin's fifth and most important Arctic voyage. He was now to follow up the beacon-light of Davis, represented by "Sanderson his Hope." He had been well trained for the work by previous navigation in the ice; and he had that love for his profession, and especially for the scientific branch of it, which made him a man after Davis's own heart. He may have been a self-taught man, but he had so far educated himself as to be able to write letters which are not only well expressed, but are graced with classical allusions. Like Davis he was in advance of his contemporaries as an astronomical observer.

The voyage of 1616 was undertaken by Sir Thomas Smith, Sir Francis Jones, Sir Dudley Digges, and Sir John Wolstenholme. As before Robert Bylot was appointed master, and William Baffin again became pilot of the *Discovery*, of fifty-five tons, with a crew of sixteen men. Baffin's papers and maps fell into the hands of Purchas, who published, in his "Pilgrimes," the great navigator's "Briefe and True Relation," and his letter to Sir John Wolstenholme. But Purchas omitted Baffin's priceless map and his journal, thus doing an irreparable injury to posterity. They are now lost, although it is probable that the very rare map met with in a few copies of the narrative of Luke Fox, may be partly taken from the work of Baffin.

The *Discovery* sailed from Gravesend on the 26th of March 1616, and shaped a course down channel; but a westerly wind coming on, she put into Dartmouth Harbour, and remained there for eleven days. Thus was the ship, destined to carry forward the discovery of Davis beyond his furthest point, receiving shelter in the harbour which was in sight of the home he had loved so well. The successors of Davis left Dartmouth on the 15th of April, a month earlier than Davis had usually sailed from the same port. The first land they saw was the coast of Greenland near Cockin Sound, in 65° 20′ N., where Baffin had been in his first Arctic voyage with James Hall, in 1612. Several Eskimos in their *kayaks* came round the ship, and were given small pieces of iron, but Bylot and Baffin did not wish to anchor so early in the voyage, having made a good passage across the Atlantic. The wind was against them, and they worked up to the northward until they reached 70° 20′ N. "Then we came to an anchor in a faire sound near the place Master Davis called London Coast." This was probably near Noursoak, on the north shore of the Waigat, or strait dividing Disco Island from the mainland of Greenland.

At sunset on the 22nd of May the *Discovery* left her anchorage in the Waigat, after a stay of two days, during which Baffin diligently observed the tides. These tidal observations gave rise to some appreher ion respecting the passage, for the rise and fall was only eight or nine feet, the flood coming from the south. Working up against a dead foul wind the old craft made but slow progress, and encountering a dead whale far out at sea,

R

some time was spent in getting the whalebone on board. But by sunset of the 30th they were fairly in sight of Sanderson his Hope, "the farthest land Master Davis was at," on the 30th of June 1587, an interval of nearly thirty years. Pushing through some loose ice, they came among islands, where Baffin and his crew had pleasant relations with some Eskimo lasses, showing them the ship, and helping them to go from one island to another, in search of their men folk. They called the group "Women Islands," a name it still retains.

From the "Women Islands" Baffin passed on to the group now called "Baffin Islands;" but finding much ice along the coast, the bold pilot steered westward, and took the perilous course of attempting the middle pack. Parry succeeded in passing through it in 1819, and Nares in 1875, but there is great danger of being beset and drifted southwards. It is always safer to keep near the shore. "Stick to the land-floe!" was the favourite maxim of experienced whaling captains. Baffin came to the same conclusion. After a short trial of the middle pack he resolved to keep near the land; and on the 15th of June he anchored in Melville Bay, under the lee of some islands off the point now called Cape Shackleton, which is 1400 feet high, and nearly perpendicular. Here the ship was visited by Eskimos in *kayaks* and *umenaks*, who exchanged narwhals' horns for pieces of iron and glass beads. Baffin therefore called the place Ho⸻ Sound, a name which ought to be restored on moder. maps, just north of Cape Shackleton, where there is a cliff frequented by guillemots.

In the last days of June the *Discovery* made the passage of Melville Bay, since so much dreaded by whalers, with little or no obstruction from the ice, and

by the 1st of July she had reached the "north water."
Baffin named a fair headland Cape Dudley Digges, in
76.8° N., and a deep bay twelve leagues further north
was called Wolstenholme Sound.   Here the little vessel
was anchored; but in a few hours she was driven out
to sea, the gale increased, her foresail was blown out of
the bolt-ropes, and when the weather cleared, they found
themselves imbayed in another deep sound, where they
anchored.   Seeing several whales, they gave it the name
of Whale Sound.   The wind soon moderated, and the
Discovery continued her adventurous course along this
far northern land, until she was stopped by the ice in
78° N., when in sight of an opening named Smith Sound,
"the greatest and largest in all this bay."   An island
between Smith and Whale Sounds received the name
of Hakluyt Island.   Here the *Discovery* was again
anchored, in the hope of finding whalebone on the shore.
But again the wind and sea rose, and they were driven
from their shelter, to beat about for two days in the
"north water" of Baffin's Bay.   When the weather
cleared up, they sighted a group of islands, which
received the name of the Cary Islands, after the ship's
husband, Mr. Alwyn Cary.

Baffin stood to the westward in an open sea, with a
stiff gale of wind, until the 10th of July, when it fell
calm.   The *Discovery* was now on the western side of
the bay, and an opening was in sight which received
the name of Jones Sound.   Here a boat was sent on
shore, and many walrus were seen on the rocks, but a
fair wind springing up, no attempt was made to kill
them.   Running southwards another opening was discovered in 74° 30′, which was called Lancaster Sound
in honour of the eminent Director of the East India

Company, who had commanded the first English voyage
to the East Indies.   Too hastily assuming this and
other sounds to be merely bays, Baffin ran southwards
along the western coast of Davis Strait for ten days, and
then standing eastward, after some difficulty from large
floes of ice, succeeded in reaching the west coast of
Greenland again, and anchored in Cockin Sound.
Several of the crew had been attacked by scurvy, and
the cook had died.   But such quantities of sorrel and
scurvy grass were now gathered and administered to the
sick, that in ten days they were all in perfect health
again.   Leaving Cockin Sound on the 6th of August,
the *Discovery* had a prosperous voyage home, and on the
30th of August she was anchored off Dover.

Thus was the wish of Davis accomplished.   His discovery as far as Hope Sanderson was extended by his
successor, and the whole of Baffin's Bay was added to
geographical knowledge.   It is pleasant to feel that Baffin
venerated the memory of his illustrious predecessor.
He always mentions him with respect, and in his letter
to Sir John Wolstenholme he generously says—"Neither
was Master Davis to be blamed in his report and great
hopes; for as far as Hope Sanderson the sea is open, of
an unsearchable depth and good colour."   Baffin's conclusion was that "there is no passage nor hope of
passage to the north of Davis Straits."   But Baffin was
wrong, and Davis was right.   In the distant future the
wishes of Davis received further development, and Davis
Strait proved to be the way to further important geographical discovery, westward and northward by Lancaster Sound, and by Smith Sound, openings which
Baffin had erroneously supposed to be merely bays.

A review of the scientific observations of William

Baffin will show how zealously he followed the example
of John Davis in this respect. We first find him, when
at anchor in Cockin Sound, engaged in an experimental
series of observations intended to obtain the longitude
by moon's culmination. In this first recorded voyage,
he mentions having taken sixteen observations for latitude and eight for variation. In his first voyage to
Spitzbergen he observed for dip of the magnetic needle,
as well as for variation; and he adopted an ingenious
method of calculating the sun's refraction. The journal
of his second Spitzbergen voyage is unfortunately lost to
us, and with it the account of his observations. But in
1615, when in Hudson's Strait, he records daily observations for latitude, and twenty-seven for variation of the
compass. He describes a complete lunar observation;
and thus has the honour of having been the first
Englishman who ever took a lunar at sea. He also
made another attempt to find the longitude by moon's
culmination, and the correctness of the deductions derived from his tidal observations was long afterwards
confirmed by Sir Edward Parry. In his fifth voyage,
when he immortalised his name by the discovery of
Baffin's Bay, Baffin was equally diligent, but his work is
unfortunately lost to us through the injudicious omission
of Purchas, and we only have his observation for variation in Smith Sound, to which he incidentally alludes in
his letter to Sir John Wolstenholme.

After 1616, Baffin, in order to obtain suitable employment, was obliged to enter the service of the East
India Company. But when he found himself under this
necessity, it is extremely interesting to find that, like
Davis before him, he never abandoned the hope of continuing his northern discoveries. He even conceived

the very same scheme which Davis so long entertained,
namely, of making the northern passage by way of the
Pacific.   Mr Briggs, in his "Brief Discourse on a North-
West Passage," says that Baffin told him "that he
would, if he might get employment, search the passage
from Japan, by the coast of Asia, any way he could."

In 1617 Baffin obtained the appointment of master's
mate on board the *Anne Royal*, of 1320 tons, Andrew
Shilling captain, in the fleet for the seventh joint stock
voyage of the East India Company, commanded by
Captain Martin Pring.   In September the fleet arrived
at Surat, and Captain Shilling was sent to the Red Sea,
charged with the duty of "settling an English trade in
those parts."   Shilling succeeded in obtaining a firman
from the Pasha of Mocha for English merchants to trade
at Mocha and Aden, and the *Anne Royal* then visited
the opposite African coast.   Baffin was very actively
employed in surveying and preparing charts both in the
Red Sea, and afterwards when the *Anne Royal* was in
the Persian Gulf.   She returned home in September
1619, and during these two years Baffin had won the
approbation of his superiors and of the Company.
There is the following entry in the Court's Minutes of
October 1st, 1619—"William Baffin, a master's mate in
the *Anne*, to have a gratuity for his pains and good art
in drawing out certain plots of the coasts of Persia and
the Red Sea which are judged to have been very well
and artificially performed."   Captain Shilling had conducted the negotiations with the Turkish authorities in
the Red Sea, with such ability and discretion that he
was selected to have command of the next fleet, consisting of four new ships.

Captain Shilling was on board the *London*, and, at his

special recommendation, William Baffin was appointed
master of the same ship. The other ships were the
Hart, under Captain Blithe, the *Roebuck*, and the *Eagle*.
Leaving England in March 1620 the fleet arrived at
Surat in November, where news had just been received
that a combined Portuguese and Dutch fleet was waiting off Jashk, near the entrance of the Persian Gulf,

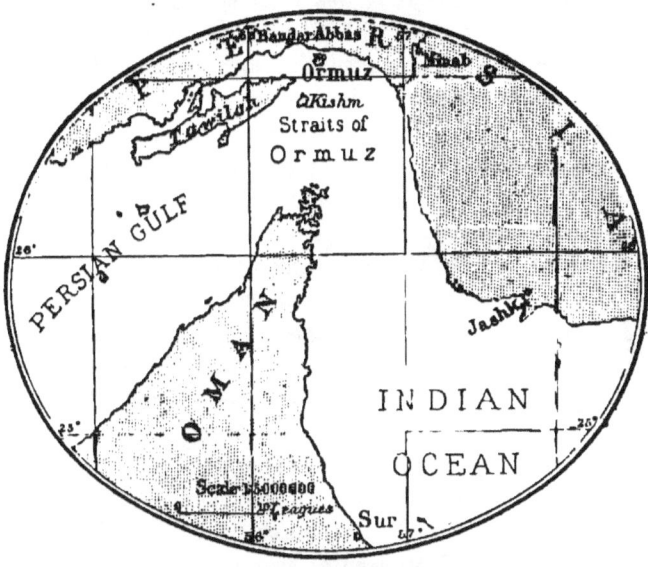

THE PERSIAN GULF.

to intercept and attack the English ships. Shilling at
once resolved to go in search of this hostile fleet, and
on the 16th of December he fell in with four of the
enemy's ships, and engaged them. The first fight lasted
for. nine hours, when both fleets hauled off to repair
damages. On the 28th a second battle was fought, both
fleets ar choring within range. But. the Portuguese first

"cried hold, enough." Captain Swan of the *Roebuck*
tells us that "about three in the afternoon, unwilling,
after so hotte a dinner, to receive a like supper, they
cut their cables, and drove with the tide until they were
without range of our guns, and then their frigate came
to them, and towed them away, wonderfully mangled and
torn." Captain Shilling was mortally wounded in this
encounter, and his body was interred at Jashk, on the
7th of January 1621, with all decency and solemnity.

Captain Blithe succeeded Shilling in command of tho
fleet; Baffin remaining in charge of the *London.* He
passed the winter, that is, the period of the south-west
monsoon, in the little port of Súr on the coast of Omân,
where there were fresh water and palm trees. Súr
received tho namo of "London's Hope," and Baffin
remained there until the 15th of August.

In 1621 tho English agreed with Shah Abbas of
Persia to drive the Portuguese out of Ormuz, by a
joint attack. The English were to have a share of
the plunder, and in future to receive half the customs of Bandar Abbas or Gombroon, the town on
tho mainland which was destined to take the place
of the island of Ormuz as a commercial mart. The
English fleet assembled at Surat, and on the 23rd of
December 1621 it arrived at an open roadstead on the
Persian Gulf near Minab, with the island of Ormuz
in sight. Here the news was received that the Portuguese had erected a fort on the island of Kishm to
protect some wells for supplying Ormuz with water.
The fort was already besieged by a Persian army, and
on January 20, 1622, the English fleet arrived. Tho
first operation was to land a certain number of guns
from each ship, and to throw up earthworks. The siege

then commenced, and, after two days, William Baffin
went on shore with his mathematical instruments, to
take the height and distance of the castle wall, so as to
find the range. "But as he was about the same he
received a shot from the castle into his belly, wherewith
he gave three leaps and died immediately." Purchas
says—"In the Indies he. died, in the late Ormuz business, slain in fight, with a shot, as he was trying his
mathematical projects and conclusions." The death of
the great navigator took place on the 23rd of January
1622. The fort of Kishm surrendered on the 1st of
February, and the fall of Ormuz followed a few days
afterwards.

In these last two chapters we have seen how the two
routes discovered by Davis, and which he pointed out as
the directions that future exploration should take, were
followed up by subsequent navigators. By way of the
" Furious Overfall" of Davis, most important discoveries
were made during the ten years which followed on his
death. Hudson discovered the south side of Hudson's
Strait, and the eastern coast of Hudson's Bay. Button
and Fox explored the western side of that great bay.
Bylot and Baffin surveyed the northern side of Hudson's
Strait, and Fox discovered the eastern coast of the
channel which bears his name. By way of Sanderson's
Hope of Davis, Baffin sailed onwards past the furthest
point of his illustrious predecessor, and discovered the
great bay which bears his own name, and also the openings or sounds which form the portals of the most
important Arctic discoveries of modern times. It was
thus that the influence of the master-mind was felt by
his successors, long after he himself had passed away.

The geographical student will find that the best and

most agreeable method of acquiring a thorough grounding in his science is, by the contemplation of the life of
a great geographer or explorer. For by this biographical
method, each coast and island, each bay and strait, is
connected with some incident in the life-story of the
discoverer or of his successors. Interest is thus given to
what would otherwise be a mere list of names, and life
is breathed into the inorganic mass. A knowledge of
the lives of John Davis and of his immediate successors,
requires an intimate acquaintance with Davis Strait and
its shores, with the east and west coasts of Greenland,
with Hudson's Strait and Bay, and with Baffin's Bay ;
in short, with all the nearer regions of Arctic America.
It is desirable that the student should be conversant
with the achievements of Arctic worthies in other parts
of the world ; because he should contemplate the complete life-stories of his heroes, and thus realise how, and
by the possession of what qualifications, their Arctic
work was done. The thorough and complete grounding
which such a study supplies, is the best preparation for
an examination of the labours of modern explorers and
of the results of their work, which will include the acquisition of an intelligent knowledge and appreciation of
the geography of the whole Arctic Regions.

APPENDIX ON THE AUTHORITIES.

———✦———

THE early years of John Davis were passed on the banks of the Dart. We derive some insight into this period of his life from Westcote's "Devonshire," from the parish registers at Stoke Gabriel, from incidental notices in other county histories, and from the writings and will of Davis himself. A careful search through the municipal archives at Dartmouth has failed to lead to the discovery of any notice of Davis, or of the fitting out of his expeditions in Dartmouth Harbour. Notices of the private affairs of Davis are given in documents preserved in the State Paper Office.

Some particulars respecting the preparations for the first Arctic voyage are to be found in the journal of Dr. Dee, and in the Minute Book of the Elizabethan Guild of the City of Exeter. The narrative of the first Arctic voyage of Davis was written by John Janes; that of the second voyage by Davis himself, with a supplementary journal of the proceedings of the *Sunshine* by Henry Morgan. The story of the third voyage is by John Janes, and the traverse or log book kept by Davis has been preserved. The whole were published by Hakluyt in his collections of voyages and travels. Davis reviewed the results of his three Arctic voyages in his "World's Hydrographical Discovery." The discoveries of Davis, with some additional names, are shown on the Molyneux Globe.

We only know the name of the vessel on board of which Davis served in the fleet which defeated the Spanish Armada; and facts relating to his service in the Azores under the Earl of Cumberland, are derived from the narrative of Edward

Wright. Incidental statements of Sir William Monson, of Sir Robert Dudley, and of Davis himself, prove that he served under the Earl of Essex at Cadiz, and in the Azores. The thrilling tale of Davis's command of the *Desire* in the last expedition of Cavendish, is told by his old friend John Janes ; and a few additional facts are supplied by the letter of Cavendish written on his deathbed, and by the extraordinary story of Knivet.

Much light is thrown on the attainments and character of Davis by his own works, entitled the "Seaman's Secrets," and the "World's Hydrographical Discovery."

The narrative of the voyage to India in the Dutch Fleet was written by Davis himself, that of the first voyage sent out by the East India Company by an unknown hand, and that of the voyage of the *Tiger* apparently by Sir Edward Michelborne. The Sailing Directions from Acheu to Priaman and Tiku by John Davis, are preserved among the Sloane MSS. in the British Museum.

Prince, in his "Worthies of Devon," was the first to write a notice of the life of Captain John Davis of Sandridge ; but he confused him with another John Davis of Limehouse, a younger man, whose life can easily be traced in Purchas, and who died in 1622. Prince was ignorant of the voyage of Michelborne, and consequently knew nothing of the time and place of the death of John Davis of Sandridge. Dr. Kippis, in the *Biographia Britannica*, repeats most of the blunders of Prince ; but, at the same time, he perceived that there must have been two Davises, for he had learnt the particulars of the death of John Davis of Sandridge from "Harris's Voyages," and if he *was* killed in 1605, Dr. Kippis saw that he could not have written a "Rutter" dated 1618, which is given in Purchas and attributed to a John Davis. In spite of the warning thus thrown out by Dr. Kippis, Sir John Barrow repeated all the blunders of Prince, and was equally ignorant of the time and place of Davis's death, although they are given by Harris and Kippis. Mr. Bolton Corney, in *Notes and Queries*, pointed out most of the blunders of Prince and Barrow. Mr. Froude, in an article entitled "England's

Forgotten Worthies," published in 1852, and reprinted in
1858, in his book called "Short Studies on Great Subjects,"
repeated all the old blunders, and added fresh ones. The
warnings of Dr. Kippis and Mr. Bolton Corney render the
inaccuracies and misleading statements of Mr. Froude altogether inexcusable. Mr. Fox Bourne, in a work entitled
"English Seamen under the Tudors," published in 1868,
gives a brief but correct account of the life of Davis. In 1880
the Hakluyt Society issued a volume containing the texts of
the works, and of all the narratives of the voyages of John
Davis, with an introduction, notes, and a critical review of
previous notices of the great navigator, by Commodore Markham. The notice of Davis, in the "National Biography," is
by Professor Laughton.

INDEX.

271

T

THE END.

GEORGE PHILIP AND SON, LONDON AND LIVERPOOL

32 FLEET STREET, LONDON.

The
World's Great Explorers and Explorations.

EDITED BY

J. SCOTT KELTIE, Librarian, Royal Geographical
Society ;

H. J. MACKINDER, M.A., Reader in Geography at the
University of Oxford ;

And E. G. RAVENSTEIN, F.R.G.S.

U NDER this title Messrs. G. PHILIP & SON
propose to issue a series of volumes dealing
with the life and work of those heroic adventurers
through whose exertions the face of the earth has
been made known to humanity.

Each volume will, so far as the ground covered
admits, deal mainly with one prominent name associated with some particular region, and will tell the
story of his life and adventures, and describe the work
which he accomplished in the service of geographical
discovery.. The aim will be to do ample justice to
geographical results, while the personality of the ex-

plorer is never lost sight of. In a few cases in which the work of discovery cannot be possibly associated with the name of any single explorer, some departure from this plan may be unavoidable, but it will be followed as far as practicable. In each case the exact relation of the work accomplished by each explorer to what went before and what followed after, will be pointed out; so that each volume will be virtually an account of the exploration of the region with which it deals. Though it will not be sought to make the various volumes dovetail exactly into each other, it is hoped that when the series is concluded, it will form a fairly complete Biographical History of Geographical Discovery.

Each volume will be written by a recognised authority on his subject, and will be amply furnished with specially prepared maps, portraits, and other original illustrations.

While the names of the writers whose co-operation has been secured are an indication of the high standard aimed at from a literary and scientific point of view, the series will be essentially a popular one, appealing to the great mass of general readers, young and old, who have always shewn a keen interest in the story of the world's exploration, when well told. It is, moreover, believed that not a few of the volumes will be found adapted for use as reading books, or even text-books in schools.

It is hoped to begin the publication of the series in September, after which a volume will be issued every few weeks.

Each volume will consist of about 300 pp. crown 8vo, and will be published at 3s. 6d.

The following volumes are either ready or are in an advanced state of preparation :—

JOHN DAVIS, Arctic Explorer and Early India Navigator. By CLEMENTS R. MARKHAM, C.B., F.R.S.

JOHN FRANKLIN AND THE NORTH-WEST PASSAGE. By CAPTAIN ALBERT MARKHAM, R.N.

MAGELLAN AND THE PACIFIC. By DR. H. H. GUILLEMARD, author of "The Cruise of the Marchesa."

SAUSSURE AND THE ALPS. By DOUGLAS W. FRESHFIELD, Hon. Sec. Royal Geographical Society.

MUNGO PARK AND THE NIGER. By JOSEPH THOMSON, author of "Through Masai Land," &c.

PALESTINE. By MAJOR C. R. CONDER, R.E., Leader of the Palestine Exploring Expeditions.

THE HIMALAYA. By LIEUT.-GENERAL R. STRACHEY, R.E., C.S.I., late President of the R.G.S.

LIVINGSTONE AND CENTRAL AFRICA. By H. H. JOHNSTON, H.B.M. Consul at Mozambique.

ROSS AND THE ANTARCTIC. By H. J. MACKINDER, M.A., Reader in Geography at Oxford.

BRUCE AND THE NILE. By J. SCOTT KELTIE, Librarian, R.G.S.

VASCO DA GAMA AND THE OCEAN HIGHWAY TO INDIA. By E. G. RAVENSTEIN, F.R.G.S.

U

Other volumes to follow will deal with—

HUMBOLDT AND SOUTH AMERICA.

BARENTS AND THE N.E. PASSAGE.

COLUMBUS AND HIS SUCCESSORS.

JACQUES CARTIER AND CANADA.

CAPTAIN COOK AND AUSTRALASIA.

MARCO POLO AND CENTRAL ASIA.

IBN BATUTA AND N. AFRICA.

LEIF ERIKSON AND GREENLAND.

DAMPIER AND THE BUCCANEERS.

&c.   &c.   &c.

GEORGE PHILIP & SON, LONDON & LIVERPOOL.

A SELECTED LIST OF WORKS

PUBLISHED BY GEORGE PHILIP & SON.

JUST PUBLISHED,

Medium 8vo, in handsome Illustrated cloth cover, bevelled boards,
gilt top, price 21s.

THE FIRST ASCENT OF THE KASAÏ

BEING SOME RECORDS OF SERVICE

UNDER THE LONE STAR.

By CHARLES SOMERVILLE LATROBE BATEMAN,

Sometime Captain and Adjutant of Gendarmerie in the
Congo Free State.

Profusely Illustrated with Etchings, Chromo-lithographs, and Wood
Engravings (Fifty-seven in all), Reproduced from the
Author's Original Drawings,

AND ACCOMPANIED BY

Two Large Scale Maps Printed in Colours.

OPINIONS OF THE PRESS.

"A highly interesting and beautifully illustrated narrative."—*Times.*

"Mr. Bateman is as skilful with the pen as he is with his brush and pencil; his style is animated, and his verbal descriptions are quite on a par with his pictures."—*Athenæum.*

"Mr. Bateman seems to be not only the right sort of man to explore and civilise savage regions, but to chronicle his adventures in them. We do not know whether to admire most his energy, his indomitable pluck, his practical common sense, his modesty, his rigid sense of duty, or his burning zeal for the regeneration of long-degraded races of his fellow-men."—*Saturday Review.*

"The whole book is well worth reading: it is instructively illustrated, and its pages present an excellent picture of life in a corner of the Congo Free State, and of death too; for in Africa as elsewhere, the foundations even of relatively slight improvements are the lives of men."—*Spectator.*

"Fair in outward seeming this handsome volume makes no vain show. With pen, as with pencil, the author evinces masterly skill in the production of choice specimens of literary and artistic excellence."—*Whitehall Review.*

"His book is of considerable interest. . . . Above all, the book is valuable for the light it throws on the influence that is being created by the Congo State."—*Nature.*

JUST PUBLISHED, Crown 8vo, 504 pp.

TRAVELS IN THE ATLAS AND SOUTHERN MOROCCO.

A NARRATIVE OF EXPLORATION.

By JOSEPH THOMSON, Author of "Through Masai Land."

Containing Sixty-eight Illustrations and Six Maps.

· OPINIONS OF THE PRESS.

"Apart from the distinct value of Mr. Thomson's volume as a contribution to our knowledge of Morocco, it is most attractively written. . . . The book is got up with excellent finish and taste, and the seventy illustrations and two maps are themselves a valuable help to the story."— *Times.*

"It is for its pictures of native life that it is chiefly valuable, the general characteristics of the country explored, and of the towns visited on the way, being well shown in the numerous illustrations from photographs by the author and others."—*Morning Post.*

"Mr. Thomson, a wilful as well as a dauntless explorer, justified the risks he ran by success; and his narrative of adventure gives us an exciting peep at the mighty Atlas, a very good idea of Southern Morocco, a stirring picture of the city itself, and graphic sketches of the Moorish, Jewish, and Berber races with whom he came in contact."—*Spectator.*

"Is worthy of being placed on the same shelf with Hooker and Ball's 'Tour.' . . . His merits as a photographer are displayed in the numerous excellent illustrations with which his pages are adorned. Nothing better have appeared. . . . But his pluck, his perseverance, his good sense, and his tact are displayed on every page. . . . Mr. Thomson's book is a most praiseworthy one. It is not only the best which he has yet written, but one of the most admirable which has ever appeared on Morocco."— *Academy.*

"The publishers of Mr. Thomson's book have set a good example by producing such a richly illustrated volume at so moderate a price. The numerous illustrations are well executed, and two good maps (a physical and a geological) accompany the volume."—*Proceedings of the Scottish Geographical Society.*

"To most readers Mr. Thomson's information concerning the Morocco Jews will be new and startling; and his well-considered remarks on the political and social condition of the country generally deserve serious attention. The seventy illustrations are a valuable addition to the book." —*Proceedings of the Royal Geographical Society.*

"The author of 'Through Masai Land' has produced another very interesting, and at times exciting, book of travels. . . . Mr. Thomson is one of those explorers who seem never to be happy unless their necks or other portions of their persons are in imminent danger of dislocation, and certainly the series of hair-breadth escapes narrated in this volume ought to have satisfied even his ambition. . . . It is not, however, merely as a very lively book of adventure that these travels are worth reading; they give a singularly life-like and detailed sketch of Morocco and its people in an unpretending and easy way, and the numerous and excellent illustrations materially contribute to its fidelity."—*St. James's Gazette.*

GEORGE. PHILIP & SON, PUBLISHERS, LONDON AND LIVERPOOL.

Large crown 8vo, handsomely bound in cloth, published
at 12s. 6d., offered at 7s. 6d. nett.

ACROSS AFRICA.

BY

VERNEY LOVETT CAMERON, C.B., D.C.L.,

COMMANDER, ROYAL NAVY;

Gold Medallist, Royal Geographical Society, &c.

WITH NUMEROUS ILLUSTRATIONS.

New Edition.

WITH NEW AND ORIGINAL MATTER, AND CORRECTED MAP.

SELECTIONS FROM OPINIONS OF THE PRESS.

" Nothing beyond the mention of the fact will be necessary to secure
a favourable reception to the re-issue in a popular form of Commander
Cameron's 'Across Africa.' Though much has happened since the
story was first written it is not out of date. Into a considerable portion of the Dark Continent traversed by the author no other white man
has yet penetrated, and what has occurred has rather tended to give
additional interest to all African exploration. In this edition Commander Cameron does justice to the explorations of Mr. Stanley in the
Congo Basin, of Mr. Johnston in the Kilimanjaro district, and the
Portuguese, Italian, and German travellers. But the·most important
part of the added matter has reference to the commercial openings now
inviting British energy and capital in Africa."—*Daily Telegraph.*

" In a second edition of 'Across Africa,' Commander Cameron sum-
marises the results of exploration in the Dark Continent since his own
expedition in 1876, and offers some valuable suggestions as to the
future of African travel and commerce. Subsequent discoveries, it is
well known, have mainly gone to confirm Commander Cameron's anti-
cipations, notably in the identification of the ·Lualaba and the Congo.
The precise nature of the Lukuga river, or creek, is still, however, a
battle-ground between geographers."—*Academy.*

GEORGE PHILIP & SON, PUBLISHERS, LONDON AND LIVERPOOL.

Imperial 8vo, price 7s. 6d.

PICTURES OF NATIVE LIFE IN DISTANT LANDS.

A Series of Twelve Illustrations (size 15 by 12½ inches), drawn and designed by H. LEUTEMANN, and beautifully printed in colours, affording life-like representations of the most striking features of the Life of tho Principal Races of Mankind.

Each Plate is accompanied by interesting and instructive explanatory letter-press, translated from the German of Professor A. KIRCHHOFF, Professor of Geography at Halle University, by GEORGE PHILIP, Junr.

The following Races are illustrated and described:—1. THE ABORIGINES OF AUSTRALIA.—2. THE PAPUAS.—3. THE POLYNESIANS.—4. THE ESKIMOS.—5. THE AMERICAN INDIANS.—6. THE HOTTENTOTS AND BUSHMEN.—7. THE NEGROES.—8. THE NUBIANS.—9. THE ARABS.—10. THE HINDOOS.—11. THE CHINESE.—12. THE JAPANESE.

An extraordinary amount of Ethnographical Information is embodied in this work.

"A book calculated to engage the deep interest of young readers."—*Daily Telegraph.*

"A capital book, from which young and old alike may learn much that is both interesting and instructive about the less known inhabitants of tho globe."—*Army and Navy Gazette.*

"The boy or girl who becomes familiar with Herr Leutemann's carefully executed pictures will have acquired a firm foundation on which to rest tho knowledge to be thereafter acquired from books of travel."—*Morning Post.*

"These graphic pictures, well drawn and coloured, illustrate the typical races of mankind."—*Spectator.*

"The volume deserves to meet with great success."—*Daily Chronicle.*

"I also advise you to look at 'Graphic Pictures of Native Life in Distant Lands.'"—*Truth.*

A New Aid to the Study of the Stars. Just Published, Printed in Colours.

PHILIPS' REVOLVING PLANISPHERE.

Showing the Principal Stars visible for every Hour in the Year. Price 2s. net.

This novel Planisphere consists of a circular disc on which the principal Stars visible from our latitude are clearly indicated. By means of an exceedingly simple arrangement the disc may be made to revolve in such a way as to show only those stars visible at any given time. In addition to this may be shown the varying time of sunrise and sunset during the whole year. The Stars are clearly shown in white on a dark ground. The Publishers invite the attention of all interested in Astronomy to this *unique* and *cheap* publication, which, it is hoped, will tend to popularise and simplify the study of the Heavens.

EDITION FOR THE SOUTHERN HEMISPHERE.

THE extraordinary success of the English Edition of this useful little instrument has induced the publishers to produce another of precisely similar construction for use in the Southern Hemisphere. It is specially arranged for latitudes 35° to 40° S., but for practical purposes it may be used in all the English-speaking countries S. of the Equator. Price 2s. 6d. nett.

"Messrs. George Philip & Son send us a 'Revolving Planisphere,' which by a simple contrivance indicates the stars visible in and near London for every hour in which absence of daylight and clearness of sky enable them to be so. The principal stars round the north pole as a centre, and extending to 28° S. declination, are mapped in white on a dark ground ; over this is a disc with an elliptic aperture easily turned by handles, and round it the twenty-four hours are marked, whilst on the circumference of the star-map are marked the months and days of the year. By turning the disc till the hour coincides with any particular day, that portion of the heavens is uncovered which is visible on that day at the hour in question. The arrangement is useful for those who desire to learn the principal stars and constellations, and handy also for amateur astronomers, who may often wish to ascertain at a glance what part of the stellar sky is visible at an hour when they purpose to look for some special celestial object."—*Athenæum.*

GEORGE PHILIP & SON, PUBLISHERS, LONDON AND LIVERPOOL.

Technical Education, Industry, and Trade.

www.ingramcontent.com/pod-product-compliance
Lightning Source LLC
Chambersburg PA
CBHW020941030726
47496CB00005B/1290